ECHOES OF SILENCE

Echoes of Silence

CHRISTY WALL

LUMINARE PRESS
WWW.LUMINAREPRESS.COM

Echoes of Silence
Copyright © 2024 by Christy Wall

All rights reserved. This book or any portion thereof may not be reproduced or used in any manner whatsoever without the express written permission of the publisher, except for the use of brief quotations in a book review.

Cover design by Erica Johnson-Smith

Printed in the United States of America

Luminare Press
442 Charnelton St.
Eugene, OR 97401
www.luminarepress.com

LCCN: 2024906303
ISBN: 979-8-88679-531-8

Thank you to the men and women who work hard in winter's frost and summer's heat, who raise cattle and work the land so that we can share your healthy meat and beautiful bounty on our family tables.

Thank you to my family who has given me endless examples of joy, mirth, and love, as well as kept me in a state of humility. Thank you to my husband who, after thirty years and nine children, still dances with me in the kitchen.

A very special thank you to Teresa Bullis, without whose faithful friendship and help this would not have been possible.

And finally, thank you to all the patient horses who, though full of strength and power, yet bow their heads before us, allowing us, even if for a moment, the privilege to share in their magnificence.

Shakespeare said it best, "He is pure air and fire, and the dull elements of earth and water never appear in him, but only in patient stillness while his rider mounts him… His neigh is like the bidding of a monarch, and his countenance enforces homage. When I bestride him, I soar, I am a hawk: he trots the air; the earth sings when he touches it…" (*Henry V*, Act 3).

Contents

Prologue 1

CHAPTER 1
Signs of Life 11

CHAPTER 2
Song of the Earth 21

CHAPTER 3
The Lion's Share 26

CHAPTER 4
Lure of Life 36

CHAPTER 5
Cool, Clear Water 44

CHAPTER 6
Together at Last 56

CHAPTER 7
Inclement Wind 67

CHAPTER 8
Horse Tales 82

CHAPTER 9
Dancing in the Aspen 96

CHAPTER 10
Cattle Drive 107

CHAPTER 11
Prayers and Promises 114

CHAPTER 12
Hearts on Fire 123

CHAPTER 13
Reading Sign 130

CHAPTER 14
The Round Pen 137

CHAPTER 15
Space of Quiet 149

CHAPTER 16
The Magnificent Echo 155

CHAPTER 17
Fair Day 165

CHAPTER 18
Abigail's Gift 175

CHAPTER 19
Rosie's Dance 181

CHAPTER 20
Secret Adventures 193

CHAPTER 21
The Cellar's Promise 202

CHAPTER 22
Joseph's Approval 207

CHAPTER 23
Pistol's Lessons 212

CHAPTER 24
Heat Wave 225

CHAPTER 25
A Bear in the Deadwood 234

CHAPTER 26
The Circle of Love 239

CHAPTER 27
The Quiet Grumbling 248

CHAPTER 28
The Hunt Which Saw Too Much 258

CHAPTER 29
Fire Storm 272

Epilogue *279*

About the Author *283*

Prologue

The February snow and howling winds blow across the endless plains. The little house with heavy wooden beams, thick walls, and earthen tile floor shudders but stands strong. It was built long ago and built to stand against the fiercest Wyoming winters. Grandma told them it used to be a church built by early missionaries. She said Grandpa found it, standing bravely on that vast 3,800-acre ranch, and impressed with its strength, Grandpa used it to build his home. There is a cross deeply etched in the wall above the fireplace, and it is where the family gathers for prayers and comfort. Grandpa used the image of that cross to brand his cattle and the Derrick brand was ever after known as the Cross Ranch.

The animals look out from the large barn nearby. All around is dark and cold, but a warm glow comes from the windows of the little home. Inside, the fire is warm and strong and fills the room with a golden light as the family inside gathers for prayers.

Papa begins: "Dear Lord, bless our families, friends, and neighbors. Please help those who are less fortunate than us. And please Lord, help Rosie's ear infection get better."

One by one, the children speak up, bringing their prayers before God. A test, a friend in need, a thanksgiving, a worry. It is a time for them to share their concerns as a family and join together in prayer.

Then Billy and Caz both say together, "And please let Papa teach us how to hunt."

Everyone laughs a little, and Mama declares that it is time for bed. Off everyone goes, jostling and joking; the three girls, Jessica, Sierra, and Rosie, to their room, and the three boys, Jacob, Billy, and Caz, to theirs. Rosie stumbles and almost falls as she walks. "I wish Susan was here. I'm so sad she is away at college," she says.

Mama puts an arm around her and says. "I know. We all miss her, but soon she will be home. Just a few more months."

Rosie stumbles again, "My ears still hurt, Mama, and I feel dizzy."

Mama hides her worry and comforts Rosie, "I'm so sorry, honey. I'm sure you are just tired and need to sleep."

Rosie climbs into bed and Mama carefully folds the blankets around her. Kissing her on the forehead, she says, "Sleep well, sweet Rosie. You will feel better in the morning, when the sun is shining bright."

But as she walks away, she shakes her head, thinking, *This is her second round of antibiotics, she should be better by now.*

The wind continues to blow across those empty acres of grass and rolling hills owned and protected by the family. The little house holds the family safe from the storm as they fall asleep, buried in their blankets and surrounded by love and faith. But those walls cannot protect them from every danger, and suddenly there is a cry in the darkness.

"Mama!" It is Rosie. Her voice is shrill and panicky. "My head hurts," she groans, "my head hurts so badly."

Mama grabs her robe and rushes to her, strangely alert but not knowing why. Not yet understanding the reason for the panic in her daughter's voice. "Is it your ears? Are they hurting?"

Rosie sits on the bed; her blonde hair is wet and matted to her head. She is rocking and moaning in pain with both hands on her head. "It's burning! Make it go away."

She has the look of a wild animal that doesn't know what is happening to her. Mama feels her forehead—she is burning up. Something is desperately wrong, and it is more than the earache.

"Paul, Paul!"

Paul hears the panic in his wife's voice, and he is out of bed in an instant.

"Paul, something is wrong with Rosie. I don't know what it is."

That man, with greying temples, resolute jaw, and thick eyebrows, is still only for a moment. That man, who has dedicated his life to providing for and protecting his family and his ranch. That man, accustomed to going out in storms to rescue birthing cows, accustomed to long hours in the sun fixing fences and helping his neighbor. That man pauses for a moment only because he cannot see this enemy. He gets dressed because he wants to be ready, even though he knows not for what.

Suddenly, Rosie lets out a guttural scream of pain. Her eyes are rolling in her head, and she doesn't seem to recognize them. Husband and wife look at each other, fear in their eyes. This is no earache, and something is very wrong. Rosie falls limp on the bed.

Papa grabs her in a blanket and says, "I am taking her to the emergency room."

Anna protests. "But the roads…they are all snowed over. And the wind …"

Papa's face is determined and resolute. "I've driven in worse. I'll take the Suburban, we can put her in the back."

Anna quickly gets dressed as Papa heads to the car. Sierra and Jessica are awake and scared. Mama quickly comforts them and tells them to pray. The girls do not notice the pallor in her face nor the worry in her eyes. She has always seemed strong, and they cannot imagine her any other way.

Grabbing her coat, Anna follows Paul down the dark hallway of the house. The fire has died down and is just glowing embers. She adds some wood and stokes the fire so the house will stay warm while they are gone. She pulls her coat close and when she opens the front door, the wind nearly sucks it off its hinges. She steps into the bitter cold, pulls the door closed, and heads outside into the storm. The snow has piled high against the house and barns. The wind is fierce, stinging her face as the snow flies through the dark.

She runs to the car, her hair and jacket snapping in the wind. Paul has just laid Rosie in the back seat and holds the door open for his wife. A quick meeting of eyes; eyes both seeking and giving courage. Each in their own way. Hers with love and his with strength. Anna climbs in and holds Rosie. She is moaning horribly and when she sees her mama, she cries out in fear and pain. Anna can barely breathe as she holds her daughter close and prays. Her petitions are like groans of her soul for she can no longer form words. She looks at her husband in the front seat, pulling out of the drive with set jaw and clenched hands. She knows he will do everything he can to get them to the hospital safely and she forces herself to breathe. The wind is harsh and wild across the open road between the ranch and town, and snowdrifts blow across the road like the ghosts of strange beasts. In a moment monstrous and powerful, pushing the car across the road and then gone.

Once they are in town, the buildings bring some protection from the worst of the wind and the roads have been cleared. Rosie is sleeping now, restless but not crying out in pain. In that moment of quiet, Anna looks out the car window, seeing her town as if she is a stranger. The motor drums on, and the car is quiet. Time seems to slow down. The town is empty and asleep, with a few streetlights putting light on the sidewalks. The Christmas lights have all been put away and the town seems dark and sad. The wind throws up the snow in sudden gusts, shaking signs and rattling anything that is loose. An old newspaper blows by, like a bat in the wind. The words "TEAR DOWN THE WALL" can be seen on its underbelly, but only for a moment before it flies off into the dark night. Anna shudders. The words feel violent and ominous.

Once in the emergency room, the nurses lay her onto a bed and they begin to ask questions. Clipboards in hands.

Safe.

Procedural.

Paul stands stoically as Anna answers, trying to stay calm. Height. Weight. Temperature. Past medications. Symptoms.

Rosie is quiet in her sleep.

Suddenly, Rosie wakes up convulsing and screaming in pain. The nurses rush to her, dropping clipboards in their urgency. She fights against them, clawing and scratching. The nurses work to restrain her, alarmed at so much violence from such a little girl. She is twisting and crying out in pain.

"It's burning! Make it stop!"

The nurses cannot hold her down, for that child has grown strong and fierce working on the ranch. Papa steps forward and holds his daughter's body while they secure her wrists and ankles. She is finally secured, still screaming and twisting like a mad creature. The nurses hurry around her with wild eyes and trembling hands. At last, they are able to give her pain medication and a sedative. Finally. Finally, Rosie once again lies quietly on the bed. Anna sits in the chair leaning against Paul, though he himself is wracked with fear and disbelief.

The doctor comes in, efficient and in control. He tells them they will do an MRI for brain imaging. Anna stands next to Paul, watching as they roll her down the hallway and out of sight. It seems like they must wait a long time for any news. The doctor returns without Rosie. His eyes are sad, but his demeanor is oddly brisk so as to keep the diagnosis far from his heart; for he is also a father. He tells them, "Your daughter has meningitis, and the infection has gone into her brain. This is what is causing the terrible pain and the crazy behavior. I am worried about brain damage. We are prepping her for immediate surgery to reduce the swelling."

The room begins to spin for Anna. She cannot catch her breath and she begins to shake. Paul carefully sits her down, fighting the nausea in his own stomach. Anna looks at her legs and hands shaking violently and wonders at it. There is nowhere to go in her mind, just blinding fear. She leans against Paul who sits beside her. He does not notice that his knuckles are white from being clenched. There is nothing to do but wait and pray.

Paul and Anna sit in the waiting room. They do not notice the hard benches straining their backs. They do not notice that night has changed into day, or that the snow has stopped, and the wind has quieted. At last, the doctor walks in, and both Paul and Anna stand up, exhausted and daring to hope. The doctor looks weary, and tells them,

"We were able to drain some of the fluid from her brain, but the infection is so bad that we are still worried about brain damage and hearing loss. Right now, we are keeping her sedated until the swelling goes down."

At the words "brain damage and hearing loss," Anna collapses into her husband's arms, and he bears the sorrow for them both, his great, generous heart holding her. Together, they go and see Rosie. She is lying in bed, unconscious, her face once again quiet and still, as if she is sleeping. For a moment it seems as if the nightmare has passed, and all is well again. The sun is shining into the room and Anna remembers telling Rosie she would feel better with the morning sun. For a moment she hopes. But the doctor interrupts her thoughts.

"There is a massive infection still pressing on her ears and into her brain," he says. "We will keep her in the hospital on IV antibiotics for at least ten days, most likely twenty-one days, until the infection is cleared."

Phone calls are made. Arrangements are decided. Papa and Mama are allowed to stay in the room with Rosie. An extra bed for exactly this reason.

Days and nights alternate meaninglessly. Papa and Mama constant at her side. Prayers, antibiotics, fluids, and more prayers. Friends and neighbors helping to run the ranch. Jacob and Jessica doing what they can to hold the home together. Susan calling from college, trying her best to give encouragement, frustrated she cannot be there.

Finally, the infection is gone and the swelling in her brain goes down. Rosie wakes up. But it is not the same Rosie. She is unresponsive and disconnected. Her eyes are hollow and distant. She does not respond to the doctors or her family. Papa and Mama are both confused and ask the doctor what has happened. What has happened to their sweet, energetic little girl?

The doctor explains, now with crossed arms and a serious face, his job done, and the beautiful little girl tucked away as a patient in his mind. "As you know, your daughter had an infection in the ears. One in two thousand get secondary complications which can include a brain abscess. We have done our best to drain the abscess, but unfortunately she has permanent hearing loss. She is deaf. The swelling in her brain can cause fever, vomiting, and altered consciousness, which is what you saw when you brought her in. With time, we hope that will go away on its own. In the meantime, it is affecting how she moves and thinks. The good news is that we cannot see any permanent damage in the brain. The damage in her ears may take away her equilibrium and cause her to be disoriented and have poor balance such that she cannot ride a horse. It may cause her to lose her direction underwater and drown because she cannot tell which way is up. All these things you will come to know in time as she heals."

Mama looks at Rosie, sitting on the hospital bed with hunched shoulders and withdrawn eyes. Her face is pale and her eyes dull. Mama's heart breaks and she wonders if anything will ever be right again. Papa, standing there with a grey face and ice in his veins, holds his wife and fights the almost suffocating grief and worry.

A nurse comes in to explain sign language, but Paul hears nothing. The room feels claustrophobic, and he has to leave. He tells Anna he is going to get coffee for them both and wanders out the door and down the hall. His heart cannot take another word. His beautiful, bright Rosie, unable to hear? Swelling in the brain? Unable to ride and swim? How can these words be true? He walks the long hallways trying to remember where the coffee is and passes a chapel built into the hospital. He stops in and prays, "Lord, help me to know what to do. Help me to make my family strong. Help us know how to communicate with Rosie. Help her brain to heal, so she wakes up. Also, Lord, you know we are ranchers, and we ride horses to do our work. Please let my Rosie be able to ride so we can work as a family. Please let me know what I need to do." He pauses then cries out with all his strength, "I will do whatever it takes, Lord." But the little church is silent and there is no response. He bows his head with resignation, motions the sign of the cross, and rises from his knees.

Walking back to Anna, he finds the coffee and pours them both a cup. It is set up for those exhausted loved ones wandering the halls. As he turns a corner, he hears echoes of joy coming from a hallway. He stops to look and sees a small family. There is a young girl in a hospital gown and they are all hugging and dancing in a circle. Their joy is contagious, and he smiles despite himself. And suddenly he is filled with a strange hope. He dares to hope this could be a promise of future joy for his own family. He shakes his head with the craziness of it, but nonetheless, his soul is filled with peace and strength. He breathes deeply and, standing up straighter, returns to Anna with the coffee. There is a new strength in his heart and a conviction that his family will once again be strong and whole. He is a determined man, and he just needs to figure out how to fix it.

CHAPTER 1

Signs of Life

Sierra sat by the fire, watching her mother make biscuits across the room near the oven. The fire felt good, for the sun had not yet heated the thick walls of their home. It was a small room, cozy and warm with a large wooden table between her and Mama. There was a pot hanging on an iron hook over the fire. Mama liked to start a stew in the morning and let it simmer over a low fire all day.

She watched as her mother rolled the dough and cut it into small circles. It was the Feast of St. Joseph. They celebrated each March with fresh-made biscuits and gravy. But this day did not seem like a feast day. Rosie had been home for three weeks, and nothing was the same. She refused to communicate or respond to anything written, and no one knew what to do. They tried to engage Rosie and tried to use a chalkboard, but she just sat there like she was in a trance. Her mother, once strong and fierce, looked old and worn down. There was no joy in her eyes and her shoulders seemed caved in, as if to protect her heart. Sierra hated to see her like that. Jacob sat at the table, whittling a piece of wood. He was much too quiet now. His usual jokes and merriment seemed lost, as if they had wandered off somewhere without him. Jessica helped her mother with cooking the sausage and making the gravy, but her beautiful singing was no more. Not since Rosie got sick. Rosie also sat at the table, her blue eyes distant and withdrawn. Her hair was brushed and pulled into a tight ponytail with a severity that betrayed the distress of the hands that bound it. Billy and Caz alone seemed untouched by the sorrow in the home and played with cars and trucks in front of the morning fire.

"Sierra," Mama said, breaking into her daughter's thoughts, "mind the stew. I don't want it to burn."

Sierra aimlessly stirred the stew. A piece of meat was stuck to the bottom and now she focused on that. A single piece of burnt meat could ruin the stew, its taste running through every part of the whole.

Papa came in. His broad shoulders were stoic, and his face was grim, the lines around his eyes etched into his tan and weathered skin. Sierra remembered so many mornings when he had come into the room with his broad smile and laughing eyes. He would joke with Mama and make her laugh and sometimes take Sierra in a big bear hug, where she could smell his aftershave and feel the softness of his big sheepskin jacket. The memory hurt her, and a tear rolled down her cheek.

She went to the window and looked out upon the land. The beauty of the rolling hills and morning light was soothing. Fog had settled in the valleys of the land and played in the treetops. The sunlight was gentle and soft. Sierra closed her eyes, letting the sun warm her face. She thought about last year when they celebrated the Feast Day of St. Joseph. It seemed like a long time ago.

SHE REMEMBERED PAPA WALKING INTO THE KITCHEN with big bounding strides. The air was warmer that day, and the snow was finally melting. There was a promise of spring and grass was growing out in the fields. Calves were being born and Papa wanted to make sure everything went well. He knew every mama out there and knew when one was having a hard time or when one had wandered off too far from the herd. Mama was cooking biscuits and gravy, and the kitchen was filled with a wonderful aroma of herbs and spices. The room was warm and cheery from the fire as it snapped and crackled in the big fireplace.

Billy and Caz sat at the kitchen table working on their math, for Mama promised them they could go with Papa if they finished. Billy chewed on a pencil as he did his addition. Musing, he asked, "Mama, is zero a number?"

Caz responded, "Of course it is—it's in your math book, dummy!"

Billy replied, "Yeah, but zero is nothing so how could it be a number?"

Caz responded impatiently, "Listen, if you don't get your work done, Papa will leave without you. It's a number, okay?"

Billy put his head back in his book and scribbled out his math, but he continued to mutter to himself about zero not being a number.

Jacob was up before dawn and had finished his schoolwork as well. He was whistling and teasing Jessica as she helped Mama cook. Everyone wanted to go with Papa and see the baby calves.

Sierra and Rosie had done their lessons the night before and were pulling on boots and sweaters. Mama laid out the breakfast and everyone ate with enthusiasm. Where did Papa think the cows would be? How many were born already? Were there any twins? Sierra remembered how happy they had all felt, there together, as if sorrow could not break through those strong walls.

She remembered Rosie crying out, "Oh! I love baby cows," and everyone nodding, for they did as well.

Then, out into the cold morning air. A spring fog had settled in the lower valleys, teasing the limbs of the trees just barely coming into bloom. The earth looked happy and satisfied, the grass rich with moisture, with little yellow and white flowers dotting the landscape. It was absolutely the best time of the year. They had brought in the horses, billows of warm air coming from their noses, still bearing the bits of alfalfa they were finishing. They threw blankets over their broad warm backs and, picking up the heavy saddles, got the horses ready.

Sierra remembered when they were younger and their father had told them, "Every cowgirl needs to pick up her own saddle." Rosie was smaller then, but she never wanted to be left behind. If Sierra could lift the saddle, so would Rosie. And so, they had struggled silently and fiercely to swing the heavy saddles over the tall backs of the horses. But now their backs had grown strong and their arms sinewy with muscle. They easily saddled the horses, put their bridles on, and stepped into the saddle. They could have ridden bareback, but today was business and they might have to help rope and hold a cow.

Together they all rode into the waiting hills. The sun slowly warmed the air, and the bridles jingled softly as the horses nodded their heads and stepped lightly. Sierra remembered with a smile how much she wanted to run that morning. "What the horses do love," she cried, leaning forward in the saddle, "is a fast run!"

But Jacob gave her a warning look and said, "You remember the rule: Stay with Papa; no running off." So, she sat back down in the saddle and settled in.

Rosie had asked, "Do you think the horses like baby cows?"

Jessica was not very nice and said, "You are only nine, what do you know? Of course the horses don't care."

But Papa had said the best thing: "They love taking us out into the fields on a beautiful spring day. They like watching the cows and keeping track of the calves. Yes, I think they do. I saw a few fresh calves in the far pasture yesterday, over by the stream. Let's go there first."

Smiling at Sierra, he nodded and then broke into a nice lope, and for a while there was only the sound of the horses' hooves hitting the ground like a lovely four-time melody. The cool air rushed over their faces, and when they slowed down Rosie looked around and laughed. "Everyone has pink cheeks and a smile on their face, even Papa!"

They had all laughed together, for there was nothing as wonderful as a lope across the valley on a spring morning while off to see fresh calves. Even Papa thought so!

PAPA'S VOICE BROUGHT SIERRA OUT OF HER REVERIE. "Breakfast is ready. Let's pray."

They prayed before their meal, asking for special blessings on this feast day, and then ate the biscuits and gravy. Jessica asked if everyone liked the biscuits, and the response was a distracted yes. No one had much of an appetite.

Papa finished and, putting down his fork and knife, said, "I need to check at the spring at the back of the property. Luke said he saw cat tracks out that way. Jacob, can you come with me?"

Jacob shook his head. "I'm sorry, I have to finish an essay for school, and then I promised Mr. Johnson I would help put in some fence posts."

Papa nodded. "Give Mr. Johnson my best, will you?" Doug and Abigail Johnson were the Derricks' closest neighbors and good friends.

Jacob nodded. "Yup, I will."

Billy got up from the table, pushing back his chair. He did not see Rosie had started to stand up, and, not hearing Billy's chair, she did not move out of the way. Billy bumped into her and she fell to the ground like a limp rag doll.

Caz yelled, "Pay attention!"

Billy yelled back, "She should have looked where she was going."

Caz pushed Billy, who then fell onto Rosie. Rosie managed to roll out of the way, just in time, but Billy was furious. He jumped to his feet and started to punch Caz who retaliated fiercely. Mama helped Rosie up and brought her to a chair. They both had tears in their eyes. As soon as Rosie was sitting, Mama yelled at the boys. "Listen here, there was no reason for that to happen! Go to your rooms and then we will think about some work for you to do! Obviously you have some extra energy!"

Both boys groaned. They knew what that meant and trudged to their room glaring at each other.

Sierra looked at Rosie, sick with sorrow. Rosie's head was down, her hair falling over her face. Sierra watched as Mama pulled it back with trembling hands. She longed for her sister's musical laugh or silly, happy comments. She sat by the fire, fuming, wondering how God could have done this to her sister. She couldn't understand why he made Rosie deaf. Wasn't he supposed to be all-good like they were taught? She clenched her jaw as the anger burned in her heart. Mama looked at her but did not know what to say. The kitchen was painfully quiet.

Sierra couldn't bear the room anymore; it felt as if the whole kitchen was choking with sorrow. "Mama," she said, "I'm going outside."

And then she ran from the room, letting the door slam behind her. Anna looked at her husband. Their eyes meeting, sorrow and worry exchanged. In his wisdom he said, "Let her go. School can wait."

A slow exhale. His strength, even in his grief, was what she needed. It was hard to know what to do, for they were all struggling, and she had no answers. All she knew to do was love her family and provide comfort. Slowly the kitchen emptied; the children to do schoolwork and Papa to the fields. Paul kissed her on the cheek before he left. She stood at the kitchen window and watched him ride away.

Anna said a prayer for him as he rode over the hills. It was all she could think to do. She was alone in the kitchen now and the silence was overwhelming. She began the dishes and stopped. Looking over the empty land, she sighed and then let the sadness wash over her.

Anna sank into a chair and began to weep. Her apron covering her face, trying to hide from her own weakness. She was so lost and confused. How was she going to help Rosie? Was her family falling apart? The joy they had known in their home seemed lost. Sierra was angry and Paul was cold. Jessica and Jacob were distant. Maybe just waiting to leave for college and get away? How was she going to bring her family back together? It seemed like the grief and fear were too much for them all. She sobbed openly, crying out to God for courage, for wisdom, and for consolation.

Suddenly she felt a hand on her shoulder. She looked up. It was Rosie. Rosie with eyes of liquid sorrow. Mama took a breath, astonished to see her there. She took Rosie into her arms, and they cried together. And somewhere in those tears, hearts began the slow process of healing. For it is in the warmth of tears that the icy hand of grief loses its grasp.

PAPA RODE OUT, GRIM AND DETERMINED. HE WAS A practical man who knew how to provide for and protect his family. He understood the mountain lion trying to feed her cubs. He understood the cattle that grazed upon the land. He understood the rain and the sun, sometimes a blessing and sometimes a curse. He even understood Sierra bolting from the house like a frightened horse.

What he did not understand was what to do with the sorrow that had pervaded his home. He did not understand why Rosie was withdrawn and did not try to communicate. They were all studying the sign language book the nurse had given them, but no one seemed to learn. He tried using a chalk board to write messages, but Rosie would not cooperate. He was angry and frustrated that they were too far away from a speech therapist. He could imagine Anna's mother being critical of him for bringing the family to live in the middle of nowhere. Nothing he did could fix the problem of Rosie being deaf. And God help him if she had no balance or, worst of all, the swelling in her brain did not go away and she didn't wake up. And so, day after day, he rode out and did what he could do—provide for his family, work with his hands, fix fences, and take care of his land and his herd. He clenched his jaw and rode on.

As he rode, the land fell away from him in a vast expanse of fields, bordered by the mountains. He breathed deeply and thanked God for the heavy winter for it brought the promise of thick grass. He felt the wind as it blew the clouds across the blue sky. He watched the hawks soar in the heavens, looking for prey. Slowly, slowly the rhythm of his horse's footsteps soothed him, and his shoulders relaxed. This was his land, given to him by his father and to his father from his grandfather. He knew every bluff, every stream, every grove like it was a piece of his own flesh. It had given him his livelihood, had given him respect amongst his fellow ranchers, and had even brought him his beautiful wife. He breathed deeply and sat lighter in the saddle. The horse felt the man's hands relax, and the horse's footsteps became more even, for in that breath the horse found quiet.

He rode for some time and then noticed that up ahead, under the shadow of a tree, the grass was matted and dark. He broke into a gallop and, coming closer, could now see the blood he knew would be there. With a lump in his throat, he stopped and dismounted. There on the ground was a young calf, newly attacked by the lion, its sides slashed. He looked around cautiously; he must have just interrupted the attack. He shot the rifle in the air to keep it away and gingerly wrapped the calf in his warm sheepskin coat. He looked around for the calf's mother but could not see her. She must have run off with the rest of the herd. Carefully placing the calf on his saddle, he mounted and then rode home quickly. He held the calf close to him and, as he rode, he could feel her steady breathing. He could feel her warmth and her fight to live. He thanked God for the chance to save this little one's life. If he made the effort to care for and protect a hurt creature, wouldn't God also make the effort to protect his sweet Rosie? And so, out under that blue sky, this small sign of life brought hope to his heart that God would also give Rosie a chance at life.

CHAPTER 2

Song of the Earth

There was yet another set of eyes, wounded and full of fire. And perhaps these eyes needed the flow of tears most. Sierra was angry. Angry at God. Angry at Rosie. And angry at herself. She could neither find the words to tell anyone nor could she make the anger go away. And so, the anger burned, unchecked within her heart.

Sierra ran and ran until her lungs screamed with pain for lack of oxygen. She ran into the hills where her father had told her not to go. That was where the mountain lions lived and had their cubs, in the protection of the craggy bluffs and thorny brush. But she did not care. Part of her wished she could die. She felt like everything she loved was gone. Rosie was her best friend and dearest confidant. Rosie was her joy when life became too serious. And now Rosie was gone, lost in those awful hollow eyes.

She finally came upon the sharp rocks. She stopped and breathed deeply the thin mountain air. She wandered through the rocks, curious. She had never gone this far, and Papa, she knew, would be mad. Suddenly, the rocks opened up and she came to a beautiful little oasis of grass, lovely trees, and a shimmering pool of water. There was a spring higher up. Its waters fell with a beautiful sound into a large deep pool which eventually ran off into a stream. She wondered if it was the same stream that went all the way to the house and then joined the river behind it. She and Rosie had always wondered where that stream came from. She took off her shoes and the grass felt soft. She lay on her back and gazed into the sky. Protected from the wind, with the sun reflecting off the black rock, the air grew warm.

She lay in the grass. Feeling the warmth. Smelling the fresh grass. Seeing the trees against the blue sky. Hearing the water lap against the earth. Her breath grew deep and peaceful, and she could feel her soul heal. Feel the anguish slip away into the deep, cool earth.

Knowing the water would be cold, she decided to go swimming anyway. She dove deep into the pool before coming up for air, gasping from the icy chill. But it was not too cold. No, not too cold. She dove again and swam lower and lower into the dark green solitude. She turned toward the sky and saw the sun shining into the depths of the water—long, languid rays of light filtering through the dark water, lighting up flecks of gold on the rocks below. It was mystical and amazing, and she felt out of time. It seemed as if the sun had found the depths of her soul as well. Overcome with its beauty, she rose to the surface. And in that moment, in that moment, her heart released its anger and despair, and she began to cry. Deep, dark tears tore her nearly in half. She struggled to the shore and clutched the soft, dark dirt, her tears flowing into the earth. She wailed in anger toward God, cried at his heartless injustice. She howled like a wounded animal who knows no God or reason. And slowly the putrid infection of her anger poured from her heart. She lay on the ground, exhausted and helpless. She wanted to lay there forever. She would not return to the kitchen of sadness. Not return to her lifeless sister. Could not, could not face her father and mother, whose eyes had lost their mirth.

She lay on the bank of the spring, the cool earth soothing her aching head. Her breathing became slow and methodical. If only she could stay in this place of peace forever. She picked up the dirt beneath her hand and let it fall through her fingers.

Suddenly there was a strange vibration. Deep below her, the earth rumbled. It carried a strange song, like a melody. She could not place it. She lay silently. Transfixed. Listening. Her sorrow and anger forgotten. And suddenly she knew—horses! It was the sound of a huge herd galloping. Her heart began to beat wildly. Her mother loved to tell stories of a wild herd of horses that she had seen when she was younger, but Sierra had never seen them, and neither had her siblings. Maybe the herd would come to the spring for water! She quickly scrambled into the rocks and hid. She was deep in the shade. She waited, holding her breath with excitement.

And then they came. Slowly at first, dancing with energy. Cautious. Ready to flee. Flashes of color. Flaring nostrils and arched necks. Manes and tails flowing like fire. Hooves striking the earth, and shrill whinnies filling the air. She gasped at their beauty. The herd stopped but remained restless, for they could smell both her and the water. The stallion approached, his neck thick with muscle. Arched, defiant, protective, and absolutely assertive. A young colt approached as well, the water too much of a temptation, but the stallion quickly turned its head and, with a snakelike quickness, bit the colt hard on the neck. The colt put his head down and went to the back of the herd.

The stallion was a deep red color with a white blaze on his nose and black hooves. His skin flashed with the sun, like a metallic cloth of fire. He came up to the water, slowly, cautiously, and drank. Ears alert, he lifted his head and looked around. The horses behind him milled impatiently. He did not like the scent of humans, but he could perceive no other danger. His decision made, he drank deeply, and his body relaxed. The next to approach was a grey mare. She came forward and also looked around with alert ears and bright eyes. And then she too drank deeply.

After those two drank and stepped aside, the rest of the herd came forward. Duns and blacks, paints, chestnuts, and grays. So many colors. Sierra was overwhelmed by their beauty and watched, barely breathing. Suddenly she had a thought: she would bring Rosie. They could sit behind this very rock and watch in silence. No need for unheard words. Just a cool swim and hopefully the horses would come.

It was the first hopeful, happy thought she had had since Rosie had been sick. It had been brought in with the flying manes and flashing hooves, like a message from heaven itself.

The horses drank their fill and ate grass. They rolled and splashed in the water like so many happy children. The sun was high in the sky and then began its long journey home. Sierra thought about her parents and knew they would worry about her. She didn't want to scare the horses but knew she needed to go home or Papa would be out looking for her. Her leg began to cramp and, without thinking, she adjusted her position. In that movement, the horses, in one motion, lifted their heads and ran off. She hurried home, anxious to tell her family. As she ran, she realized she was smiling. She laughed out loud at herself, and that laugh was another ray of light in that once-dark soul.

As she approached the house, she saw that Papa had come home for lunch; his horse, Bandit, was tied to the hitching post. She burst in the door like a fire of light and hope. She did not see her eyes sparking with fire, her cheeks flushed from running and excitement. She did not see her face full of joy. All she saw was that Rosie had turned toward that great burst of energy and her eyes were full of something. Life. Curiosity. Hope. Their eyes met with such a force of love that everyone in the room felt it.

"I saw the wild horses!" she cried out.

CHAPTER 3

The Lion's Share

Everyone turned to her and asked questions at the same time.

"Where were you?"

"What kind of horses?"

"What did they look like?"

"Were they the wild horses Mama told us about?"

Mama looked up, alert, curious, her melancholy forgotten, like a child who has found a favorite toy, once lost. Mama said in a whimsical voice, "Well, my goodness. I thought they were gone for good, looking for forage across the far mountains." Then she said proudly, "Those horses are very special, you know, and the ranchers are proud of them. They are allowed to roam freely across the land and are protected by law. They are direct descendants of the original Colonial Spanish horses; they are part of our heritage."

Though they had heard it before, the family was enchanted by Mama's description, for now it seemed real to them. Sierra described the stallion, his thick, arched, muscular neck, how he pranced around the mares and protected them so nobly. She described the baby horses playing in the water and the beautiful mares of so many colors. Sierra looked up at Rosie and saw that she was watching her, trying to understand. Sierra grabbed the chalkboard and wrote "Wild horses." Rosie's eyes flew open, but the conversation continued, and no one could write fast enough.

Papa noticed. It was the first time Rosie had shown interest in anything. He smiled at his family, and his eyes sparkled for the first time in a long while. He had another surprise to share with the family on this blessed feast day, for he knew how much his daughters loved caring for young calves. When the talk about the horses calmed down, he said, "Well, I have some news as well. I brought home a baby calf that needs some care. It was attacked by a lion. I sewed it up and no bones are broken and none of her organs are damaged. I think she will be okay. Jacob is in the barn with her now. I looked for her mama, but she must have run off at the attack. We can return her to the herd when she can eat grass."

As everyone cried out in happiness about a new little one to care for and love, Papa wrote on the chalkboard which they were using for Rosie. "I found a baby calf that needs caring for." He showed it to Rosie, but she did not respond. Papa turned away slowly and put it down with a grim look on his face.

Mama took a breath and waved to the rest of the children. "Let's go out to the barn to see."

They all marched out to the barn, like it was a parade. Sierra looked at Rosie, inviting her, pleading with her. The two sisters stared at each other for a long moment—one lost, the other full of life. At long last, Rosie stood up and followed Sierra to the barn.

Jacob sat in the barn surrounded by wound ointment, bandages, and a bottle of penicillin. The calf was standing and drinking from a bottle full of fresh cow's milk. Everyone gathered around the brand-new calf, commenting on how small it was.

Papa reminded them, "You know how it is—that baby needs to be fed every four hours. She needs her bandages changed." He looked at Billy and Caz. "You two are going to help with the feeding as well. And that means in the middle of the night. We all take shifts."

Rosie stood back, watching. Papa looked at her, willing her to fight. Willing her to come forward. Willing her to live, like this baby calf. She saw that look and came forward. Mama looked at Rosie with tenderness. The tears that morning had brought their souls into a beautiful bond. Fortified by her father's will and her mother's love, she came forward and admired the baby. Life pushing past death.

When the baby was fed and sleeping peacefully, they all went into the house for lunch, talking about the baby calf and the horses and what an exciting day it was. Rosie watched everyone speak, but after her initial excitement, her attention faded away. She could not understand what was being said, and the words flowed over her like silent birds into the sky.

Papa saw this and asked, "Is everyone practicing their signing?"

Mama answered, "I'm having a tough time learning. Sierra, Jessica, how about you?"

Jessica nodded. "Yes, Jacob and I have been working with Caz and Billy. But Sierra won't even try."

Sierra looked up, ashamed and angry at Jessica for telling them. Papa gave her a hard look and said, "Sierra, you need to start trying." Then, looking around he said, "We all need to work harder to learn sign language."

Everyone nodded. It was a difficult thing figuring out a new language.

Billy and Caz had finished lunch and were now playing a card game. Billy put his hand to his forehead and imitated horse ears with his fingers. Rosie pivoted and looked at him. Suddenly everyone was quiet and watching them. Did Billy actually sign? Had Rosie understood? Rosie looked at Billy with a smile and a nod. She made the same motion back to Billy. Billy nodded quietly and went back to his cards. Everyone watched in silence, filled with hope. Mama started to hum as she washed dishes, and Papa kissed her on the cheek. Perhaps they had not lost Rosie after all.

But there was a warning that had to be given. One unpleasant job that still had to be done. Papa stood up and said, "I'm headed out. Sierra, come with me, please." Sierra followed him. She knew what was coming. Once outside, Papa looked at her sternly and said. "Where did you see those horses?"

Sierra put her head down. She wanted nothing more than to lie, but she could not. "By the spring in the bluffs."

Papa's jaw flexed, like it did when he was angry. "I thought that's where you were. I've told you not to go there for a reason. Just yesterday, I found cat tracks. There were some big tracks along with some small ones too. A mama lion and her babies. Sierra, they need food like the rest of us. She is very dangerous right now."

Sierra looked up at him, feeling like he was taking the last hope of joy from her. She had to say something even if she was going to be punished for being disrespectful. For Rosie, she would take the punishment. She just couldn't keep silent. "Papa, the horses will come back. Maybe they will scare the lions and keep them away. Please let me see them again! You saw how Rosie was excited about them. I could tell her about them. I'll learn sign to do it." She did not dare tell him about her plan to bring Rosie.

Papa looked at his daughter with concern but with admiration as well. She was already twelve and very strong-willed as well as passionate. She was so much like her mother. He was quiet and thoughtful, for he too had seen Rosie's reaction. It was the first sign of hope he had that Rosie might come back to them. But he shook his head. No, he could not risk the danger. He knew too well the power of that cat and how easy it would be to kill his daughter.

"That's not how lions work. They cover large distances looking for small prey to take down. My answer is still no."

And then he walked away. His shoulders were back, and by the way that he walked, Sierra knew he was angry. But Sierra was so sure, so very sure that this was a way to bring Rosie back. And that smile in the living room was confirmation. There was hope and she would fight for it.

Lunch was over and there was more work to be done. Paul rode off with Bandit, his strong, calloused hands gentle on the reins. There was little need to direct the horse for Bandit seemed to read his mind. Those two had worked together as partners, day in and day out, for sixteen years. As he rode, he fumed.

"I've seen what those lions can do. Can't Sierra understand I want to protect her?" And then the quiet, unbidden thought, *But Rosie. My God, what if that is what will bring her back?*

He was angry and conflicted. He came to a swiftly running river and, while crossing, Bandit slipped a bit, getting them both wet. Paul sat quietly in the saddle, knowing his balance was the best help for Bandit to find his feet. It was a cold day for being wet, but Paul did not notice. Bandit recovered his feet and crossed the river. They lunged up the side of the steep bank and then stood for a moment while Bandit caught his breath and Paul surveyed the view. Beautiful white and grey clouds soared across the landscape. There was a strong, cold wind, but Paul did not mind. The wind suited him. It was a beautiful land, rugged and open. The range was covered in thick snow but, down here, the spring grass was just beginning to show. It was a sign of hope. There would be feed for his cattle. Looking at it always brought Paul peace of mind. Suddenly, a butterfly landed on his horse's neck for an instant and then flew away. It was such a strange thing to happen, and it brought a memory to his mind.

IT WAS A FEW YEARS AGO. THEY HAD NEEDED TO BRING *the cattle in before branding. He had all his children with him and Anna too. They had been riding along the edge of the river canyon. Rosie stayed with him, while the other children had ridden ahead with Anna. He loved to watch his wife and children ride. They were all good riders and understood the cattle. He chuckled. Sierra and her horse Ginger were like a grass fire on a windy day! But Rosie…Rosie, she was something else. From the beginning, she had always fought to be as good and strong and fast as her older sisters. And when she rode, she rode like she was part of the horse. Rosie, enjoying her father's company, now interrupted his thoughts.*

"Look, Papa, how the light falls over the canyon walls, like it is reaching for the bottom."

He smiled at her, and they stopped to look out over the canyon. It was beautiful in the evening light with the sun falling around it, bringing a soft, rosy glow. The canyon was very deep, and a river ran far below them. He looked at her and said, "Let me show you something."

He yodeled, and his voice, sounding like a beautiful harmony, went across the canyon and then came back to them. She laughed and tried to imitate him, singing out across the space. She looked at her father in awe as her voice came echoing back to her. She wondered aloud, "But my voice is so little. How can it make it all the way across this canyon and back again?

He remembered telling her, "Your little voice is magnified by the walls of the canyon. Isn't God wonderful to give us such a voice through nature? Most of the time nature reflects who we really are, and that reflection can teach us a lot—like a storm that makes us realize we are weak. But sometimes God surprises us, and he lets us be more than we are. When I ride Bandit, I am borrowing his strength and power, his speed and agility. My horse magnifies my ability and allows me to be more than what I am. Always treat your horse with respect and kindness, for this gift is given with trust."

She nodded and petted her horse's neck, thanking him. Then she yodeled again over the canyon and they both smiled as it came back to them. Just then, a butterfly landed on Bandit's neck and sat there for a moment, its wings shimmering in the setting sun.

Rosie laughed happily and said, "Look, Papa, it wants you to see how pretty it is."

HE SIGHED DEEPLY. SHE, OF ALL THE CHILDREN, COULD make him smile, could make his worries evaporate. He prayed, as he had so many times, "Lord, show me how to help Rosie."

Bandit flicked his ear back, hearing the voice of his master. He could feel the weight in the saddle and the heaviness of the hands.

Back at home, the afternoon sun sent long rays of light through the house, filling it with warmth. The children sat with their schoolwork, some at the table, some on the couch, and some on the floor. Sierra was on the floor in front of the fireplace and tried to concentrate, but memories of the horses galloped through her mind. Sierra looked up in the now-worn sign language book how to say "horse." She laughed when she realized Billy's "ears" were exactly right. When Rosie looked up, Sierra made the sign. Rosie's eyes flew open and looked at her with a question. Surprised, Sierra nodded and signed "many horses." Sierra smiled, and Rosie smiled.

That night, Paul and Anna lay in bed together. They were both quiet and thinking. Finally, Paul spoke up.

"I think we need to keep working on sign language and hope Rosie learns to read lips. I don't think the chalkboard works except with quick, important messages. I almost feel like it's a crutch and Rosie misses out on so much just looking at what we can quickly scrawl."

Anna nodded, "I think you are right. I wish there was a speech therapist that we could go to. I'm trying to talk with her, but she just doesn't respond."

Paul took her hand and said "Let's pray right now. Dear Lord, please help Rosie. Please help the swelling in her brain to go down. Help her to want to connect with us. Help us to know what to do to help her. Help me with my temper, Lord. Please inspire Anna with what to do every day. Amen."

Anna whispered, "Amen."

After a pause, Paul said, "I'm sorry, Anna. I've thought about it, and I don't want Sierra to go to the spring. You know how dangerous it is. That is right where I found that torn calf."

Anna shuddered. She had only seen the stitches after the calf had been treated by Paul and Jacob. She understood he was worried and understood he wanted to protect them. But she was so desperate for Rosie to connect to something, and how could she forget that moment of joy on Rosie's face when she understood the wild horses had returned?

She said, almost in a whisper, "But what if that is the answer? What if that is the very thing that brings Rosie back?"

"I understand. I do. I saw Rosie's face too. But Anna, it's not worth the risk. I have seen what those cats can do. You and the girls just cannot go there."

"Paul, you've taught me how to use a rifle. I could protect both of us."

He was quiet for a long time. And then he spoke so low that Anna could barely make out his words. "I cannot lose anyone else. It would break my heart."

She understood what he meant, for they both felt like they had lost Rosie.

They were quiet in the dark, their intimacy wrapped in the comfort of their bed and the stars through the window. He could feel her next to him and hear her breathing. The silence was all around, bringing a peace only the night can bring.

Paul looked at his wife, admiring her face barely outlined in the starlight. She was tough and she was beautiful. Just like his daughters. He spoke. "Remember how the girls would fight over things? I remember one time I had to separate them all. What was that over?"

Anna laughed. "I think it was a scarf."

Paul nodded. "That's right. Rosie took it from Jessica and refused to give it back. Jessica just stood there, crying. Then, Sierra tried to defend Jessica and suddenly all three girls were in a fight, and none of them talking to each other."

Mama laughed and rolled her eyes. Having daughters was its own special challenge. So much different than the boys who just slugged it out and were best friends again.

Paul was quiet and then said, "Rosie is fierce when she wants something bad enough." He paused, thinking in the dark. And then he spoke up, "I think we need to find something she cares about."

Anna was very quiet, lying beside her husband. Waiting.

Finally Paul spoke. "Maybe I can take you and Sierra. We will go together, and I can watch over you."

She nodded and kissed him happily. Wrapping his arms around her, he said, "I love you, darn it, and I would die if you were hurt."

She nodded, knowing that he was doing everything he could to protect and provide for their family.

But out in the darkness, a lion prowled the earth. She too had to protect and feed her young. Her ribs were thin, for she gave everything to her hungry cubs. Her meal that she had worked so hard to take down had been interrupted. She needed meat and would not rest until she found it.

CHAPTER 4

Lure of Life

The goats were due to have their babies. They had been bred in October as the days were getting cool and the trees were turning orange. Today was five months exactly. Mama was ready. Billy and Caz were very excited because this was the first time they would be showing goats at the fair. Mama was going to help them pick out the best ones.

There were five goat nannies who were pregnant. Mama had the birthing basket ready with gloves, lubricant, and rags. This was in case they needed to step in and help. Most years the babies were born naturally, nursed on their own and began their first steps within moments. But sometimes a baby presented in the wrong direction, or a nanny got too tired and needed help. Even thought it was freezing outside, Mama slept with the window a tiny bit open and one ear alert. Sure enough, deep in the morning, before light, she heard the plaintive cry of a little one. She ran down the hall and cried, "The goats are having their babies!"

In a moment, everyone bolted out of bed, putting on jeans and boots and jackets. Rosie saw everyone getting ready and looked at Mama. Mama looked right back at her, challenging her, hoping that Rosie would join them. Rosie lowered her eyes, and for a moment Mama thought the look had been too much. Too much pressure. But then a movement and Rosie too was getting dressed. Mama smiled in the darkness. Out they went, each with a lantern in their hand.

The cold hit them and they sucked in their breath. There were mounds of snow piled in drifts as the wind had blown them. The stars were always brighter in the cold, and they winked in the night sky. They could see their breath and hurried to the barn.

They were glad for the warm protection of the barn. Jessica brought a bucket of warm water and molasses from the house—a fragrant drink for the nannies that would also give them much-needed sugar. Sierra and Billy dashed off to get flakes of rich alfalfa hay. The brand-new baby goat cried again in the night and a coyote howled far away in the mountains.

In the fresh straw there was a red-and-white-spotted nanny licking off a kid that had just been born. It was determined to stand on its wobbly legs while the nanny's harsh tongue invigorated and encouraged its movements. The kid was beautiful, with a deep red coat and bright white patches, like both his parents. The nanny stopped and began to circle, almost stepping on the kid. Rosie instinctively rushed in and moved it away. Everyone was focused on the birthing, but Mama noticed the movement in Rosie. A spark of life. Her love for the baby goats overcoming that awful, dull spirit.

The nanny stopped and pushed. They could see the dark bag begin to emerge and then slide in again. The nanny pushed again, and now they could see two tiny hooves inside the bag. But something was wrong. They all waited and held their breath. The nanny pushed again and this time they could see a little more—there were two hooves but no little face. The kid was presenting breech. Rosie started to move forward, anxious and worried. Mama touched her on the shoulder and said, "Give her a moment." Rosie nodded, understanding the intention, for they had been birthing goats together for as long as she could remember.

Rosie stood back and they all waited. The nanny pushed again, and in one gush, the kid came out. The nanny began to lick the thin, clear amniotic membrane off the face, and soon her baby was breathing, making sweet little sounds and working on standing. The nanny seemed at rest. Billy and Caz knelt in the thick straw and brought the babies' mouths to the teats full of warm colostrum. Soon the tails were wagging happily, which was the sign to all that the babies were nursing. The rich colostrum giving life and strength to those young bodies.

They found comfortable places to sit in the barn. They would wait a while and see if she had more babies and if she needed help. It was still early; the sun was not up and the other nannies were preparing for labor. Breakfast seemed a long way off and could just as easily take a moment to doze off. Mama sighed happily as she laid her head against the thick wood of the barn her husband had built. She treasured moments like these. The straw and wood gave a warmth and fragrance to the air and kept the chill of the morning outside. The nannies munched their hay and made pleasant sounds as their bodies prepared, for they were waiting too. The light from the lantern cast a warm glow, softening features and illuminating her circle of children and their happy faces. Rosie's face was calm and attentive. It was the first time Mama had seen her like this and her heart swelled with happiness. And hope.

As they sat and watched, two more nannies gave birth without a problem. One of them had triplets and the other had a pretty set of two. They heard another cry from a young brown doe, and they looked at each other, chuckling at how fast the babies were being born. But this was how birthing day went, for the buck had covered the girls in one day and so they would all give birth on the same day. There were two more nannies left to give birth.

They chatted happily, trying to guess what color the new babies would be. Jessica and Sierra talked about past births. Jessica said, "Remember the baby that we thought would die, and all we could do was put her by the fireplace to stay warm?"

Sierra responded, "Yes, and after delivering two more goats, we came back and she was standing and ready to nurse?"

Billy asked them all, "Remember the time when we came home from Mass and all five nannies had given birth?"

They smiled in the soft light, warm memories keeping them company and binding them together as a family. Rosie, however, stayed in the shadows, wrapped in silence, her eyes large and luminous. She could watch the goats as well but could not enjoy the sharing of memories.

The red-and-white nanny began pushing out her third baby. They could see two little hooves and a nose first, so they tried to let nature take its course. The brown doe cried out again. This was her first birthing, and she was having a hard time. They could see she was pushing and nothing was coming out, so Rosie went and got the gloves and the lubricant. There was a moment where Mama's eyes met hers, a moment of peace and hope and goodness. And then the crying doe. Mama nodded. Now was the time.

Rosie had the smallest hands, and she was very careful about not hurting the mother. She put on the gloves, rubbing lubricant into the fingers, and carefully slid her hands into the nanny. With the next push, Rosie was there, helping. Guiding. Pulling ever so gently. The baby goat was tangled with her brother and Rosie carefully and quickly untangled legs and helped bring out that new kid. The baby fell to the ground and the mama goat began to lick it, encouraging the new kid to stand. She was brown like her mama, but with a stripe on her side. The baby was coughing and sputtering. Sierra helped wipe off the nose and mouth but still the baby began to wheeze and sputter. Before anyone could praise Rosie for helping the nanny with her babies, they realized the baby was starting to go limp and cold, for it could not get any oxygen.

Mama knew what to do. She went out into the middle of the barn, where it was wide open and there was no chance of hitting anything. She grabbed the baby by the back legs with one hand and with the other, supported the body. Then she spun in a circle. The centrifugal force pulled the mucus from deep in the lungs out through the nose and mouth. Mama stopped spinning the baby, and still the baby coughed and wheezed. She did it again, but this time when she stopped spinning, the coughing and wheezing had stopped. Soon that baby was up, standing with her mother and nursing happily, her tail wagging. Everyone breathed in relief.

Now, the doe was pushing again. She was having more trouble and Rosie put on new gloves and lubricant and helped again. The next, who had been tangled with its sister, was tail first. He was brown with white hooves. They helped clean the baby and brought it to his mother to nurse. Within moments, a third baby was born, with bright red spots like his sire, but this one was born healthy and strong and all on its own. Dawn was well on its way; through the windows of the barn they could see the sky turning beautiful shades of pink, rose, and yellow. Everyone looked at each other, happy, tired, and hungry.

"What a morning!" cried Sierra.

And before another word could be said, the last nanny began to push. They all laughed for the craziness of it—so many babies born in just a few hours! She delivered two babies without incident, both white, and then began to push again. A third baby, red with a white stripe on its side, was born and began nursing. The fourth baby was a big male with a red head and white body. Thank goodness he was born easily and that the young mother had four happy, hungry babies fighting for her milk.

They stopped and counted the frisky little babies, now all standing and trying to hop in the thick straw. Fifteen! They were so many colors, with thick, rich fur and little tails that wagged as they drank milk. Rosie stood with them, looking with pride and love at the kids she had helped bring into the world.

They discussed which ones had the best conformation. The first one born, with bright red spots, was big and strong and also very flashy looking. Caz chose him and everyone agreed it was a good choice and would get the judge's attention. Billy took a long time and finally chose the last one born, the red-headed baby. He was big and stocky as well. They had high hopes for the babies this year at the fair. Seeing them nurse and hop around, the mothers munching their hay, full of contentment, everyone felt it was a morning well done.

Mama said happily, "Let's get cleaned up and get some breakfast!"

They walked together to the house, the sun now bright on the horizon, the piles of snow sparkling and winking in the morning light.

They all hustled inside, leaving boots and jackets in the front entryway in a happy mess. They headed to the sink, washing off all the traces of birthing. Jacob surprised them with breakfast—scrambled eggs, bacon, and toast from Jessica's homemade bread. Papa had started the coffee, and the house was rich with the smell of good food, sweat, and hay. Everyone talked at once, telling Papa of the births. Papa smiled at his beautiful family, and Mama read clearly the look of love directed at her. Yes, life was good. For a moment Rosie and her deafness had been overlooked by most.

It was only Papa who noticed that in the chaos and excitement of the moment Rosie was quiet and had become withdrawn. There was no place for her in all those words and expressions of joy and happiness. No room for her to tell how she had helped the goats give birth. And even though her heart also was filled with joy, in the loss of expression she retreated into her own eternally quiet place.

That night Paul and Anna talked about Rosie. Anna told him again about how Rosie had helped the goats give birth. Paul was quiet for a moment and then said, "Anna, she needs to start talking. There is no reason she cannot talk. I know her voice will sound strange, but she should be talking." He paused for a long time and then said, "I miss her voice. She was always so full of joy." And then he spoke very quietly. "I feel like my heart closed when she stopped talking. I try. I try very hard not to blame God."

Anna lay in bed quietly. She could hear the bitterness in his voice, understood the battle he fought just to keep his faith. And, more importantly, she knew he was speaking more to himself and to God than to her. She lay beside him, praying for him quietly, letting him know she was there.

CHAPTER 5

Cool, Clear Water

May came bright and warm. Anna woke up with the sun, renewed with energy and hope. She stretched in the warm sunlight and thought, "Susan will be here on Friday. Just five days and I'll have all my children home under one roof!"

With a happy heart, she gave herself the luxury of looking out the bedroom window and enjoying God's splendor. It was a beautiful morning, with the clouds tinged in rose and the sun filling up the earth. She stretched in bed for just a moment longer then got out of bed and dressed. She went into the kitchen to make breakfast and saw Paul had not left yet. He was filling a mug with coffee and preparing to go out. He kissed her and said, "Let's schedule the branding for next week. Can you call everyone? The ground is dry and it's warm enough and it will be great to have Susan here."

Anna nodded. "It will be nice to ride with Susan again. It feels like it's been a long school year with her gone."

"Yes ma'am. It will be great to ride together again," Paul said before chuckling. "She's a pretty good hand, like her mother."

Anna kissed him, but then said, "Well, that's good because I'll need to stay home with Rosie."

Paul was quiet. They would have this conversation later—now was not the time. He leaned in to kiss her goodbye. "I'll see you tonight, my love. Have a good day."

He walked out of the house, but just before closing it, Paul popped his head back in the door and said, "Oh, can you take Pilgrim and Apache out on a ride with the boys and warm them up?" She smiled at him and nodded.

Sierra and Jessica started breakfast and Jacob came out declaring, "Susan is coming home at the end of the week!"

Billy and Caz erupted in shouts of joy and started a silly dance. Jessica and Sierra turned to each other, grinning. They had all been counting the days. They loved Susan and missed her. She was like a second mother to them, always kind and helpful, with good ideas of fun things to do.

Mama laughed at Billy and Caz's reaction and said, "After breakfast, we are going to finish chores and get our school done for the year."

She turned to Rosie, sitting at the table, withdrawn and dull. Rosie had not been counting the days, for she had lost too much time being sick. She wrote on a chalkboard for Rosie, "Susan is coming in five days. We will finish school today." She held it up for Rosie to see.

Rosie looked away. She was angry. Her days felt dark and lonely, and she did not know how to find hope or strength. She had moments of happiness, but the silence suffocated them like overgrown weeds in a garden. She did not know how to overcome the awful silence, the awful inability to connect. She felt small and helpless and all the attempts with the chalkboard made it worse. It made her feel like she was in a strange, funny house, like the ones at the fair with warped mirrors. And so she deliberately ignored the chalkboard and looked away. It did not matter that Susan was coming home. Nothing would be the same and nothing mattered.

But that turning away was a new reaction and not lost on Mama. She realized in that moment that Rosie was being obstinate. This was new. It was willful and an entirely different kettle of fish, for Mama understood stubborn. She put the thought aside to contemplate later and, turning to the others, said, "All right, let's work hard. We are so close, we can finish today."

A cry of joy erupted from everyone. They had not only been counting the days for Susan to come home but also counting the days for school to be finished. No one wanted to do school when Susan was home, so if they worked hard her arrival marked the beginning of summer. They hustled to get their schoolbooks and sat at the table.

Everyone paused and quieted as Mama started with a prayer. "Come, Holy Spirit, fill the hearts of the faithful."

The children responded, "And enkindle in us the fire of your divine love."

And in a moment, schoolbooks were opened and pencils grabbed like swords ready to go to battle. Mama looked around the table, pleased with her children. They were good students and hard workers with different strengths and weaknesses. She loved teaching them, loved to see how their minds worked, and loved discussing things until their eyes lit up with understanding. She always tried to encourage young mothers to homeschool, telling them, "If you love teaching your child to walk, how much more will you love teaching your child to know and to think?"

Looking at Rosie, she thought, *And you, my dear, will be a very different challenge.*

"I think we were discussing St. Paul when he said we have to run the good race," Jessica said then, interrupting her mother's thoughts. Anna turned and looked at Jessica, as though she was reminded of a truth.

"Hmm, yes. Running the good race." Mama then read two scriptures out loud.

"'Therefore, since we are surrounded by so great a cloud of witnesses, let us rid ourselves of every burden and sin that clings to us and persevere in running the race that lies before us while keeping our eyes fixed on Jesus, the leader and perfecter of faith.' That is Hebrews twelve, verses one and two.

"'However, I consider my life worth nothing to me, if only I may finish the race and complete the task the Lord Jesus has given me—the task of testifying to the gospel of God's grace.' That is from Acts twenty twenty-four.

"Who can tell me about the cloud of witnesses?" she asked after a moment.

Billy spoke up and said, "They are the saints that are in heaven who help us."

Caz, not to be outdone, said, "And our guardian angels."

Mama smiled and nodded. She knew very well that they were all being helped and encouraged by that cloud of witnesses.

She asked, "And how do we rid ourselves of burden and sin?"

Sierra looked up, "Confession. By the way, when are we going to confession? I need to go."

There was a modest nodding of heads around the table.

"We will go this Friday," Mama said. "I need to go too."

With that everyone sighed. Renewal and help were on the way. Sins forgiven. Sins of anger and despair. Sins

Echoes of Silence

of pride and lack of charity. These were common in all families, for sacrifice and kindness are needed for a home to run peacefully. But God in his mercy welcomes all his children and forgives them. Giving them each the grace to start fresh and begin new.

"All right then, this afternoon I want each of you to write something on those two quotes. Jacob and Jessica, I would like two pages with cross-references from other sources. Sierra, you can write two paragraphs. Billy and Caz, you will copy the Bible quotes."

She then wrote on the chalkboard for Rosie, "Please copy this Bible phrase," and tried to decide how and if she would enforce it. School with Rosie was not going well at all.

"Okay, let's go on to your math assignments."

Everyone pulled out their books. Most of them could learn the lesson on their own and only needed to ask questions once in a while. Mama took out her knitting and began to knit. The rhythmic click-clap of the needles brought a soothing sound to the children as they worked on their problems. Mama was pleased to see Rosie working, chewing on her pencil and writing. She breathed deeply, thankful for that little bit of progress. Mama relaxed in her rocking chair and began to daydream.

MAMA SMILED AS SHE REMEMBERED A DAY OF HOME-schooling. *The children were younger.*

"Let's see," she thought, "Jessica was twelve, so that was four years ago. It was a different time back then; Susan was home and sixteen years old. Jacob had been as mischievous as ever as a fourteen-year-old, and Billy and Caz were only four and two. How could time have gone by so quickly?"

She remembered she had been teaching Jacob algebra. It was so different from addition and subtraction, and the unknown numbers were confusing him. He was so practical. He kept asking what the x was for, not settling for an unknown quantity.

Mama laughed just a bit, and everyone turned and looked. They saw their Mama, with soft eyes and a smile on her face, knitting needles turning and clacking away. It was comforting to see her at peace, with a smile, and so they stayed quiet and enjoyed the moment. Rosie saw them all turn to their Mama, and she turned too, for once out from under their gaze. Looking at her Mama, free from pain, gave her such immense relief that she sighed deeply, and her body relaxed. Sierra heard the sigh and she too sighed. Jessica started to hum a beautiful chant, and Jacob's deep voice joined her. Just like that a wave of happiness surrounded the family, that deep breath from Rosie causing an echo of peace from one to the next.

Mama noticed none of this and continued in her daydream.

Jessica, she remembered, had slipped out while she was working with Jacob. She had gone to the window and looked out and saw Jessica head out to the horses. She watched as Jessica took Apollo and put a simple rope halter on him. Many years ago, she had rescued and trained Apollo. He was an orphaned and wild colt, but with her patience and training he had turned into a wonderful horse, even if he was still a bit wild. Mama smiled, watching him stand quietly and patiently, his fire controlled.

As Jessica led him around the house, Sierra and Rosie came up to her.

"Watcha doing?" said then-six-year-old Rosie in a small, sweet voice.

"I'm riding out back."

"Can I come too?" asked Rosie while Sierra looked on with big eyes, wanting to come as well.

"Sure," Jessica said with an excited smile. "I'll help you get on."

Jessica reached out to tiny Rosie, who half-climbed and was half-lifted onto the back of the patient horse. Mama could only smile as Apollo, who had caused so much trouble, stood quietly with half-closed eyes. Now Sierra wanted to get on too.

"Let's see," thought Mama, "Sierra would have been eight."

Sierra didn't want to pull off Rosie, so she went and got a lawn chair and used it to climb up the side of the horse.

She watched from the window, hand over her mouth, as Sierra balanced on the arm of the lawn chair and, with the help of the other two girls, climbed upon the back of the waiting horse, not even flinching when the chair fell over just as Sierra stepped off.

Successfully nestled on his broad back, the three of them had gone down the hill while Apollo stepped as carefully and gingerly as he could, carrying his precious cargo. That same horse had once been out of his mind with fury and fear, and there he was carrying her three girls as though his life depended on it.

THINKING BACK, MAMA WONDERED WHAT ADVENTURE they had had that day. Wondered what school had not been done. And knew it all didn't matter. That adventure was like gold in their souls.

Sierra broke Mama's reverie, slamming her pencil on the table and breaking it. "I hate algebra! I just don't understand why x's and y's can't be combined!"

Mama came over to her and explained how it worked and they worked through the problems together. When they were done, Mama said, "Look, it's okay you don't understand. But you can't just fall apart when things don't go your way."

Sierra glared at her and went back to her math. Mama shook her head and thought, *That girl has got to get her emotions under control.*

Mama went over to Jessica to see how her math was going. Her paper was perfect, with straight lines of figures and numbers written in such exactness that the page was actually beautiful. But only a few problems had been finished. Mama thought about what to say and finally said, "You are doing a beautiful job, Jessica. Just don't forget that you need to finish the problems by the end of the day." Jessica nodded silently.

The boys had scrawled figures in wild lines, but they were doing their problems correctly. And Mama thought, *Oh, if only they had some of Jessica's form.* She showed them on a scratch paper how to line up their numbers and the boys looked on with sincerity. However, it would be some time before they could master the control not only of the pencil but of their minds.

Mama took a breath and went to look at what Rosie was doing. For the past three months, she had done nothing. Every day, Mama was faced with a blank page and soulless eyes. But today! Today Rosie was doing her math! Mama's heart quickened for it was fair and honest work. Mama put her hand on Rosie's shoulder to encourage her. Rosie jumped, for she had not heard Mama and was focused on her math book. But Mama's hand stayed quiet on her shoulder and at last could feel Rosie relax into it. Mama smiled and nodded, and Rosie understood that Mama was pleased.

Finally, they broke for lunch. Sandwiches were made and devoured and everyone begged for a break outside. It was a lovely day, and they all decided to go to the river and do their reading there. Many a book had been lost or ruined by a day on the river, but what did it matter? God had provided such beauty, there was no point in wasting it. They packed up some snacks, schoolwork, towels, and water. And off they went. A parade of love. Billy and Caz found sticks and began to battle, the sticks making sharp sounds in the quiet air. Birds singing, Jessica humming, Sierra pointing out the butterflies. Rosie walking beside Mama, reaching out and taking her hand. Jacob, caring the bulk of the goods, knowing he would miss these adventures in a way he could barely express. It was a little parade; down the hill and around the grove of cottonwood trees, the hills rolling away from them, the sky bright and blue with soft clouds. Dragonflies dodging around like flashes of light, catching bugs and lighting up the air with color.

They arrived at their favorite place. They called it Sweetwater because the water was sweet and clear. There were little gold flecks that had fallen amongst the rocks at the bottom, and they liked to think the sweetness was from the gold. It was a part of the river that ran behind the house, where water spilled into a natural basin of rock and the water was deep. The sunlight cast streaks of light through the water, lighting up the shiny, smooth rocks below. Reeds grew along the edge of the river, softening the sunlight. There was a sandy beach where they tossed their towels, placed the chairs and unloaded their snacks. They ran for the cool water, diving in enjoying how its coolness contrasted with the warm sun. Mama sat back in her chair, watching her children splash and play like so many bright fish. They were all natural swimmers, with strong backs and sinewy arms. Jessica splashed Sierra, then Sierra threw herself at Jessica and down under the water they both went, tanned arms and legs flying above. The two came up for air, grinning broadly. Jacob got into a wrestling match with Billy. Caz, determined to free his brother, climbed on Jacob's broad back, causing them all to tumble into the water.

Rosie sat with Mama on the shore, quietly watching. She was thinking about the water. And Mama was thinking about Rosie. Seeing Rosie deliberately turn away was the first indication that Rosie was aware. She had also started doing her math. It was her first real glimmer of hope that Rosie's brain was healing. Now they just needed to figure out how to break through her willfulness. Maybe she was scared. Or stubborn. Or who knew what else. But the brain was in fact healing and that was a much better scenario. Mama's mind began to turn as she contemplated this new perspective. She was filled with excitement and could not wait to tell Paul!

So, when someone splashed Mama, she jumped and, with a twinkle in her eye, rushed into the water and began splashing everyone. Billy and Caz jumped on her and then

Jacob tried to pry them off. Mama fell into the water and came up laughing. Deep belly laughs echoed in the canyons around them. Everyone started to laugh with her, and Sierra and Jessica now jumped on her as well. Mama, who was usually so kind and gentle, became fierce as she fought everyone off. Everyone began to laugh and shout in glee as they fell in and out of the water. They had not seen Mama have fun like this for a very long time.

Rosie watched, torn between wanting to go in and be a part of things, but scared of the silence and the sudden movements. While everyone was laughing, she walked up the river a bit. Mama noticed but did nothing, playing with the children, yet watching Rosie out of the corner of her eye

Rosie walked to the water's edge. The water was quiet here and protected by rocks. She stepped into the water. It was cool and clear and felt wonderful. She looked at her toes wiggling in the soft sand and clear water. She saw the ripple of her toes spread out upon the water. It reminded her of when she and Papa had sent echoes across the canyon. She tried to remember what he had told her.

"The little thing made great by God."

Her eyes softened and a smile played around her face, the memory of her father and his sweetness lightened her sorrow just a bit. But it was the memory of what he had said to her that tugged at her mind like an answer trying to be found. And that little puzzle wore away at her anger, just a bit, like water wearing away at a rock. She stepped out of the water and joined her Mama, now sitting in the chair and drying in the warm sun.

At last, Mama said it was time to go. As they all gathered to leave and began the walk back home, Rosie realized that her anger was not quite so consuming. She remembered how excited she had been about the wild horses, and now she wanted to know more. What she did not realize was that the swelling in her brain was subsiding and with that she was not only able to think more clearly but also to take some control of her emotions and her thoughts as well. Walking home as evening brushed the land, there was a new feeling in her heart. She had hope that there was an answer to her dilemma, and that if she just looked hard enough, she would find it.

CHAPTER 6

Together at Last

Today was the day! The long-awaited day. Susan was coming home from college for the summer. The house was full of excitement and preparation. Rooms were being cleaned and organized to make a place for the oldest sister. She had been missed—her smile, her take-charge attitude, her calm in the face of the storm. She was always the one to make up games to play or tell stories. And oh how Mama had missed Susan playing the piano while Jessica sang along.

Lookouts needed to be posted so that they could let everyone know when Susan's car was coming down the drive. Mama decided that Billy and Caz would do it, mostly because they were getting underfoot and making a mess.

Mama quickly organized tasks. She and Sierra would work in the kitchen, cleaning and making dinner. Jessica would be in charge of making Susan's bed and cleaning the room they would be sharing. Mama, with her new insight, deliberately handed Rosie a tray of silverware and told her to set the table. Even without the words, the intention was clear. To Mama's surprise, Rosie simply nodded and began to set the table. Mama stood and watched while Rosie's back was to her. It was good. Rosie was helping and that was new.

Mama went around the house to make sure everything was in order. She stopped at the door of the girls' room and watched Jessica. The room was far from finished.

"Why isn't this done?" Mama asked.

"I've been working on it," Jessica defended herself weakly.

"Jessica, you need to learn to work more efficiently and with more determination. Now hurry up. We want Susan to feel welcome and she will be here very soon."

Jessica worked more quickly, but even as she did she grumbled under her breath, "Why should I work quickly? What is wrong with slow and steady?"

Suddenly the dogs started to bark and the boys started to yell, and before anyone needed to announce it at all everyone knew that Susan was coming up the drive. Rosie watched from the window inside the house. She was scared that Susan would not love her. Scared of what Susan would think of her. A tear filled her eye and slowly fell down her cheek. If she could have run away, she would have. She did not want to go outside, so she just stood in the doorway and watched.

Susan slowed the car and took a deep breath. She would not have admitted it, but despite her excitement she was feeling dread. She wondered what Rosie would be like. Would she look different? Would she act much different? She prayed for courage, squared her shoulders, and got out of the car. She was immediately met by three dogs and two brothers who nearly knocked her over with their joy. She looked up and saw Mama and Papa standing there, looking pleased and proud. They each hugged Susan happily.

Sierra came running from the barn to hug her sister, her brown eyes filled with happiness and gratitude. A warm hug was given and received, and both sisters looked at each other. Susan seemed older and calmer, Sierra seemed on edge and a little ragged. Susan thought, *It must have been hardest on her, Sierra and Rosie had been inseparable.*

Jessica came out of the house, having just finished the beds. Susan rushed to her and gave her a hug. Jessica was older, more mature, with bright green eyes and long brown hair. Susan couldn't help but notice she was becoming a lovely girl. Jacob also came out from the barn, and right away she noticed the change in him. He seemed taller and stronger, but also more resolved. His jaw was firm, and his eyes steady. She could only guess how hard it had been to take care of the family while Mama and Papa were in the hospital with Rosie. It was the first time she really thought of him as a man. It seemed strange to think this about her younger brother.

Finally, Susan looked up for Rosie and saw her standing in the shadow of the doorway. Susan was sick with grief. Who was this sister? The old Rosie would have bounded down the steps and thrown herself into Susan's arms. Her pink cheeks and flashing blue eyes would have sparkled with excitement and joy. She would have been telling stories a mile a minute even as she was running out the door. But this Rosie only stood there looking lost and silent. Tears came to Susan's eyes, and everyone noticed. Mama smiled at her, demanding courage, for courage would be needed. Papa's eyes grew resolute as he said, "We have a room waiting for you, and Mama cooked a fine meal for us. Afterward, we will show you a new little surprise in the barn."

In the kitchen there was a symphony of activity. Everyone but Rosie was in the kitchen at the same time, cooking, preparing, and cleaning. Papa put on some music and Mama gave out orders like a conductor.

"Papa, can you check the meat? Jacob, get those dishes washed. Jessica, finish the cake. Sierra, work on the salad. Billy, dry the dishes for Jacob. Caz, help cut up vegetables."

Papa checked on the meat and declared it was ten minutes to dinner time. There was a hum in the air as everyone worked, almost dancing around each other in a well-known pattern of movement. Rosie sat watching everyone, starting once again to retreat into herself. Susan, seeing this, handed her a vase and a loose bunch of flowers that Jessica had picked. The intention was clear, and Rosie began working with the flowers, the aromatic bloom filling the air and light filling her soul. Yes, it was good to have Susan home.

Over dinner there was the excited exchange of stories. Talking about the wild horses and the baby calf. Asking about old friends. Asking about new friends. Mama and Papa watching their daughter, now a young woman, almost finished with college. Rosie sat and watched and then retreated. Susan noticed and did not know what to do. Mama noticed and did not know what to do. Papa noticed and his jaw flexed anxiously. But everyone else was just glad Susan was home and they were all together again. It was a feeling of completeness and security and maybe everything would be all right.

At last, Papa finished eating and sat back, enjoying his family together around the table. He said, "I'm glad you are home Susan; we need your help. We are branding and castrating next week and we will need to bring in the herd from the high pasture."

Susan smiled happily. She loved bringing the cattle in, riding the land far and wide, and bringing them all to the holding pen. She loved seeing the new babies hop and jump with their gangly legs and sweet faces. The wildflowers were out now, and all the world was fresh and green. After the cattle were collected, sorting, branding, and castrating were next. It was a long day of work, but everyone worked together—horses, men, women, and even the ranchers' children. It was like a well-oiled machine. These ranchers had been working cattle since they were children and so everyone understood what to do. The horses were cow-smart and understood how to dance around a young, spirited calf, sometimes kicking and leaping in the air. Afterward, the women put on a bounty of food. Everyone had an appetite and ate and talked happily. It was a time of community and hard work. It was a time that united them together and forged bonds that would last generations. Susan was proud to be a part of the ranchers' life and hoped she could continue to live like this, raising her children to throw a rope, ride a horse, and sing songs while the coyotes howled to the moon.

The family was in good spirits as they did the dishes together. Papa put on some music and, taking Mama's hands, soapy and wet, he started to dance around the kitchen with her. A slow, gentle waltz. At first, she resisted him, her mind still on the dishes, but his hands were strong and guided her gently around the room. As they circled in the kitchen, her body relaxed into his and her eyes softened. The children stopped what they were doing and watched, mesmerized. Papa whispered something in Mama's ear, and she threw back her head and laughed with sparkling eyes. She moved easily with him, and the kitchen melted away.

Jacob watched and murmured something he had heard. "Evil is thwarted by the love between husband and wife."

Susan watched them and thought about Joe, for she still had to tell the family about him. Jessica watched, enchanted and longing to find love. And, as for the youngest four, they felt happy, for within the arms of their parents' love, they knew they were protected and safe.

That night, they all gathered together for prayers. All nine of them in the living room, sitting on couches, on the floor, intertwined like a human wreath of love. Mama and Papa on the small couch, her body tucked close to his. Jacob, Billy, and Caz sat on the floor by the great fireplace. Susan sat with Rosie, Jessica, and Sierra on the couch, and they curled into each other, arms and legs wrapped. Rosie sighed, a deep and profound sigh. For that act of love and sisterhood made her feel connected and loved. Mama heard the sigh and looked at Papa. Papa had not seen it or heard it, but he saw Mama's look and he too relaxed, almost imperceptibly. And slowly a ripple of peace went around the room like a silent wave of hope.

After prayers, everyone sat quietly in the room by the fire. Its embers glowed softly, and Rosie's eyes started to flutter. She fell asleep, buried in that wreath of love. No one wanted to leave, they wanted to just stay there. Papa put another log on the fire, and they watched dreamily as the flames burst into strength and light filled the room.

Susan said, "Tell us the story about Apollo, Mama."

Everyone chimed in and said, "Oh yes! Tell us a story!"

And Mama, feeling happy, began to tell one of her favorite stories. "Once upon a time…"

Billy and Caz made a bed of blankets and pillows and promised themselves they would not succumb to Mama's rhythmic voice and enchanting storytelling. Jacob leaned back against the couch and closed his eyes. He didn't like to admit it, but he too loved Mama's stories.

"There was a fierce and glorious mare, she was the color of nutmeg, and the heat of ginger…she was pure air and fire."

Jacob mused, "From Shakespeare." And Mama nodded.

"She gave birth to a beautiful golden colt. He was the color of the sun and just as strong and wild as his mama. He lived in a herd that traveled all through a vast land of grass and fresh water. It was a good life. He fought with the other colts, and they frolicked in the water and ran races in the tall grass. But one day, a terrible thing happened. A mountain lion, hungry and needing to feed her babies, jumped from a high rock, landing on his mother. She was taken down instantly. The herd took off running. The young colt was confused. Should he stay with his mother or run with the herd? She gave one last look at him as she lay there dying and nickered at him. But he did not understand that she wanted him to flee with the herd.

"When she finally stopped moving, he turned to look, and his herd had gone. He wandered the hills looking for the herd but could not find them. He came upon another herd, but they rejected him. He had grown too strong and was a threat to the stallion leading them. He was cast out, alone and very afraid. He became more and more wild, having to protect himself from predators and run from anything he could not fight.

"One day, he wandered into thick woods looking for grass and stepped in between two logs. One of them rolled, just enough to trap him. He panicked and tried his best to escape, but the log was too heavy, and he could not free himself. He was alone, away from water, and there was no food near him. He knew he was going to die.

"Just then a young girl came upon him. He did not know if she was a predator, so he thrashed and screamed at her. 'Get away! I will kill you!' But she saw that his leg was trapped and saw the dried blood from the wound it had made. She came to him softly, quietly, whispering. He did not understand. She was different from anything he knew. He stopped thrashing and stood quietly, shaking in fear. She came closer and brought her face close to his. He closed his eyes and breathed in her breath. It was good and sweet. She breathed in his breath, and he felt close to her. Then she reached out to rub his neck and sweet memories of his mama grooming him filled his heart. His body relaxed and he sighed.

"She worked to free him. His leg was not broken, and he found he could walk. Not knowing what else to do, he followed her, trusting her. They came to a stream with some grass. He drank and ate greedily, for it had been a long time. She sat with him for the afternoon, sharing her apple with him. When she walked away, he did not know what else to do but follow her.

"She gave him a name, Apollo, and gave him a large pen with plenty of food and fresh water. He had other horses to run around with, and he thought he could be happy there. But, once in a while, he could hear wild herds of horses going by and his heart ached for his old life and for his mama.

"The girl spent many hours teaching him to walk with her, to take a bridle and finally to ride him. But he had a wild spirit deep in his veins. He tried his best to listen to her and do as she asked. Some days he could not, and he bucked and ran too fast. She worked hard with him, making the right thing easy and the wrong thing difficult. He loved her very much. When she had her own babies, she let him smell them and he kept a careful memory of each one. He did his best to protect each of her little ones, carrying them on his back and keeping them from danger.

"But the fire was hot in his veins, and he longed for the wild plains where he could run free. One day, he was out with her, and he saw a beautiful wild mare. He wanted to go to her, but the girl kept him away. He reared and bucked, arguing with her, but he finally settled down and walked away as she wished.

"The girl, you see, she knew. She saw. Every day he stood at the edge of his pen, looking for that mare. She ran by sometimes in a great herd of mares and Apollo called out to them. 'Take me with you!' But they did not stop. Apollo raced around his pen, looking for a weak rail, but the pen was made true and strong and so he was trapped. The girl saw his sadness. When they rode out together, Apollo did as he was asked. But when she was in the house, he longed to be free.

"One day, the fence broke. A tree fell onto the rail and suddenly he realized he could leave. The girl came out. He looked at the girl whom he had known for so long and who had saved his life long ago. Then he looked at freedom. He stayed out of love, but she could see the longing in his heart. She fixed the fence and he stayed.

"Seasons came and went and one day in the late spring, when the grass was long, and the wildflowers bright, a herd of mares came by and stopped by his pen for they had lost their stallion and could see in Apollo his strength and courage. The beautiful mare was with them. Apollo was all majesty and strength as he pranced around his pen. The woman saw this and her heart grew sad, she could see he wanted to go with them. Apollo had loved her and taken care of her for many years, and she decided it was time to set him free. So, while the herd was still there, she went out to him. She put a halter on him and led him out to the fields. The two of them walked together for the last time. He was excited about the mare but walked quietly with the woman he loved. Finally, she stopped, took the halter off him and with a last touch, she set him free. For a moment, he paused, his muscles bound, ready to run, but he put his head in her arms and breathed deeply her scent. And then he flew into the wild plains, joining the herd of mares.

"Every once in a while she saw him, surrounded by pretty, golden babies. She knew he was bringing them to her to show her. She knew he still loved her but was living the life he was meant to live.

"And…" Mama paused and looked around the room with a mischievous smile, "he lived happily ever after. The end."

Everyone clapped. They loved the story of the wild colt, but they loved the story even more because Mama did and that made them happy.

Papa said, "What a story you tell, Mama!"

Susan asked, "Would you ever let Apollo go wild again?"

Mama answered whistfuly, "I don't think so, but I see the look in his eyes sometimes and I wonder if he wants to go. I can always feel that he is still wild and behaves only because he loves me. But he is also getting old, and I don't know how long he would survive in the wild. It is fun to think about him running a herd of mares and making pretty golden babies."

They all sat there for a little while longer. Rosie, Caz, and Billy had all fallen asleep, for the night had grown long and the fire was now only embers. There, in the dying light of the fire, under the ancient cross, the little family sat, enjoying each other's company, enjoying the warmth, and enjoying being together at last.

CHAPTER 7

Inclement Wind

The next morning, Paul woke up Anna with a kiss. "Let's go on a sunrise ride."

She stretched, yawned, and smiled at him. "Yes! That sounds wonderful."

As she got dressed, Paul handed her what they called a Cowboy Sandwich—two pieces of toast, a fried egg, and some sausage. She took it one hand as he handed her a cup of coffee in the other.

"Let's go," he said. "Apollo and Bandit are saddled."

She smiled and kissed him, with egg still on her face. "My goodness, you are the dashing hero this morning!"

He smiled mischievously and they went outside into the cool night air and then into the barn. Finishing her coffee, Anna put the coffee cup down on an old worn table. She made a mental note to bring the growing collection of abandoned cups back into the house. Mounting the horses, they rode out just as the sun was touching the horizon.

The wind was fresh and cool, and the horses had a spring in their step. Out through the yard, past the gate, out into the open land, Anna burst into a fast gallop, her hair blowing out behind her. Paul laughed to himself and urged Bandit to catch them. Bandit was all brown and the girls made fun of him for looking boring, but Paul had not chosen him for his color. His horse had excellent cow sense, was easygoing, and had an incredible work ethic. But he was also fast, with a broad chest and piston-like legs. He surged after Anna and Apollo. And when Anna heard the pounding of hooves close to her, she turned and there was Paul with a grin a mile wide and flashing eyes. He passed her easily and she followed him, both their horses slowing now. They came to a rise and stopped, overlooking their vast land. The stars had slipped away now, and the sky was rosy and pink. The wind picked up and Anna turned to him, her chest heaving, her eyes sparkling, and her hair blowing loose around her face. Paul could not help himself. Pulling her close, he kissed her passionately. She fell into his arms, and both the horses had some work to do to keep their riders in the saddle.

They were quiet for some time, watching the sun rise, until at last he spoke. "I want you to come with us to bring the cattle in. I want all of us to go. This is what we do as a family."

She was silent and he watched her face, watched the anger tighten her jaw, watched her eyes narrow. He knew this was coming and it was why he had brought up the conversation like this: on horseback, out in the open. "What about Rosie?" was all she said in reply.

He responded in quick tones, trying his best to make her understand. "Listen. I know. But you have to understand that we can't put our lives on hold for her. I don't know if she still has swelling in her brain. I don't know if she can ever ride a horse. I don't know if she will learn sign language or try and talk to us. None of this I know. But we have our livelihood, our jobs, our ranch. I would like you to come with me and all the kids and Rosie needs to stay behind. Can you ask Abigail if she can stay with Rosie?"

Anna protested. "I told you I think the swelling in her brain is going away. I think she is being stubborn. Can't I work with her? Can we postpone it? Is there another option?"

Paul shook his head. "No, we need to bring the calves in before they get too big. We cannot bring Rosie. It is too dangerous right now. You know there is a risk of storms and flooding rivers. It's not the way to introduce Rosie back to riding. I want to do it in our yard when its quiet."

Anna was quiet. Over the years, she had been through some rough spring river crossings with the cattle. It made sense that this was not the time to see if Rosie had her balance back. Finally, she spoke, the words coming out slowly and painfully. "I know you are right." Then she said, "It just makes me sad to leave her behind." Before Paul could say anything more, she turned Apollo around and said, "Let's go home."

They rode the rest of the way in silence. Neither of them needed to say anymore. It hurt them both to leave Rosie behind.

They arrived home, unsaddled the horses and went into the house. Anna was quiet as she cooked breakfast. Papa announced that in two days they would be riding out to bring the cattle in. Everyone cheered. They loved going out as a family and bringing in the cattle. They loved sleeping overnight out under the open sky and cooking food in the Dutch ovens. Mama usually brought things for S'mores, and Papa made sure to pack good food.

Papa announced to the children, "Friday we will be bringing in the cattle." Everyone cheered."

Rosie just glared at him, furious that he had to communicate that way, furious that she was left behind, and furious that she could not hear the plans being made. She had always loved going out to bring the cows in and didn't understand why she was being left behind. She got up and walked to her room, slamming the door shut, taking satisfaction in the motion but hearing none of the sound. Mama sat very still, working hard to keep her emotions hidden. Papa got up and started on dishes. No one said a thing.

Mama spent the next day packing bags. They would borrow packhorses from Doug and Abigail. Luke Maverick and his son Cody were coming. Luke and his wife Carol were good friends of Paul and Anna, and Cody was Jacob's friend. Luke offered to bring a horse for Jacob and an extra horse in case something happened. Anna made sure they had full chaps and slickers to protect them from rain. She packed enough food for two days, bringing the Dutch oven for cooking over the open fire. She packed two tents—one for the girls and one for the boys—if it rained, but if it was clear then they liked to sleep out under the stars. She packed a change of clothing and a first aid kit.

Paul hooked up the horse trailer and that night Anna and Paul drove Rosie to Abigail's house. Rosie was sullen and quiet. When they arrived, Anna spoke with Abigail, thanking her profusely. How could she prepare Abigail for what it would be like to care for Rosie? But Abigail could see everything as soon as the threesome walked in the door. She had four daughters and understood moody and sullen. She hugged Anna and told her not to worry, it would be all right. Two of her daughters were Rosie's age and they would try and play with Rosie. If Rosie didn't want to play, well that was her choice too. Paul spoke with Doug, and they loaded the packhorses in the trailer. Anna did not want to leave. She went to Rosie and wrapped her in her arms. Then, pulling back, she looked her in the eye and said, "I love you." A tear formed in Rosie's eye and Anna carefully brushed it away. She wrote on the chalkboard, "I will be back in two days. You be good." Rosie nodded and Anna was thankful for that. Paul took her hand and Anna gave one last hug to Abigail and walked away, brushing the tears from her own face.

The next morning the family arose just as dawn was lighting the sky and saddled the horses. Papa packed the food, clothing, and camping gear for the packhorses. The two horses stood there quietly, with wooden frames like two x's on their backs. On the wooden frames, attached with straps, were large canvas bags. These bags would carry all their gear and food. Papa was thankful he could borrow those horses from Doug.

Luke came with his son Cody, a pack mule, and two extra horses as promised. Doug arrived with his horse dancing in excitement. It was young and still a little green. He traveled light, and so everything he needed was in packs tied to the back of his saddle. Two hired cowboys arrived, looking as rough and wild as the horses they rode in on. They traveled light as well and had their gear packed on their saddle. Paul had assured them he would bring enough food and supplies for everyone. It would only be one night out on the land, for it was all they needed to bring in the cattle.

Once the cattle were all gathered together in the home pen, Papa was going to tag and brand all the new babies and castrate the young bulls. It was a time for him to look at all his cattle, make sure they were doing well, tally the new babies, and start making decisions on which ones would go to market in the fall.

As last-minute packing was done, there was a lot of joking and laughing. For it was a time of camaraderie and the kind of challenges they all looked forward to—crossing riverbeds, searching for lost cattle, and sudden storms. These were the challenges they lived to overcome, these were the challenges that could be seen and controlled. It was the things they could not control that worried them, like the weather and cattle prices.

They rode out with the sky starting to turn pink and a brisk wind coming down from the mountain. Papa led the way. The morning felt fresh and clean, and everyone was in good spirits. Out past the stream they rode, past a beautiful glen of aspen, up around the bend where the land rose high and one could see for miles. Finally, they started to see groups of cattle, but they would ride to the farthest end of the property first and then start them all toward the house.

The hours went by peacefully and quietly. Billy and Caz playing games in the saddle. Sierra, Susan, and Jessica riding in a little group, talking and laughing. Papa came back and rode beside Mama. As they rode, Anna worried less about Rosie and started to relax. *He's right*, she thought. *This is our livelihood, this is what we do as a family. It's good for us to be doing this together, and Rosie will be okay with Abigail.* She prayed, "Please, Lord, let her have her balance and be able to ride with us. Please let her try and talk to us. Please help her to trust us and be willing to try. Please God, let her be okay."

Paul called for everyone to stop for lunch. Anna had made sandwiches, and though most had brought their own, Anna had enough for everyone to spare. She also brought dried apples from the cellar and some homemade cookies which were well received by everyone. Lunch was quick as they still had far to go. After lunch, Anna and the girls packed up and they were off again. They passed more groups of cattle and Paul made mental notes of how many he had seen and how many more remained. He noticed they were all huddled in tight groups under bluffs and below trees. Usually they would be scattered around, grazing. The wind felt strange to him, and he had a bad feeling about it. Paul rode over to Anna.

"We need to cross a river up here. I am going to check it out first. Just wait with the kids."

This river collected water from the surrounding high bluffs, and he knew this river could go from mild and sweet to a raging torrent in a matter of moments. He was worried about the rain he knew was coming. He looked up at the sky. It was clear and blue, but it was tomorrow that he was worried about. Paul studied the river and found a shelf in the earth where it was higher than the rest. The shelf was sturdy and so he had Anna and the boys cross first. Even as they did, Pilgrim stepped in deep sand and lost his footing for a moment and fell forward into the river. Caz lurched forward but stayed centered in the saddle as Pilgrim found better footing and continued across. Anna shuddered to imagine Rosie crossing the river. It was just too dangerous. She had been foolish to think this would be a good idea for Rosie's first ride, but it just broke her heart to leave her behind. As she watched the rest of the children cross, she was glad they had spent so many hours in the saddle, for they were able to help the horses navigate the rocks and sand and stay centered in the saddle when the horses took a misstep and stumbled.

As the sun was setting, they finally came to the end of the property which was cut off by a sheer wall of rock. There were two bluffs that perhaps had been one solid rock wall, but the wind and rain had long ago worn out a cleft between the two. The entrance was cut off of by falling boulders, and so the hundred or so cattle seeking protection from the wind stayed on the outside of the wall. This is where they would stop for the night. The wind was kicking up and the rock gave them some protection.

They tied up the horses to a rope tied between two trees and set up camp. The sky was clear, and everyone decided to sleep out under the stars, even Anna and the girls. They gathered wood and started a few campfires. Everyone brought their own food, but Papa had plenty to share. They cooked steak on an open grill and potatoes and vegetables in the Dutch oven.

As dinner cooked, Papa went to Anna and the kids. "Come here while it is still light. I want to show you something."

They followed him as he walked toward the cleft in the walls. They climbed over the boulders and found themselves looking up the side of the wall, about sixty feet tall. Papa pointed to man-made markings, some engraved and some painted. They looked very old and strange. Papa said, "I remember my grandpa telling me about these. He thought they were most likely carved by the Natives who lived here, maybe two hundred years ago, maybe a thousand years ago."

Sierra gasped and cried out, "A thousand years ago! That's amazing!"

Mama said, "Most likely still here because they are protected from the wind and the rain."

Papa nodded and told them solemnly, "Even though they are on our property, the drawings are not ours. They belong to a long-ago civilization, and we are the caretakers of them."

Anna and the children stood and looked at them, amazed. Susan and Jessica traced their fingers in the grooves. Some of them looked like animals and some looked like strange words. It was amazing to find this on their property, and they considered themselves blessed by the people that had lived there so long ago.

Finally, dinner was ready. As always, it tasted far better after a long day's ride, with the wind blowing warm and a sky full of stars. After dinner, Anna brought out the makings for S'mores and the men pulled out their flasks. Doug brought out a harmonica his father had given him. As they lay by the firelight, gazing up at the stars, Doug began a favorite Eddie Arnold tune, "Cattle Call," and everyone joined in, howling and yodeling, their voices echoing across the valley while coyotes joined in.

> *The cattle are prowling the coyotes are howling*
> *Way out where the doggies bawl*
> *Where spurs are a-jingling a cowboy is singing*
> *This lonesome cattle call*
>
> *He rides in the sun*
> *Till his days' work is done*
> *And he rounds up the cattle each fall*
> *Singing his cattle call*

The fire slowly died down to embers. The moon rose and tiredness overtook them all. They lay on their bedrolls and fell asleep looking at the vast heavens and wondering about the God that put them there.

In the middle of the night, the wind started to blow. They heard the sound of it before they registered what it was. It came roaring across the plains, throwing up against the wall. The horses pulled at their rope as dust rose up in great billows, and coffeepots, left on campfires, rolled across the dirt. Paul had only seen such severe wind gusts a few times in his life. He knew they could all fit, both horses and riders, in that cleft between the walls. Further back, it actually became a cave as the two bluffs ran together. He ran to get Anna and the children and brought them in. The men followed him without words, for the wind was so loud he could not shout above it. The horses wanted nothing with the wind, so as they were led over the boulders, they slid and climbed willingly. The cows were happy enough pressed up against the shadow of the wall, lying down, lowering their center of gravity. They knew the weather and how to make it through. After everyone was safely between the walls and protected from the terrible wind, Paul walked back to Anna and helped her settle in. They had a lantern so they could see in the dark.

Suddenly Sierra shouted, "Look at the drawings! They seem like they are moving with the lantern's light."

The family stopped and looked. Some of the drawings showed up in bright relief with the light and the shadows. Then Jacob pointed and said, "A cross! Just like the one in our house."

Everyone turned and looked. It was indeed the same unique shape. It could only be seen, now, from the light and the darkness converging in that place. Jacob was quiet, for it inflamed a yearning in his heart that he was trying to discern.

Before anyone could respond, the wind picked up with a frightening sound, howling around them like a great lion trying to take everything with it. They prayed that the rest of the cattle had found places to protect themselves.

Paul understood now why he had seen them collected in the protection of bluffs and trees. Paul found out later the wind gusts that night topped seventy miles an hour. But the family was safe between those two great walls of rock. And there, once again, under the protection of the cross, the little family huddled down, said their prayers, and fell asleep. Finally, around six in the morning, the wind stopped, and it was silent outside. There was a collective breath from the group, not even realizing the burden of the wind's howling.

As daylight dawned, they could see the skies were dark and foreboding. That wind had brought in very heavy storm clouds. Paul spoke to the men. "It looks like we are going to be hit badly. We need to get across that river before the storm hits."

They had all been thinking the same thing and were working quickly to pack up. They stowed everything away in the canvas bags, placing tarps over them, lacing them down tightly. It would do no good to have them flapping in the wind. They put on their slickers and cinched everything down tight. As they mounted their horses, Paul gave instructions. "Anna, take Sierra, Jessica, and the two boys and watch out for runaway cattle. I hope there is no thunder. The last thing we need is a stampede. Jacob and Susan, you ride with Luke. Cody and Doug on the other side. The hired hands will be in the back, and the rest of us will ride out front."

Everything packed and secured, they urged the hundred or so cattle hunched against the wall to start moving out. It was some doing to convince them to move, but they finally managed with a lot of calls and smacks of the lasso. As they started across the broad valley, they picked up the stray groups of cattle who were happy to join the group. They looked like they had a rough night, but none of them had been hurt. They became a long slow train of cattle with riders on either side turning back any cows that bolted. Fortunately, the wind had died down. Paul urged everyone forward. He wanted to get across that river before it rained. They all had the same thought, and they pushed the cattle as fast as they could. They made it to the river just as it started to rain.

Every man there knew what was at stake, they knew the capacity of that river. It was a large group that needed to make it across and everyone was worried the water would rise quickly. Paul sent Anna and the children across first. Already the river was getting swollen. Pilgrim and Apache, carrying Caz and Billy, went first. To the boys, the river did not look much different than yesterday except that it was a little higher, but Papa knew better. Trusting their papa, they urged the horses forward. As they crossed the deepest part, the cold water reached up to their legs, pulling at them as it rushed past. But the horses were strong and forged forward. They made it across safely. Anna breathed a sigh of relief, thankful that Rosie was not with them. She and the girls were next, but Apollo, Ginger, Rain, and Dash, carrying Mama and the three girls, were young and very strong. They surged across quickly, lunging over the stones and jumping through the water. The girls sat their horses well and so helped the horses across.

The rain was coming down heavy now and everyone could barely see. Mama and the kids stood on the other side of the creek, praying and trying to hide beneath their slicker hoods. It was cold and windy, and everything was wet.

The men all hollered and pushed the cows across as the river became more swollen and more angry. They shouted at the cows while the horses tossed their heads and stamped their feet pushing at the cows. As the last of the cows made it across, Doug, Luke, and Cody brought up the rear. They had very good horses who carefully worked their way through the fast-moving water. At the deepest part, the horses had to swim. The men clenched their jaws against the bitter cold, hung on to the horses, and willed them across. Suddenly, everyone on shore started to shout. A large log was coming down the river, bumping and being carried by the white water. Doug and Luke just made it to shore, but Cody was the third and the log was headed straight toward him. Cody saw the log and urged his horse forward, but in his excitement, he became reckless. He leaned forward, and that sudden change of balance was too much in the fast-running stream. His horse stumbled. Just as he did, the log hit him and his horse, knocking the two of them over. Doug and Luke were on shore now and Luke threw a rope to his son. It went straight to Cody. He reached up and managed to grab it and they pulled him out. As he climbed up on shore Luke ran to him. "Are you hurt?"

Cody shook his head. "I'm fine."

The horse was another story.

Sierra gasped and said to Jessica, "Oh! I hope they can help Buckeye get out."

Mama looked at Sierra severely as if to say "Quiet."

Buckeye went downstream for a ways, fighting and struggling against the water, looking for a foothold. They knew that the horse would have to find footing himself. They could not help him. The water was too fast and there was too much debris to throw a rope. Everyone watched horrified, praying he would find solid footing and had not been injured too badly. Doug, Jacob, and the two hired hands stayed with Anna and the cattle, while Luke, Cody, and Paul rode down the river to see if they could help the horse at any point. Finally, the water slowed at a shallow point, and Buckeye, finding footing, managed to make it out on the bank. He stood on the shore, panting and exhausted. They ran to look at him. Cody ran his hands along Buckeye's legs, and announced to them all happily, "Some cuts and bruises is all, but no broken bones. He'll be alright."

And everyone nodded in approval. However, he was too exhausted to carry a rider. The reins had been torn off from catching on debris, so they put a rope around the horse and led him back to the group. Everyone cheered as they showed up with the horse walking beside them, and for a moment the rain did not matter. They took one of the spare horses and Cody saddled him up. His reins were gone, so he took some extra rope and made reins with that. And just as they had finished all that, the storm passed and the sun came out. Everyone looked to the sky, took a deep breath, and said a private prayer of thanks.

Paul cried out "Let's go!" and they started moving again. Everyone was ready to get home. Doug and Cody took the front and spread out on either side of the cattle. Paul rode out to a bluff and stood watching the trail of cattle walking, heads down, exhausted and wanting to go home. He had his own way of counting and figured there were about twenty head missing. He rode back down to the cowboys and told them, "Over by that bluff, where there are trees near the river, there are some cattle that took cover there."

They rode off to bring the cattle back to the line. Everyone was happy to take off their slickers and tie them behind their saddle. The sun felt good on their shoulders and slowly they began to dry off. The two cowboys returned with twenty head and now the herd was in one group.

Paul rode up beside Anna and reached out and held her hand. It had been a rough ride, but they were going home now. Anna looked at him, with both fear and resolution in her eyes.

"Come with me," Paul said. And they rode up to a high bluff so they could see across the land. "Look," Paul said as they watched the long line of cattle walk across the wide green fields. "This is what God has given us."

Anna nodded as they watched the long line of cattle walk across his green fields. They were drying in the sun now, shiny with health, fat, and with good confirmation. He kissed her and they were well pleased with all that God had given them. The inclement wind had moved on for now and the sun shone brightly on the Cross Ranch.

CHAPTER 8

Horse Tales

The June air was warming the earth. The grass had grown long and thick. Papa had made enough profit from last year's cattle sales to put a fresh load of hay in the barn and that made him very happy. Vegetables were in abundance, the fruit was growing heavy in the orchard, and Mama talked about canning them all for winter. The streams and river by the house rushed happily by. It was a time of hope and renewal. Sierra and Mama were in the kitchen, with Billy and Caz playing nearby. The family had committed to learning sign language and Rosie was learning too. Jessica and Susan were out in the barn feeding the animals before breakfast. They had made plans to go shopping in town and have lunch with girlfriends.

Papa came out to the kitchen, kissed Mama, and said, "What do you think about going to the spring today? I will take you and Sierra. Maybe the herd shows up, maybe it doesn't. But I have a bit of a break today to take you. Get breakfast done and the kitchen clean and we will go."

Sierra turned to Papa, with an open mouth and flashing eyes. "Yes! Oh yes! Can we?"

Mama smiled and said, "You heard Papa, as soon as breakfast is done and the kitchen is clean. Jacob, can you stay behind and watch everyone?" Mama asked while Sierra started scrambling eggs. Jacob nodded.

Caz looked up and said, "But I wanted fried."

"Nope. Everyone is getting scrambled. Billy, can you make toast for everyone?"

Billy said, "Wait, I'm not ready for breakfast."

"No matter, breakfast is being made. Take it or leave it."

Billy and Caz looked at each other. They might as well eat now, they thought. They had a long list of chores to do, weeding the garden being one of them, and they were not looking forward to their day. Sierra hummed and whisked around the kitchen. Mama smiled. Sierra could see Rosie watching them. Rosie knew something was up as well, and Sierra promised herself, again, that she would be taking Rosie out to the see the horses. But, oh! To go with Mama and Papa! My goodness, she hadn't even dreamed of doing such a thing. She was nearly shaking with excitement.

Finally, breakfast was done and the kitchen cleaned. Sierra took out Rain, a feisty, small, palomino-colored mare, and Mama took out Apollo. Papa, of course, rode Bandit. While they saddled the horses, Papa took the rifle and ammunition and secured them in the saddle. He hoped he wouldn't have to use the rifle, but he would be ready just in case. The three rode out. They walked some and then broke out into a lope across the fields. They went through thick grass which came up to the horses' bellies, past the grazing cows, past the stream that went to their home, and even saw a family of foxes out hunting. Mama rode beautifully and Sierra watched her with pride. She loved her mama and hoped she could be like her when she grew up. The air

Echoes of Silence

rushed through their hair, and it felt glorious. Finally, Papa slowed down and they all slowed down to a walk.

Walking side by side, Mama turned to Sierra and said, "Before I married your father, I loved following the herd and watching them. In fact, I met him when I followed the herd to this spring we are going to. Your father was out hunting some cats that had attacked his father's herd and he ran into me at the spring. He was very angry at me and shouted, 'What are you doing here?' I thought it was because I was on his property and thought he was very rude about it. But actually, he knew about the cats and was worried about me."

Sierra smiled. They all knew their father's story. It was a beautiful fall day and he had left home to hunt the lions that were stalking his family's cattle. He heard a noise in the rocks. He thought it was the lion and, loading his rifle, he crawled around for a better view. There, instead of a lion, was the most beautiful girl he had ever seen.

Papa spoke up. "She looked half-wild, with long, black hair blowing in the wind, flashing dark blue eyes, and rosy cheeks. I was astonished, I can tell you. But, even worse, scared I might have shot her."

Mama continued. "So, instead of saying something nice, he yelled at me."

Papa's eyes sparkled as he said, "I tried to make amends when I saw her at Mass on Sunday but then she wouldn't have anything to do with me. Man, I had to work hard just to get her to talk to me and go on a date with me."

Mama smiled at Papa, and he smiled back. It was good to remember those days and remember when they had first fallen in love.

They arrived at the spring and Papa said, "Let's tie up the horses here on this tree. The herd might be curious about visiting them, and you two can go here behind these rocks, where it is cool. I am going to go up high where I can keep a watch."

Sierra asked, "Can we swim?"

Papa shook his head, "No our scent will be too near where the horses want to go. I saw their tracks earlier. I hope they come around for your sake."

And with that he took the rifle and climbed to higher ground, leaving Mama and Sierra alone. They found a nice place to rest, and after a while Sierra asked her mother, "Do you like being a mother?"

Sierra could hear Mama smile. "Oh yes. It is amazing to love your husband so much and to feel like your love is so strong that a child is created in your womb. Only women experience the miracle of a child growing inside you, feeling it kick and turn, being able to sing to it."

Mama paused and Sierra knew she was remembering being pregnant. Sierra had watched Mama in the evenings, just sitting in a rocking chair and quietly singing to her baby in the womb. She loved that memory.

"But what about the diapers? And the kids getting sick? And yelling at the boys when they don't do work? Do you like that part too?"

Mama laughed. "Well, diapers are not my favorite part, or cleaning up throw-up. But those sacrifices are worth it. Watching your child grow and become strong, each child so unique and beautiful, those sacrifices seem like nothing. Each child is different and amazing, like all the flowers we see in the spring. It's wonderful to see and rejoice in God's creativity."

Sierra had to ask. She was afraid, but she had to do it. "What about Rosie? Do you like being a mother to Rosie?"

Inside, Mama's heart hurt. She didn't understand why this was being asked. Was it because she was so sad? Did she, in any way, show she didn't like being Rosie's mother? It was good that Sierra asked so she could at least clarify. She said a quick prayer that her answer would be sufficient.

"Yes, of course I love being Rosie's mother. When I became a mother, whether I realized it or not, I accepted all the joys and sorrows of motherhood. All the good and the bad. My job is to take the gift of life which God has given me and help that soul become the best it can be, to glorify God with what God has given it. This is true with each child. Every child has their struggles, their strengths and weaknesses. So, I rejoice in the strengths and help guide and direct where the child is weak. God is doing the same with me, you know. Now, what happened to Rosie, I cannot understand God's will, but I do know that now I have to help her learn how to go through her life being deaf. It is difficult and I'm not sure how to do it, but God knows how to do it. So, I pray, and yes, I cry, but he will show us all what he wants Rosie to be. And honestly, honestly, that is going to be amazing too. So, yes, I love being a mother to Rosie, even if I'm not sure how to do it."

Sierra nodded. It was a good answer, and she thought she understood. But what assured her the most was the love and the strength in her mother's voice. That was what she needed to hear. That her mother thought Rosie was going to be all right. She leaned heavily on her mother's faith, and this helped her faith.

Sierra settled into quiet and Mama was thankful, for she knew that her daughter had found rest and courage in her answer. She made a quiet prayer of thanksgiving for the words she had been given. And there, in the warm sunshine amidst the falling water and sparkling pond, mother and daughter sat in happy repose.

They saw dust rise up in the distance. They both watched as the horses approached. They came languidly, with the little ones scampering and playing and the rest eating as they walked. They were a beautiful mosaic of color as they moved. When they got close enough, Sierra and Mama hid behind the rocks and waited. Sierra cast a look at her mother and was surprised by the childlike look of joy in her face. She caught a glimpse of what her mother must have been like as a young girl and felt suddenly very close to her. She thought she would have liked being friends with her back then.

Papa watched from above. He thought about Rosie and wondered if she would ever be able to ride a horse again. He thought about all the times he had ridden with her, and he could not bear to think they were over. He watched his wife and daughter talking, laughing, and sharing. It was good to see them happy like that, and again he wondered about Rosie. He took a deep breath and thanked God for the blessings that were his and prayed again for Rosie's healing.

As the herd approached, he was struck by their beauty. It had been a long time since he had seen them. The ranchers were proud of these horses and their Spanish heritage. He suddenly remembered his grandfather telling him that the missionary fathers who had built their home used these beautiful horses to travel from ranch to ranch bringing the sacraments and friendship. He smiled, thinking of his grandfather, a feisty old man who had been stronger than he looked. Grandpa had taught him how to carve wood on those long winter days when there was not much that could be done. They would clean the guns and oil the leather for the horses, and then Grandpa gave him his first knife and a piece of soft wood to whittle. He told stories on those long winter days, and one of them was about the wild horses from Spain. His mind lingered on the memory, and finally, in the quiet of the sunlight, he reconsidered his decision to let his wife and daughters come out here. His wife, he reminded himself, was smart and good with a gun. If he put aside his fear, he knew he could trust her. He smiled a bit and thought, "Goodness knows I sure don't have time to sit up on a rock every time they got the notion to go out."

The horses arrived, stamping and milling about—first the bay stallion drank and looked around, then the head mare, and then the rest of the herd. The colt, which had been reprimanded before, stayed back, his lesson learned. The horses drank and then relaxed in the grass, eating and some lying down, resting. The babies experimented with the water—first a step, then quickly back into the grass. Then, curiosity being too much, they went back to the water's edge, took a step, saw their hoof disappear, waited for calamity, looked at the other horses standing on the edge, eating grass under water, and, reassured, took another step. Soon the babies were splashing in the water and frolicking with each other. The sunlight sparkled on the drops of water and the horses' colors flashed red, black, grey, and gold.

Another horse appeared on the horizon. It was a dark grey, with black legs and a black mane and tail. It was young and lean, with many cuts on its flesh. He stopped and stood there, silently, head up. The bay stallion immediately turned and neighed a warning. The herd, in one fluid movement, went behind the stallion, the head mare tucking the horses into a tight circle. The bay stallion came forward, his neck arched powerfully, and his muscles so bound that he practically floated above the earth. The grey was also a stallion, though younger and obviously without a herd to protect him. He was desperate for water but also for companionship. Flies tortured the poor horse as he tried to bite them and get them off his festering wounds. This desperation made him willing to fight, though Sierra could see he was not as powerful as the bay.

She looked over at her mother and Mama whispered, "The young grey horse is a colt, probably three or four years old. He's been kicked out of his herd and is now looking for a new herd. He knows he needs some mares, but he is afraid to take on the older and stronger stallion. He has been wandering without protection and you can see every time he tries to join, he gets kicked out. Now he is desperate."

"Like Apollo?" Sierra asked and Mama nodded.

The grey reared, letting the bay know he was willing to fight. The bay ran towards the grey, with his neck like an arrow, ears back, teeth bared, charging with the full force of his weight and strength. He tore into the chest of the rearing grey. The grey turned on his hind quarters to get away from the blow, but not fast enough. The wound was ugly and bleeding. As he turned, he kicked at the bay and made contact on the left shoulder just as the bay moved away. The bay reared this time, but the grey did not pivot fast enough, and the sharp hooves of the bay slammed down on the shoulders of the grey. The grey turned and again kicked out at the bay, but the bay knew what was coming and moved away in time. The bay bit at the grey's hindquarters and sent him running. The herd relaxed and returned to grazing and drinking, while the stallion stood a long time watching the grey disappear into the plains.

"I don't understand, Mama," Sierra whispered. "Why was the bay stallion so mean? What is that grey stallion going to do?"

Mama said, "It is the way of things. The stallion must protect his herd. That grey wanted to steal his mares and start his own herd. One day the bay stallion will get old, and he won't be able to protect his herd and a younger colt will come and take it away. When I was a young girl there was a young colt, black as night. I watched as he tried to steal the mares but could not. But he was smart and strong enough to keep trying, and one day he was the stronger and the older stallion had become the weaker, and soon he took charge of the herd. Now it is the bay that is in charge. Horses need a leader, that is how they find safety. It is the way of nature that the weaker gets cast aside and the stronger takes care of the herd. Otherwise, they have no protection against predators. Always remember that when you are riding you must be the leader. When you show the horse that you are in charge, the horse feels safe. If you are afraid, then they must protect themselves, and when they are afraid, they can put themselves in danger."

"How do you show them you are in charge?"

"Watch that mare over there, the black-and-white paint. See her baby?"

"The little paint by her side?"

"Yes. Watch how she carefully nuzzles it and makes sure that he is walking just where she is walking. Not ahead of her and not behind her. She has that baby at her side so a predator only sees the mother, and not the baby. It is for safety. But also, by controlling his footsteps, she is showing him that she is in charge. He feels safe, knowing she is watching over him. That is how he knows he belongs.

"Now, see that grey mare with the black baby? He is a little older, looks like a yearling. He is a little more brave and adventurous. She needs to show him that she is still in charge. Watch now—he is wandering away from her. See how she reaches out her neck, with her ears back and bites his flanks. She is telling him, 'Get back here!'"

The young colt came back to his mother, but in a while he wandered off again. Mama and Sierra watched, fascinated. The second time, the mother had only to look at him with ears back and the colt returned to her side.

"You see how quickly he learns? When we train horses, we act like their mama. We can't bite them or kick them, but we can use our legs or the reins to give them a little bite. Not to hurt them, but to direct them and let them know we mean it. They want to be directed, and if we are consistent they will stop fighting us and be calm under our direction."

Sierra pointed to a young horse that was outside the herd. It was a beautiful Appaloosa with brown spots, but it was obviously frantic, circling the herd. "What is going on?"

"That is a two-year-old colt, I'm guessing. He has done something wrong, maybe started a fight, I'm not sure, and the head mare has sent him outside the herd. He is very worried because he knows he cannot survive outside the herd."

Sierra nodded, remembering the grey horse.

"So," Mama continued, "he is running around the herd, circling it, checking to see if any of the mares will let it back in. Now watch, his lip will go soft, and start to flap a little. Then, he will lick his lips and lower his head. This is how he says, 'I'm sorry. I will do better. I will obey you. You are in charge of me.' Now watch the head mare."

The head mare stopped and squared up to the colt. The colt stopped also and dropped his head, still licking his lips.

Echoes of Silence

The head mare lowered her head and stepped back. Slowly and respectfully, the colt walked toward the herd, and the horses moved, making room for him.

Sierra laughed quietly. "That was amazing!"

Mama nodded, smiling. "If we ever need to train a horse, we will imitate the head mare. That is what horses know from nature and what they learn from the herd."

They noticed a young filly; she was a beautiful blue roan with a black mane and tail. She was pushed away by one mare after another. She was about a year old, with long legs, little ears, and a pretty face.

"Do you think she has a mama?" Sierra asked.

Mama watched for a while and finally said, "I'm not sure. She is still young to be without a mother."

It was late afternoon now, and Papa came down from above. "It's time to go."

They got the horses and started the ride home. They were rejuvenated in body and soul. On the ride home, he took Mama aside.

"I think it's okay if you take the girls. You are a good shot and I know you will watch them."

Mama smiled. Smiled for his trust, smiled for his kindness, and smiled because she knew he loved her more than anything.

They arrived home and Papa went off to the barn where Jacob had been working on a broken tractor as Mama and Sierra went inside. Jessica was making fresh bread and Susan was sitting at the table with Rosie and a fresh bouquet of hydrangeas. They were surrounded with paper and paintbrushes, the afternoon light filling the room. Rosie had a beautiful hydrangea half-finished on her canvas. Susan looked up and smiled, Rosie looked up and smiled, and Mama's heart could not have been more full. Susan, in her lovely, generous way, had opened up a door in Rosie's mind and through that door came much longed-for light.

Just then Caz and Billy burst in the doors, bringing three very dirty dogs with them. The dogs ran into the table, spilling a water jar and ruining Rosie's painting. Everyone jumped at once, and soon there was a mad scuffle of dogs running everywhere. Susan and Rosie were jumping and pushing back chairs, Jessica crying out in dismay, Mama and Sierra trying to save paintings which now looked like modern art with paint running down, and the two boys headed for the fridge. Finally, everything settled down and Sierra started talking about the horses. She looked up at one point, and Caz was signing away, with Rosie watching him and then alternatively turning and watching Sierra's lips. Jessica was very excited about the horses and kept asking questions.

"Please, Mama, can I go next time?"

Mama smiled at Jessica and said, "I think that would be lovely." Then she stood up and said, "It's time to get dinner ready. Sierra, there is a roast in the fridge, can you put it in the oven? Billy and Caz—let's go to the garden and we can pick some fresh vegetables. Susan, if you could pick up the painting project? Jessica, thank you for making your wonderful bread. I quite feel like celebrating tonight. Rosie—you set the table."

Rosie did not hear that bit of instruction, and Mama well knew it. But she thought it would be good for the other children to know that Rosie was being given a job as well. Mama took out the silverware box and brought it over to where Rosie was sitting. She looked Rosie in the eye and Rosie nodded.

As the afternoon light filled the home with a soft glow,

the roast filled the kitchen with the aroma of herbs and savory meat. Everyone was hungry and waited for Papa to come in for dinner.

Jacob came in with Papa just as the sun began to fall below the horizon. They washed their hands and faces in the big kitchen sink, and Mama handed each a fresh towel. Dinner had been placed on the table—thick slices of roast, potatoes, fresh vegetables from the garden, and milk from the cow. On the table was Jessica's homemade bread, and the water sparkled in lovely glass pitchers. The sun fell low through the windows, filling the room full of light. Everyone sat down, and Papa said prayers before the meal.

"Bless us, oh Lord, and these thy gifts, which we are about to receive from thy bounty, through Christ our Lord. Bless those who have no food and who are less fortunate than us. Amen."

Food was passed around, and conversation filled the room. Papa said the baby calf was doing well, and he would soon be introducing it to the herd. There was still plenty of grass in the fields and even though they were forecasting a hot summer, so far all was well. Mama and Sierra told everyone all over again about the horses, and Mama gave Papa a look of such love that everyone felt it in the room. Susan said she and Jessica had gone shopping with some friends, but afterward she and Rosie had decided to paint. Papa looked at Susan and then looked at Rosie. Rosie smiled such a shy and beautiful smile. A tear came to his eye, and he scolded Mama for too much onion in the salad. But everyone knew, and everyone felt happy on that warm summer day.

There was no fire that night for the room was still warm from those long evening rays, but the cross, etched into the stone a long time ago by a holy priest, was there. The sun fell across it, making its lines darker and more pronounced. They all sat for a moment, thinking collectively that this wall had been part of a church. That their home was sacred and safe. And that even though tragedy had struck, so had blessings abounded.

Papa began, "In the name of the Father, and the Son, and the Holy Spirit…"

CHAPTER 9

Dancing in the Aspen

There were whispers of drought, but no one wanted to believe it or even say the words out loud. Surely there would be rain. Papa came into the kitchen soberly and told the family, "Doug asked if we could help move the cattle from his higher fields down into the lower field where he still has grass. His higher fields have been eaten down too far and the grass is gone. There is nothing left for the cattle." Papa winced. It was too early for the grass to be gone. Doug had a very big lower pasture, and he hoped it was enough to feed the cattle until the fall sales. "I told him he would have the Derrick family in full. Early to bed tonight, tomorrow we will be there at dawn. Abigail will make a big dinner for us."

Anna said, "I'll call her and see what we can bring."

After Papa left with Jacob, Mama turned to the girls. "I need to work with Apollo. Do you want to join me?" The girls nodded happily. A day with Mama on the horse was a great day. "Billy and Caz, you can come too. Get out Pilgrim and Apache and you can get their muscles loosened before tomorrow."

Susan immediately realized Rosie could not go with them. Not wanting anyone to feel badly, she said, "Mama, I need to do reading for school over the summer. Can Rosie and I stay home?"

Mama looked at her with gratitude. "Yes, yes of course."

"Hurray!" cried Billy and Caz. "We don't have to do chores!"

Mama smiled and reminded them, "There will be enough time for chores later. Girls, get Dash and Ginger. I want to give you a bit of a lesson as well."

Dash was a big black gelding with a white blaze on his nose. He was sure and steady but quick on his feet when he needed to be. Ginger, a red mare with four white socks, was the fastest of all the horses. Sierra loved riding her at full speed across the plains.

When Mama went out to get Apollo, she was upset at leaving Rosie and Susan behind. She wished it didn't have to be that way. Apollo immediately sensed her mood, and as soon as she entered the pen, he ran away from her. The girls watched quietly as they put the halters on their horses and took them out of the pen.

Okay, thought Mama, *we are going to make this a lesson.* She called out, "What do you do if your horse runs away?"

Jessica, who was always so calm, never had that problem. Sierra, on the other hand, always had that problem, her energy often sending the horse off bucking. Today was better because Ginger and Dash were friends and so when Dash didn't run, neither did Ginger. Apache and Pilgrim were so old everyone had lost track of how old they were, so the boys had no problem catching them. They had already put bridles on and were sitting on the horses bareback, throwing a baseball back and forth. The two horses sat there with half-closed eyes, looking entirely pleased at being needed. Pilgrim was an old black horse whose lineage was wholly unknown. He was Papa's horse back when he was young. Apache was just as old, an Appaloosa with red spots, and no one remembered anymore where he had come from. It seemed like he had always been on the ranch.

Mama said, "Sierra, what do you do?"

Sierra answered, "Send the horse around the pen until he stops."

Mama answered, "Yes, you are right, but remember we talked about joining up when we watched the colt in the herd? That is what I am doing now."

Suddenly it all clicked for Sierra. While Mama sent Apollo around the pen, Sierra explained to Jessica what she had seen in the horse herd. Jessica was sad she had made other plans that day and so she just listened quietly and watched her strong mama work with Apollo. She looked like she was dancing with him. Mama would lean to the left just a bit and he would run to the right and then she would change the direction of her body and he would follow.

Mama said, "Remember, the body doesn't lie. Your mouth can lie, but the body tells the truth. Horses listen to what your body is saying. They are a perfect reflection of who you are and how your body moves. Remember that we ask the horse, who is magnificent and strong, to bow his head and obey us. And so, even more, we must bow our heads and obey God. But you see, what we ask of the horse is greater for we are small and imperfect. But God is all-powerful and all-perfect. All the more should we obey him. Remember that when you ask your horse to obey you, and ask with humility."

Finally, Apollo stopped, licked his lips, and when Mama relaxed her posture he came towards her. It looked like magic, and the girls watched her, amazed. Mama stood quietly, and this horse who had just a moment ago been running from her put his nose to her face. When Mama exhaled, Apollo breathed in. Then, when Apollo exhaled, Mama breathed in. As though they were exchanging souls. Mama rubbed his neck and slowly put the halter on. And then without a word, she walked out of the pen, and he followed her, meek and quiet, licking his lips.

Mama saddled her horse, but the children rode bareback. Mama sat in the saddle for a moment, looking at her sons and daughters. They were good riders, and she was proud of them.

She said, "I want you to be mindful when you ride. Think about what you are doing and what you expect the horse to do. You are responsible for every footstep of all four feet."

Apollo started prancing, eager to be off.

"Watch Apollo. I have not asked for any of his feet to move. I am going to back him up because that gets the thinking part of the brain working. He doesn't back up naturally and so he has to think about it. Also, I can get all four feet to do what I want at once." She sat back in the seat, pulled back on the reins slightly, and squeezed his sides. "I am just going to bring the reins to my body and tuck with my hips. That movement with my hips activates his hindquarters, which he needs to use to back up. I squeeze a bit with my legs which gives him some movement."

With very little obvious movement from Mama, Apollo tucked his head and backed up. The girls could see Apollo change from being energetic to quietly thinking.

Mama said, "Okay, now you back up your horses. They are trained well, so they will respond if you give them the right cue."

Sierra pulled back too much and her horse, Ginger, backed up quickly and they ran into a bush.

Mama admonished her. "Nice and easy, Sierra. Less energy. Take two steps and then lift the reins and sit up. Think about where your horse's feet are."

Sierra tried again and Ginger listened. She took four steps back, but at least they didn't run over anything.

"Okay, Jessica, you try."

Jessica's horse, Dash, was not dashing anywhere, and Jessica looked very frustrated.

Mama said, "Jessica, you are not tucking your hip and you are not squeezing with your legs. You can't just pull back on the reins. Try again and think about what your body is doing."

Jessica tried again and this time Dash took one careful step backward.

While Mama had been instructing them, Apollo had taken many steps in every direction. He was eager to go and did not understand why they were just standing there. But Mama very calmly put him back in the same spot each time. Finally, Apollo realized it was easier to stand quietly rather than take a hundred steps to nowhere.

"Make the right thing easy and the wrong thing more work," Mama reminded them. "All right, we are ready to ride out. Billy, Caz, let's go."

They all went off together, the five of them, and Susan watched from the house, feeling a little sorry for herself. She would have liked to go too, but what would Rosie have done alone at home? She got out a book to read. Rosie, seeing that Susan was reading, went and found a book and the two of them ended up enjoying an afternoon of reading. It was a luxury Susan had not had time for since she started college. As she read, she remembered why she loved reading so much. She made some tea and brought out some cookies they had made the day before. Rosie's face softened and a smile played around her lips as she sat by Susan, reading and munching on a cookie.

MAMA SAID THEY COULD HELP PAPA BY CHECKING ON A group of cattle tucked in by a rise in the land with the stream below it. There was a little grove of trees on the stream's edge and cattle liked to hide in that shade. Papa wanted them to count how many were there. They veered to the left and headed toward the stream. As they rode, the earth spread out around them in waves of green wheat grass. The tips of the grass were just starting to make the pods that would soon hold wheat for the cattle. The wind blew the lush grass, and it seemed to have a life of its own, blowing one way all across the plains and then changing direction with the wind. The sky seemed big and wondrous, full of big white clouds slowly floating by. The hawks soared high in that endless sky while the flowers still dotted the fields by the water. It was an amazing and beautiful day. They rode quietly, soaking up the beauty of the land and feeling the rhythm of the horses walking. Pilgrim and Apache started out stiff and slow, but as their muscles relaxed they kept up a good pace and tossed their heads like the happy cow ponies they once were. Jessica and Sierra talked happily, and Jessica asked about the wild horses.

"They were so beautiful," said Sierra. "We have to see if Papa will let us go together."

Jessica nodded. "I'd love that!"

The two had little races when the land opened up, and once, when they finished, they brought the horses close together and traded places while the horses balanced the acrobatic girls on their backs. Finally, they came back to Mama and the boys.

Jessica asked Mama, "What was it like growing up in a shop? Did you like wearing nice clothes and living in town?"

Jessica thought it sounded wonderful. She didn't like the hard work of a ranch.

Sierra cried out, "Oh! That sounds terrible. Being stuck in a house all day! Nowhere to run and play."

Mama laughed at the difference between the two girls. There were some people who loved living in town, loved the organization of it, the nice houses with manageable yards. The grass lawns and the gardens. She thought for a moment about how to answer.

"Well, I loved living in town as a young girl. It was all I knew. I love my mom and dad. My mom was very beautiful and came from New York, which is a very big city. You know, she was wealthy and famous. She met my father when he was shopping for his store. He was well-read and had a quick wit. He completely charmed her. So much so that she was willing to move to Wyoming for him. There was no other way she would have lived out on a big ranch away from other people; living in a small town was strange enough. I think she had a hard time adjusting. My mom taught me how to dress and do my hair, how to choose good fabrics, and how to sing. She said every girl should have a charming hobby."

Here the girls laughed. Jessica asked, "A charming hobby! What is that?"

"Oh, like playing the piano or singing. Something to charm a man."

Sierra asked, "Did it work? Is that how you charmed Papa?"

Mama laughed. "No, not at all. Did you know that I met you father when he was a young boy?"

The girls cried out excitedly, "No, tell us!"

Billy and Caz had wandered off with the horses. Mama called them back and then began her story.

"He came into the store, and he was about twelve. He had curly golden hair, like an angel, and bright green eyes. He looked very mischievous and knocked over a jar of candy. His father was strong and handsome. I remember my mother getting all fluttery around him and my father glaring at her. Papa's father got very mad at Papa for knocking over the jar of candy. He paid my father for the jar and the candy, and I remember Grandpa telling Papa he would have to earn the money. I think Grandpa was a harsh man."

The girls listened eagerly. They had never met their grandparents, as both had died early, so they always wondered about them. They thought about what Mama said for a while and then Sierra asked, "So Papa was mischievous? Tell us more."

"Well, after he got yelled at, he looked at me with this big smile and actually winked at me! I always thought it was because he liked me. I even wonder if he knocked the jar over to get my attention."

Everyone laughed at that.

They came upon the stream and a little grove of pretty aspen trees, with their tall white trunks and fluttery green leaves. It was what Mama had been looking for.

"Okay, we are going to practice weaving in and out of these trees. I want you to focus on using your legs to direct the horse. Imagine you are dancing, and when you want to go to the right you turn your hips. This turns your shoulders which changes the pressure on the reins. It also changes the pressure on your legs and even the position of your legs. So, if you turn to the right, your right hip pushes back against the horse's hindquarters, your right leg will move back just a bit, and your right shoulder and arm will pull to the right. So, without tugging on the reins, your whole body communicates to the horses the direction you want to go."

The girls tried it and laughed awkwardly as their horse kept going straight and they had to use the reins to avoid bumping into a tree. Mama tried it and at first Apollo tossed his head, but she corrected with a slight tap of the reins, and soon he had his head down in a beautiful arch and she was weaving in and out of trees. They calmed their minds and tried again. Mama said, "Think of the natives who rode without saddles or bridles while they hunted buffalo. Think how much control they needed to have just with their bodies. Pretend you are hunting in this forest using both your hands to manage the bow and arrow."

That was just the inspiration Sierra needed, and soon she and Ginger were weaving around trees. Jessica tried again, somewhat exaggerating the motion, but finally Dash understood as well. The three of them wove around the trees. It felt like they were dancing there amongst the beautiful, tall, slender trees, the leaves fluttering in the wind and the blue skies up above.

Pilgrim and Apache would have nothing for it, and no matter what the boys did those horses stayed put. They had put in their time doing fancy footwork and were done. Billy and Caz found a big pinecone and started throwing it back and forth. The horses sat quietly in the shade, happy for the break.

Mama said, "When you turn around the tree you want to make sure you can see the horse's inside eye just a bit. That means he is collected and is carrying himself well. We don't want any snakelike necks that are overextended. You do this by holding the reins with even pressure, not too loose." They all worked on this for a while, then Mama said, "Apollo started off arguing with me and not really listening. Now, he is soft as butter, and it seems like he can read my mind. We just needed to get his thinking brain on and also to remind him I am the boss. Now, I will have a good ride tomorrow moving those cattle."

It was a lovely lesson. They let the horses graze as they unpacked their food and sat under those beautiful trees by the stream. They talked and laughed as they ate the bread Jessica had made, the cheese from their dairy cow, the fruit and vegetables from their garden, and the beef from their livestock. They each thought about how thankful they were for these moments as they rested their heads against the trees and looked at the blue sky contrasting with the sun through the leaves and listening to the gurgle of the stream. Finally, it was time to go. They packed up their things and headed back, the horses relaxed and obedient.

Susan and Rosie, meanwhile, had finished reading and decided to cook a nice dinner. Susan patiently showed Rosie what she wanted done and Rosie willingly helped. By the time everyone got home there was a fine dinner of grilled pork chops, mashed potatoes, and a fresh salad from the garden.

Papa came in from helping the neighbors get ready for the next day. He had a big appetite, as did everyone. Papa said prayers and they began to eat and talk about their afternoon, sharing the afternoon in the aspen and how Mama taught them to dance with the horses. Papa looked at Mama with a smile and she smiled back. The girls noticed that exchange, even Rosie, and they grinned at each other. Jacob was quiet and thoughtful, and Rosie noticed that as well. She looked at him with questioning eyes, but he did not notice.

After dinner, Papa pulled back his chair and said "We will be ready to ride at five o'clock. We'll ride out to the Johnsons'. It's only a mile if we go the back way."

Susan asked, "I'd like to go."

Papa nodded and said, "Sounds good. I'd love to have you there. An extra hand is always needed."

Mama nodded, smiling. She knew there would be few times she could ride with Susan and was so happy that Susan could go.

Jessica, realizing Rosie needed someone to stay with her, asked, "Is it okay if I stay home tomorrow? I want to make some bread for the fair." She added excitedly, "I'm trying a new recipe with fresh herbs, Rosie," and she looked at Rosie with an encouraging smile. "Can you help me?"

Rosie turned away without responding and Jessica ignored her.

Mama just looked at Jessica and said, "Thank you. I really appreciate this. Can you get the salads ready by tomorrow afternoon?"

Jessica nodded and said, "I'll bring the bread too and see how everyone likes it."

"That sounds wonderful. We will leave while you're asleep but we'll be back around four in the afternoon to pick you both up."

Dishes were done, prayers were said, and everyone went off to bed, ready for an early morning.

CHAPTER 10

Cattle Drive

Well before light, Papa woke everyone up. Mama was already in the kitchen making breakfast burritos which they could eat on the way. Sierra took her burrito and stepped outside. She stopped for a moment, looking at the night sky. The moon had set long ago and the stars were so bright they filled the night with light. She thought about the people that had been able to find figures in such a wild array of light. She had seen them in books: beautiful swans, wild horses, fierce warriors. But to her, it looked as though someone had thrown out wild seeds of light on a black velvet earth.

"Let's go, let's go," Papa encouraged.

They went out to the horses, who greeted them with soft nickers and warm breath from their nostrils. Sierra loved how warm Rain felt and wished she could ride bareback. But today was business, so she saddled her up and was soon ready.

The horses were ready to go. They knew there was something going on, and they stepped lightly and tossed their heads.

Papa looked over at Pilgrim and Apache, proud that they were coming along and carrying his boys. Pilgrim had been his horse when he was learning to work cattle with his father. Papa mused, *Me and that old boy have been through a lot together. He has seen a lot in his life.* He was thankful Anna had taken the time to ride him gently the day before and took good care of him so he could be carrying Caz. He knew Pilgrim would not only know what to do with the cattle but would protect Caz if there was any trouble. *A good horse is worth his weight in gold*, Papa thought. Soon, dawn began its slow arrival, and as the sky turned a light rose color they arrived at the Johnsons' ranch.

The Johnsons' brand was the "Shooting DJ" with an arrow under the letters "DJ." Many of the brands were generations old and carefully recorded each spring. They were a source of pride to each ranch and recognized around the state. They joined the others in the front yard. Doug was saddled and ready to go. There were about eight other cattlemen and a few neighbors there to help as well. Luke and Cody Maverick were there, and Jacob rode over to Cody.

"How is Buckeye doing?"

Cody rubbed the neck of his horse and said, "He's doing fine. I had to work on his legs some, but the swelling went down and he's ready to go."

When everyone had arrived, Doug began giving direction. "We will go out in groups of three and start collecting the cattle and bring them down to the lower field."

Doug sorted out groups, with Anna and the girls in one group and Billy and Caz with Papa. Jacob, Luke, and Cody rode together. Everyone was in good spirits, talking and joking. After a few hours, they had collected the cattle from the high ground and were on their way down the mountain. They stopped for a quick bite to relax a bit and to let the cattle rest.

As she ate, Mama wondered how Jessica and Rosie were doing at home together. But she had little time to worry. It was already time to go. The next part of the drive was rough as they were headed through some heavy rock outcroppings and then they would cross a river. After that they would be out in the open land which was nice and easy.

They made it through the rocks, but as they approached the river an older cow decided she didn't want any part of it. She split off with about fifteen head following her. They went right past Mama and the girls back up through rocks and to the higher pasture. Mama cried, "Let's go! We need to go get those cattle!"

Mama, Susan, and Sierra rode off after the cattle. It was hard to see very far with the tall rocks. They rode up and down small gorges and rock outcroppings. It was hot in those rocks and rough riding. Suddenly they saw the cattle in a low riverbed, looking for shade and water.

Susan cried, "Mama, you want to go right or left?"

Anna took the right and Sierra and Susan took the left. The terrain was very rough with heavy rocks and brush, and the horses had to pick their way through it. But Ginger was fast and quick, and so Sierra was able to fly across the rocks and around the trees. Mama thought, *She shouldn't have done that; she is going to come upon the cattle too quickly and scare them.*

Apollo was angry about picking through rocks and tossed his head to argue. But he was sure-footed, and he and Mama made their way, hoping to cut off the cow's progress back home. Suddenly, Sierra rode up to the cows too fast, and they bolted.

Mama yelled, "Sierra, you must go slower and not scare the cows! Now we have more work to do!"

Sierra nodded and went forward, but she was tiny and on a small horse, so while she slipped under thick branches, Mama had to duck and weave. She was glad for her work in the willow trees the day before. Mama saw Susan on the left side of the bank, ready to cut the cattle off and move them toward the herd.

It was clear Sierra would get to the cattle first. Mama called out again, "Go slower!"

Sierra threw a hand in the air as she rode ahead, and Mama did not know if it was a sign of acknowledgment or disrespect. She grimaced at her daughter and continued through the rocks and trees.

Suddenly they saw the cows resting in the shade and their spirits rose. She called out, "Sierra, move them to the left, Susan is across the bank ready for them."

Mama and Sierra surrounded the cattle slowly and managed to walk them forward. They were joined by Susan. By now the cattle were hot and tired and ready to drink from the river and cross it to join the herd. As they approached the group of men and cattle, there was plenty of calling back and forth amongst the separated cattle and the lost group. Mama and the girls rode behind them, happy that all had been made right. Papa looked back at Mama with admiration.

MEANWHILE, AT HOME, JESSICA SET TO WORK ON HER bread. It had been rising the day before and it was ready to be mixed with herbs, worked into rolls, and baked. She thought rolls would be easier than cutting from a loaf at the Johnsons'. She loved this part of making bread and stood in the kitchen feeling the velvety dough work through her hands, the sunlight pouring through the kitchen window and the smell of fresh herbs in the air. She thought about Rosie.

She remembered a few years ago when she and her sisters had been fighting. Her father sat them all down at the dinner table. He looked each one in the eye and then said, "Look around you. These are the people closest to you. This is your family. These are the people who will always have your back. Cherish each other and treat each other with respect and kindness." He said it not only as a promise but as a command. He was so fierce that night, and Mama too. Jessica and her brothers and sisters had looked around. They each realized Papa was right. They nodded their heads and let their anger go.

Jessica sighed, but this was tough. Rosie could be so stubborn and hard to work with. Jessica wanted to work with her but didn't know what to do when Rosie ignored her. She worked quietly, rolling the dough and when she looked up, noticed that Rosie had come into the kitchen and was watching. Jessica held out a handful of dough, offering Rosie the chance to help, but also offering so much more: friendship and acceptance. Rosie came and together the girls worked with the soft dough, forming it into little balls. They put the rolls into one of Mama's pans and placed it in the oven. Afterward, the girls looked around at the kitchen covered in flour and herbs, and then looked at each other and smiled.

AT THE JOHNSONS', THEY HAD ALMOST MADE IT TO THE lower pasture and had only to cross a river. They set the cattle off at a slow pace over the shallowest part. It was later in the year, so the water was not too deep or fast. Papa was in front and hollered at the head cow until she went in. He rode beside her to keep her going. Climbing out on the bank, Paul helped push the cattle past the river to a wide bank of grass where they could rest while the herd finished crossing.

Finally the cattle had all made it across. They opened the gates and sent the eager cattle into the lower pasture. There was plenty of green grass and fresh water. When the cattle were safely locked in, the Derrick family cut across the mountain range and rode home.

Jessica had been faithful, and the food was ready for the picnic. She had a few nicely made salads and the rolls smelled amazing, just out of the oven. They packed the food in the Suburban and all drove to the Johnsons'.

There was already a long table laid out, surrounded by a crazy collection of chairs. The sun was lower in the sky and the air cooler. Long rays of sunlight fell through the trees, bringing a golden glow to the afternoon. Abigail and her daughters loved to put out a beautiful table and everyone felt honored to be included in their feasts. On the table there were plates, silverware, and tall glasses that sparkled in the falling light. One of the wives had brought fresh flowers and was putting them in vases along the table. There was a long, white, gauze table runner that fell all the way down on the grass. It was a beautiful setting. The work was hard, but this was one of the best meals they would eat. Everyone brought food to share, and it was laid out on another table, like a huge buffet. The men were grilling steaks and burgers, all from their own beef. Beer was passed around in plenty, and good spirits arose as tales were told of this cattle drive and others from the past.

They sat, friends and neighbors, long into the night. Little ones fell asleep in little nests they made of blankets, and songs were sung with coyotes joining in. This was the glue that brought the community together. Hard work and joyful times. They were there for each other in times of need and celebrated in times of joy. It was a special time, and they all knew it.

At long last, they headed home. Rosie and the boys slept in the back seat of the Suburban. In the quiet of the night, Mama reached out and held Papa's hand.

CHAPTER 11

Prayers and Promises

It was one of those lovely July nights where the air cooled and the sun bounced from one mountain range to the next. The sky lit up, with colors of rose and blue causing all the earth to be under a pink halo. The family went outside and decided to say their evening prayers under that beautiful sky.

"Hail Mary…"

The sky slowly darkened, and the stars began to appear one by one. The moon came out, soft and hesitant at first, and then brighter and brighter. The mistress of the night sky. She heralded the stars who came at her bidding, and they surrounded her in adoration. The horizon stayed a soft dusky gold for quite some time, and the little family watched as every tree stood out against that horizon.

"Full of grace…"

They breathed deeply the cool evening air and prayed. The familiar words of the rosary, falling like a soft rumbling stream, different and yet the same. Papa reminding them of Bible quotes for each decade.

"The Lord is with thee…"

Together their breathing slowed and bodies relaxed. The night air grew cooler, and a hush grew over the land.

"Blessed are you amongst women…"

Somewhere a cow lowed to her calves and dogs howled to the beautiful moon. It was a time they all treasured. Rosie heard none of this, but she sat in a rocking chair and took in the beauty of the skies and coolness of the evening.

After prayers ended, they began to share their days. Their hopes and struggles. Susan quietly mentioned there was a boy at college, and while Billy and Caz laughed and hooted Mama and Papa knew it was better to listen and not ask too much. Mama was excited for her oldest and first daughter, and Papa was protective. But questions and such would come later as Susan was willing to share. Jacob, however, did not have Papa's prudence and asked who it was. Susan shared a name: Joseph Bollinger. Mama smiled for she knew the family. They were a good family, hard workers with a strong faith. Jacob cried out, "Oh! I know his younger brother! We played football together at school. His brother's a good guy, so maybe I won't have to beat up Joe."

Papa listened, not convinced. He ruefully realized no one would be good enough for Susan. She was his first daughter, and he did not want to lose her. But he had another burden on his heart and after the conversation found a lull, he mentioned it. "I'm afraid we are headed for a drought. I went to our Cattlemen's meeting and that is what all the signs are showing. The springs are lower and continue to go down, and it's too early for that. We need to pray for snow in the mountains to fill the reservoirs. If we don't get snow, I'm afraid I'm going to have to sell our stock early."

The lighthearted mood disappeared immediately. Mama's silence was heavy as she took her husband's hand in hers. He squeezed it, his fear and worry transferring from one to another. She said quietly, "I was wondering. I've noticed the grass already getting brown in places."

Billy asked, "How does snow help? It doesn't give us more grass for the cows to eat."

Jacob, wanting to show he understood, responded quickly, and Papa let him answer. "When you raise cattle, you always have to think ahead. You have to know you can feed the cows when they are pregnant and that you can feed all those calves when they are born. You can't just let them starve. So, if we don't have water coming from the springs high up in the mountains, there isn't enough grass in the fields. Then we need to sell the cows early or not breed them. Or sell the calves when they are young. Either way, we lose money because we have to sell the cattle early, when they are light, or we buy hay and feed them until the fall. The worst thing is to do nothing and then the animals starve and die. So, you have to take a look at what your field conditions are way ahead. We need snow all winter, but an early snow will help renew the water table. Then we can keep the cows, breed them, and have a good hope there will be enough grass to feed them and their calves in the spring."

Papa was satisfied with the answer and nodded in the dark. Billy, meanwhile, had found a toad and was playing with it. No one knew if he had even listened to Jacob's answer or not. He turned to his family and said, "This toad here, he needs rain to live. But he doesn't look worried. He just finds a nice wet place and lives there. Do you think he knows if snow will come in September? Maybe he came here to tell us it will."

Everyone laughed a bit, but the young boy's wisdom was not lost on his family. Papa murmured, "Look at the birds of the air, they do not worry…"

Jacob laughed and said, "Christ should have told us about the toads."

Susan responded, "No, he gave us Billy for that."

Everyone laughed.

Mama said, "Well then, we will start praying for an early winter. Can we make it through until spring with the hay we have in the barn? What if we have snow in September? How about that?"

Papa laughed despite himself and said, "You can't order weather, like one orders a new dress."

Everyone laughed with him. It was a laugh that relieved the fear in their hearts. A serious drought could bankrupt them. It had happened to other ranchers they knew, and it was gut-wrenching to watch.

Papa said, "Okay, if you put it that way, snow in September would be excellent. I do have enough hay in the barn to get us through spring, thanks be to God."

Mama said, "Okay then, I will find a good prayer for that snow, and we will pray it every night."

Papa chuckled ruefully. It was no use arguing with Mama when she was on a praying mission, and he let her faith carry him. He was the only one who had seen the devastation of a drought when he was a boy. His father was stubborn and had done nothing and so the cattle slowly starved. The sight of cattle starving and watching helplessly as the mountain lions and birds ate the flesh off bare rib cages had been seared into his mind forever. Because of that time as a young boy, he always did everything he could to have hay saved up in his barn. It was always his first priority after the sale of the cattle. He never wanted to see that again. Growing up in the city, Anna had not seen drought like he had. Perhaps their store had less income because it was the ranchers who came in to buy the merchandise, but she had not had to face what he had. Her faith seemed simplistic to him, but who was he to judge the power of God? He would pray with her, but he would also fight with everything he had to protect his family. They sat out in the darkness of the night a little longer. The companionship of the family drawing around them. Finally, yawns replaced conversation and they drifted off to bed and sleep. Peaceful under the stars and the strength of family.

The next morning, Susan woke before dawn, wanting to enjoy the coolness, for she knew the day would be very hot. She quietly left her room, trying not to wake her sisters, and went to make a cup of coffee. It was dark outside and there was a warm breeze which felt good in the cool night. On the front porch she sat in a rocking chair and let her mind go quiet. It had been a difficult month at home. The changes in her family had been profound and there was so much sorrow. She let her mind run quietly over different moments as she rocked rhythmically in the chair. The motion was soothing, and she let her breathing quiet. The stars began to fade, ever so gently, and she knew the dawn was on its way. Soon, the horizon took on a faint orange light. Ever since she was a child, she loved watching the dawn. The orange just touching the base of the mountain, putting in black relief every tree. The sky at the horizon, a soft orange contrasted with the dark black of night, still hanging on. When the breeze settled, she was a bit chilly, but she relished that chill. The warm breeze spoke promises of a heat which she did not like. The sky took on a rosy hue and she sipped her coffee peacefully.

She heard a sound, and then realized that Jacob had come out to join her. He chose a solid chair; one a friend had made from local trees. A gift to them after Rosie's illness. He too sipped a cup of coffee, and the two, brother and sister, sat in the dark, quiet and reflective.

Finally, Jacob spoke. "What is college like?"

He was a young man and fighting to rise to the standards of his father, whom he admired very much. But in this question, in the dark, with his big sister, his voice had a vulnerability in it that surprised even him. He wished he could take back the words as soon as he had said them.

Susan was quiet for a moment. She heard the vulnerability as well and she treasured this moment, where she was once again the big sister that could protect her brother, even if just for a moment.

"Well, it is a lot of fun," she started. "I've made some really good friends, and I love my classes. We are talking about really important subjects, like why man exists and how to be a good person. I love the practical classes too, the math and the science. My favorite class, no surprise, is music. I've aways loved music but I didn't realize it was mathematical."

Jacob laughed a bit and said, "Well, I'm not sure I'd find that as interesting as you. I can't play piano worth a darn. It made Mama so mad."

They laughed quietly in the darkness, childhood memories running through their minds.

Susan spoke again, "Remember the pipe that broke behind the wall and we didn't know it? We had to pull out the boards from the wall and everything was moldy. Remember Mama frantically calling out orders to take everything out of the room? She was like an army general."

Jacob laughed. "Yes! Oh my gosh! Mom was terrifying and Papa was just violently ripping out wood. He was angry because it was the part of the house from the old church. He didn't want to destroy it. I remember pulling out half the wall and all the things in the room that were near it. There was so much mold and rot."

Susan shuddered at the memory. "I remember Papa pulling out the baptism gown that we had all been baptized in. It was completely rotten and covered in mold and Papa had to throw it out. Mama's face just…" Susan searched for the word. "She was so so sad. I never even thought about that baptism gown until that moment. Mama just stood there with tears running down her face. I was so sad watching her. "

Jacob nodded, for that moment had changed him as well but for a different reason.

Susan continued. "But I also realized that it was in that moment that I understood how special that gown was, and I suppose even how special baptism was. I realized it mattered."

Jacob nodded beside her. It was light now, and he could see the side of her face, struggling to explain her thoughts. He wanted to hear what she was trying to say. It seemed very important to him to know her thoughts. They didn't have many moments like this, and he was glad he had woken up and gone outside.

Susan continued, "At college, it feels like nothing really matters. Everything is nice, pretty. Clean. All your meals are there. There is a lot of fun and I have really good friends. But almost because it is so easy, I start to forget that anything matters. Coming home and seeing Rosie…" She paused, then continued, "That was really hard. Much harder than I thought it would be. It hit me that it mattered what I did, like *really* mattered. Helping Rosie with school. Being here to help in the house. I don't know, just being here. It's funny how suffering shines a light on what matters. And when everything is just fun, you lose track of that."

There was a time of quiet. The birds began their morning song. They could hear the animals rustling in the barn. All the world was fresh and waking up. The sun began to seriously warm the air and Susan was already thinking about the cool house.

Then Jacob spoke, his voice low and very serious. It was strange and different, for he was the most mirthful of the family. "I understand what you are saying about suffering. But we have to remember to offer our sufferings to Christ. Sometimes I sit in my room and hear Mama cry. It breaks my heart like you cannot imagine. Or I will walk in the barn and Papa is on his knees praying with a face that wears every line of sorrow on it. Seeing Rosie with her hollow eyes just guts my soul. Susan, it has been so hard living here. I don't want to admit it, but I've wanted to go to college just to get away." They laughed ruefully because they both knew Jacob had tried everything to get out of going to college. "But Susan, we have to offer up those sufferings to Christ, and by uniting them to him, we can make up for what is lacking in Christ's suffering and help to save souls. There is no other way to live with Rosie's deafness. Or all the hardships we know. They can bring good. The greatest good. We have to remember that."

Susan nodded as she rocked. "You are right. Remember that book we read, *The Greatest Battle*? We have to give our suffering to save souls. We can't forget that."

Jacob nodded quietly. He was thinking of something more. Something he was having a hard time putting into words.

The two of them watched the colors of the sun take over more of the sky, going from orange to a soft pink. The coolness of the night started to warm just a bit. The air felt wonderful on their arms and faces.

In the silence, Jacob spoke. "When we were tearing the room apart, remember when we found the crucifix hidden in the old church wall? It was very old, and we imagined that a priest had hidden it there and then it had been plastered over. It struck me that we wouldn't have found it if we hadn't torn down the walls. It made me think that beautiful treasures can be found if we are only willing to tear down the wall of pride and attachment to worldly things."

It was actually the moment he had thought about being a priest, and this was the closest he had ever come to talking about it.

Susan didn't know what to say. Now the sun was up in the sky, and it was getting warm. She pushed his arm and said, "Aren't you the sudden philosopher."

Jacob rolled his eyes, grabbed her rocking chair, and rocked it quickly back and forth. They both laughed. Susan said, "Let's make breakfast for everyone. Biscuits, bacon, and eggs!"

CHAPTER 12

Hearts on Fire

Mama sat at the old table and looked at her home. It was summer, and now was the time to do something about all the neglected projects that she had put off all year in order to teach the children. She almost rubbed her hands together gleefully—now some cleaning would be done!

She took out some paper and started to make a list of what she wanted done. She did not let herself reflect on how she did this every year, and yet every year trips to the river, visits to the city, cattle drives, and round-ups often took priority. Nonetheless, every year, after school was out, she had high hopes of deep-cleaning the house and repairing broken things. Perhaps this year they would organize the bookshelf. Yes, a nice, cool task in the heat of summer. She sipped her coffee and enjoyed the quiet of the morning, watching the light play on the tall, golden grass outside her window.

Sierra came out to the kitchen, rubbing the sleep out of her eyes. "Can we go see the horses?"

Mama put down her coffee cup and was just about to

speak when Caz came bounding out of his room. "Us too! We want to go too!"

Oh dear, thought Mama. *The wild horses would never come with so much commotion.* She turned to Caz, "How about if we all go to Sweetwater instead? You both can take your fair goats and work with them as we go?"

Caz nodded happily and went to tell Billy. Sierra looked at Mama and then said, "I'm going to stay home and bake with Rosie. Would that be okay?"

Mama, excited about the idea of Rosie baking, did not notice the way Sierra's eyelashes fluttered, as they did when she was evading truth. Mama said, "Oh! I think that is wonderful! I'll take whoever wants to go to Sweetwater and you can bake with Rosie."

As it turned out, Susan and Jacob decided to go shopping in town, and so it was Jessica and the two boys who went to the stream with Mama. As soon as everyone left, Sierra turned to Rosie and signed "Horses." Rosie's eyes lit up like they had not done since her illness.

Sierra went out and saddled Ginger and Rain, carefully tucking the rifle in Ginger's saddle scabbard. Sierra did not know Rosie might have impaired balance. Did not know she could lose her orientation underwater and drown. Papa and Mama had not told anyone for fear of alarming them, but also because they did not want to believe it was true. "Time would tell" was what the doctor had said. So, they waited and they hoped, watching Rosie, looking for trouble with balance, afraid to let her swim or ride.

But Sierra knew none of this. She brought out the saddled horse and watched as Rosie mounted without a problem. They were going to spend the day riding and swimming, just like the old days.

Rosie's eyes flashed with excitement as she mounted Rain. Sitting in the saddle felt amazing, and the strength of the horse filled her with energy. She remembered suddenly what Papa had said about borrowing the horse's magnificence. For the first time, she did not feel small. She did not feel helpless. She felt fast and strong. Those feelings were a sweet elixir to her heart.

Sierra started off at a walk, but the horses sensed their excitement and started to jig, trotting in place and tossing their heads. Sierra looked back at Rosie, looked at her big smile, her secure seat, and thought, *Rosie can still lope. She's only deaf.*

Sierra broke into a gentle lope. Rosie could not hear the cadence of the hooves hitting the ground, but she could feel the rocking of the horse and feel the wind in her face. She felt alive and free. She closed her eyes for a moment just enjoying the feeling of riding again. She thought again about what her Papa had said long ago about God surprising us when nature makes us feel grand. Galloping across the field on her favorite horse definitely made her feel grand! Sierra looked back and saw Rosie riding, a huge smile on her face, the wind in her hair and her cheeks bright with excitement. Her heart swelled with joy.

Finally, they came near the spring. Sierra stopped and went to help Rosie down, but Rosie glared at her and got herself down. Sierra tied the horses and took the rifle. Rosie followed as Sierra went behind the rocks and they sat on the cool earth and waited. It was a warm day.

Since that day at Sweetwater, Rosie had wondered what it would be like to go swimming. She was worried about the water. She had showered, so she knew it was all right to get her ears wet. She didn't know if going underwater would be bad for her ears. As she lay in the sun with Sierra and felt hot, she finally decided she would get in the water, though maybe she would keep her head out of the water. She stood up and walked to the edge of the spring. Sierra watched, knowing intuitively that this was a big moment for her, even if she didn't understand why.

Rosie stood at the water's edge. The sun beat down on her. She knew the water would be cool and refreshing. She had so many memories of swimming with her family. Finally, making the decision, she jumped in the water, making sure to keep her head above the surface. It felt amazing. She floated on top of the water, looking up at the sky and the clouds floating above them. She felt suspended in time and space, with no cares or worries, no missed words or stories untold.

In that moment of suspension, she gathered her courage, took a deep breath, and went under the water. She opened her eyes and saw the sun filtering through the dark green, saw the rocks below, and for the first time felt entirely free. In a world of no sound, her loss of hearing was forgotten. She floated under the water for as long as she could and then came to the surface laughing. Sierra had been watching, worried, not knowing what to look for, but ready to pull her out of the water if Rosie looked in trouble. So, when she came to the surface laughing, Sierra was filled with both relief and joy. She jumped in the water and splashed Rosie, and Rosie splashed her back. They laughed and swam some more. As Rosie swam, she felt the pull of the water against her muscles, something given, something returned. She felt alive and strong. Finally, happy and exhausted, they got out and lay in the sun, feeling the warm earth beneath them. The puzzle turned around and around in Rosie's head. What was the key? Her father had told her something important that she needed to know, and she needed to remember it. The horse magnified her. Something small made grand. What was the other part of it?

Suddenly Sierra felt the earth's movement. She turned and looked at Rosie, willing her to feel. Rosie's eyes flew open. She could feel it! They stood up and watched the horses come across the plains, and then as they got closer went and hid behind the rocks. Rosie gasped with the beauty of them all. Sierra was so proud and happy for bringing Rosie. The bay stallion came, bringing the mares and babies. The young horses played in the water, pawing at it, then sinking into its coolness and rolling around. The mares drank and ate the green grass which was plentiful around the spring. The bay stallion found high ground and watched. Sierra looked at Rosie and her face was full of wonder and joy. There was so much beauty that she forgot she could not hear. The two girls watched a mare direct her foal: moving her hip and the foal responding with a movement. A flicker of an ear and the foal returning to its mama.

They saw the blue roan filly. She stood alone, looking at the other mares. They watched as she ate, distracted and wary. Sierra signed to Rosie, "I think she is still alone." And Rosie nodded, then signed, "Maybe we could train her, like Mama trained Apollo."

And then the stallion called. The herd gathered together and then in a moment were gone. A wild splash of color, dust, and wind, and then silence. Rosie and Sierra looked at each other, the memory of such beauty and strength reflected in each other's eyes.

Together they rode home. Swimming and riding freed Rosie's soul, and she knew, for the first time, she would be all right. If only she could tell Mama!

They returned home with happy hearts and decided to bake Mama's favorite chocolate cake. They were just taking it out of the oven when Mama opened the front door. "I smell something wonderful," she cried out happily as she came into the kitchen. "It smells like chocolate cake! My favorite!" She swallowed them each up in a hug and kissed them. They wiggled out from her hug, Sierra laughing and Rosie with a big smile on her face.

That night after dinner, the family sat around the old cross in the wall and began their prayers. Papa asked for petitions.

Susan prayed, "For those who are suffering, Lord, please give them relief."

Mama added, "That we get snow for the land and the cattle."

Jacob prayed, "That I know God's will for me." Papa looked at Mama and she looked back at him.

But before they had another thought, Sierra interrupted with a question. "When can Rosie go swimming?"

Mama stayed silent and Papa answered for them both. They had been waiting for this question, dreading it. Dreading the answer even more. Papa answered carefully, "The doctor said she may lose her orientation and drown, so we have to start her slowly and see how she does."

Sierra answered, not at all aware of the dread in her parents' hearts, "I'm pretty sure she will be fine. Let's go swimming on Sunday."

Mama and Papa were silent. Silent with fear. Silent with hope. Finally, Billy, getting frustrated, said, "Let's finish prayers. God, please let Rosie go swimming and be fine."

And Caz responded, "Amen."

That night, Paul and Anna sat outside on the porch in the quiet of the night. They watched the stars fill up the sky. The night air was cool and felt freshening and calming. Mama rocked in her favorite chair and the rhythm of the wood against the wood porch was soothing. Finally, Papa spoke. "Have you seen any sign that Rosie has no balance? Watching her walk around and sitting—she seems fine. I think we need to start pushing her."

Mama took a breath. She had been waiting for this moment. "I think you are right. Let's put her on Apache and see how she does. He will take care of her."

Papa responded, "Put her on Pilgrim. I like that old horse."

And Mama nodded with a smile on her face.

CHAPTER 13

Reading Sign

Now that Sierra had something she wanted to talk about with Rosie, she set upon learning to sign with determination. She studied the signing book and tried to sign with everyone. The two boys were surprisingly good at it and soon the four youngest could be seen signing enthusiastically. When Papa saw this, he gave Mama a look that said, "We had better catch up, so we know what they are saying."

In fact, the girls were making plans on when to go see the horses next and what they would do with the young roan filly. Mama saw "horses" used again and again and she could only wonder what was going on.

As breakfast was being made, Susan announced that she was staying home and organizing things for school. Jacob and Papa were working on fencing. A tree had died from lack of water and had fallen on the fence. Mama had an idea for the day. She asked Jessica and Sierra if they wanted to go to the spring. Jessica was very excited to go. She was still upset she hadn't gone the first time. Mama avoided looking at Rosie and didn't sign because she didn't want Rosie to know. No, she wasn't ready to take Rosie. They needed to make sure she could ride. And, whether she wanted to admit it or not, that lion that had shredded the calf was still in the back of her mind. It was too much of a risk.

Mama took out the rifle and ammunition and put them both in her saddle. She and the two girls rode out: Mama on Apollo, Jessica on Dash, and Sierra on Ginger. There was a long look between Sierra and Rosie as they walked out the door, but it was a look of promise. "Don't worry. We will go out again. I will take you." Rosie trusted her and was willing to wait.

As Mama and the girls rode off, Rosie stood and watched them disappear into the distance. She saw a movement out of the corner of her eye and turned to look. Caz had his hand behind his back and something in his hand moved quickly. Billy stood next to him so Rosie could not see what it was. She signed "What do you have there?"

Caz couldn't sign with his hand behind him, but Billy could. He signed "nothing."

Rosie shook her head as if to say, "I don't believe you."

The two backed away and then suddenly jumped as a giant toad managed to escape from Caz's grip. The two boys started chasing the toad across the yard, jumping and missing. The toad was jumping as fast as it could to save its life. Rosie laughed out loud. She did not hear the laugh, but the boys did. They stopped and looked at Rosie, their smiles huge. Rosie looked back at them, a little surprised; surprised she had laughed, surprised she could not hear it, surprised at their reaction. She signed back "Looks like that toad outsmarted you."

The boys ran off after the toad, but more than that, they ran off to celebrate their sister's laugh.

But there was another sign. An entirely different sign. Mother and daughters rode out to the spring. Apollo was very jumpy and disturbed; Dash and Ginger began to prance as well. And then they saw it. A lion sign. Scat. Track. Blood. A sign of a battle. And then they came upon the horse. A beautiful black mare, with her neck torn so badly she could not stand. Her body covered in long claw marks and bites. Mama said in a severe whisper, "We need to go—we've interrupted her meal." She grimaced. "I have to put the horse down." Mama took out a bullet and noticed that her hands were trembling. She took a breath, quieted herself, loaded the gun, and shot the suffering mare. The shot of the rifle echoed in the canyon and hurt their ears and hearts.

They turned the horses and left as fast as they could. Jessica was quiet and very pale. Sierra was crying over the mare, her tears blowing away in the wind. She realized she hadn't really believed her father about the lions. Finally, with some distance behind them, they slowed to a walk. The horses had known, they had smelled the lion and wasted no time putting distance between them and the spring. They were covered in sweat and their mouths full of foam. They danced at a walk, with bridles jingling. Mama and her daughters exchanged looks. Horror. Sadness.

Anna realized, really for the first time, what her husband had been worried about. What he had been tracking so long ago when she was a girl. Realized in a moment what he had seen with the calf. Realized his anger and his worry. They rode the rest of the way in quiet.

Mama went inside and focused on making dinner, making sure Rosie and the boys were all right. Jessica and Sierra spent a long time brushing the horses and putting them away. They quietly processed what they had seen. Susan and Jacob came home, and Susan, sensing the mood, played a melancholy sonata on the piano.

That night at dinner, Papa signed, "What happened today?"

Billy and Caz began signing quickly about a toad, and then Rosie joined in. Papa was thrilled to see his three youngest signing away. It did not matter that he only caught a few words. He smiled broadly at them until he glanced at his wife and daughters, who were silent and dark. He gave a questioning look to his wife, who just shook her head. Meanwhile, Jacob and Susan joined in as well. They were more hesitant with their signing, but Jacob tried to say he had spent the day with his friends and Susan tried to say she was buying a birthday gift for Jessica, and it worked out just fine that Jessica couldn't read Susan's sign.

When dinner was finished, Papa paused and looked at his family. His eyes sparkled and he had a smile on his face. The children looked at him, delighted and waiting. Papa announced that Rosie would ride Pilgrim. He signed as he said it and Rosie smiled, partly because he got it jumbled up, partly because she was happy to finally ride with Papa, and partly because she knew she could ride. A ripple of excitement went through the room, and they quickly cleared the table and stacked the dishes for later.

If anyone expected Rosie to be scared, they were wrong. Papa saddled up Bandit and Pilgrim and everyone went outside to watch. Mama put aside her memory of the black mare from the morning and stood and watched. This was a big moment, and she was equally scared and excited. Papa went to help Rosie mount the horse and was surprised when she hopped on easily. Papa looked at Mama with surprise and pride. The two, father and daughter, sat in the saddle for a moment, Pilgrim's head up, proud, as though he knew what a special job he had. Papa and Rosie rode around the yard, and Rosie sat easily in the saddle. Everyone cheered and clapped, and Papa's heart just burst with pride in his daughter. Suddenly, Rosie broke into a lope and Mama gasped, but Rosie sat quietly in the saddle. Papa easily caught up to her and together they slowed to a walk.

Papa cried out, "Rosie is fine! She has her balance! That old doctor was wrong!"

And his trumpeting voice was heard by all. Rosie watched her father and was filled with joy and pride. Mama laughed despite herself and after they put the horses away all paraded back into the house to finish the dishes. There was a lot of commotion in that kitchen, and for the first time Rosie helped dry dishes instead of sitting at the table left out. Jessica started singing and Jacob joined in, for even though he said he had no musical talent, he had a beautiful, deep voice that blended with Jessica's haunting high notes. Then Papa, in a burst of high spirits, started to sing an old Irish song he learned from his grandpa, and then everyone joined along and danced as they cleaned. There was plenty of soap on the ground as the dishwashers clapped along. Mama forgot about the morning ride and swished her hips to the song as she cleaned the counter. The little house was filled with joy, and Rosie was right in the middle of it all.

Later, as Paul and Anna prepared for bed, Paul could not stop talking about Rosie's riding. He was so relieved she could ride. He had been so worried that she would be an invalid. While Paul was speaking, the memory of the horse suddenly filled Anna's mind. Paul, noticing her change in mood, asked, "What? Are you worried about Rosie? Don't! She was amazing!"

Anna shook her head. "No, she rode beautifully. And did you see how Rosie was in the middle of the kitchen cleaning while we all sang and danced?" Paul nodded his head, his heart bursting with joy. She swallowed hard, afraid to tell Paul, afraid of what he would say, and still horrified by what had happened. She sat on the bed and looked up at him. "We went to the spring. We interrupted…" Anna broke off for a moment before trying again. "There was a mare. I had to put her down. She was so torn apart. It was a lion. It was awful."

Paul sat down next to her, his heart so filled with joy, there was little room for fear. "But Anna, you brought the rifle. I'm sure that lion heard that shot and took off. You did the right thing."

"Yes." Anna looked at him, feeling his strength. "Yes, and we rode away quickly. But Paul, what if—"

Papa responded firmly. "Listen to me, Anna. That day I found you at the spring. That day you caught my heart. That day that changed my life. I saw lion tracks and was hunting that lion when I saw you. You took my breath away; I was so scared you would be hurt. I have been haunted by that fear because that lion is big, and she is dangerous.

"But Anna, this is what I realized tonight. We have faced some terrible hardships and sorrow. But God is good. He has been with us. He is healing us and making us whole. We have to remember that a greater Father is watching over us. I never thought I would see my family singing and laughing like I did tonight. I was so worried Rosie could not ride, that she would be an invalid. But look how wonderfully she rode!" He took her in his arms and said, "Anna, you are safe. You brought a rifle; you saw the lion tracks. You are wise and strong. Tonight, my love, I saw a greater sign, the sign of God's love in our lives. There is no greater sign than that."

Anna kissed him, and as he held her, she was strengthened and found hope.

CHAPTER 14

The Round Pen

It was lightly raining outside and windy. The children sat around the table, restless. Mama knitted and Susan played the piano. But no one could sit for very long. Sierra was sketching aimlessly while Jessica worked on a new recipe for her bread for the fair. She interrupted Susan's piano, saying, "I don't know what to do! The herbs just sink to the bottom of the loaf! I can't figure out how to make them even."

Susan stopped playing and asked, "Well, what about if you roll the bread?"

Jessica said nothing but began to roll the bread out, wondering if she should cook it differently. Billy and Caz were playing chess, but that quickly turned into a wrestling match when Billy took Caz's queen. Rosie gazed out the window pensively and Jacob sat at the table, agitated, throwing a saltshaker back and forth between his strong hands.

Restless, Rosie got up and went to see what Sierra was sketching. She gasped, for Sierra had horses, beautiful horses, galloping all over her page. She had captured so passionately the arched necks and open nostrils, the wide eyes full of expression. She signed to Sierra, "What about the filly? Did you draw her?"

Sierra nodded and flipped the page. There was a beautiful rendition of the blue roan filly with her high hips, scraggy mane, and wild-flowing tail. She had even captured the brambles that had been caught up in it.

Rosie signed, "What should we name her?"

Sierra signed back, "How about Pistol? She is silver like Papa's pistol, and I bet she's fast." Rosie nodded. They were both still, and then Sierra signed, "I bet we could train her. Should we ask Mama?" Rosie nodded again.

Sierra sat up and said, "Mama, there was an orphaned filly, a blue roan, could we train her?"

Mama looked up from her knitting thoughtfully. When she trained Apollo, she had worked with a very old trainer who had studied horses for a long time. He was different from the cowboys who just roped a horse and jumped on his back until he quit bucking. He was the one who had showed her how to watch the herd and how the alpha mare trained the young horses.

"We can do the same," he told her. "The horses communicate with body language, with pressure and release. If we can imitate that, then we can talk to horses."

She had learned much more than training horses; she had learned self-knowledge and self-control. She learned how to trust and how to lead.

Yes, she thought, *this will be a good lesson for the children and help teach them some virtues.*

She smiled and said, "All right, yes, I think that is a good project for us all. Jacob, can you set up a round pen under that old oak tree by the stream? There is already water out there. Set up a pen next to it with a gate. I would like it to be made of old tree logs so it looks natural. The logs must be set deep into the earth so it will be strong. It's a big job and I am happy to pay you. How long do you think that will take?"

Jacob looked up. The timing was perfect. He needed to think and there was nothing like working the hard ground to give him some time to work through his thoughts. "Can I ask some of my buddies to help? Could you pay them too?"

Mama nodded. "Yes, that would be fine. There are plenty of old trees from the fires we had a few years ago."

Jacob nodded and got up. He called his friends and they decided to start right away. Summer was half over, and they were bored and restless.

Out in the heat, Jacob and his friends measured out the arena and the pen. The arena was a good size: sixty feet in diameter and the pen forty square feet. They took the truck and went to pick up the fallen trees. The bark was burnt, but they picked logs with healthy wood on the inside. They cut the logs to ten feet and trimmed off all stubs and branches. They piled them in the old ranch trucks and delivered them to the spot they had picked out.

Back at the site, the boys began the hard work of digging into the ground. They had shovels and pickaxes for the hard earth and rock. Soon there was a methodical sound of metal on earth. The boys, each of them, worked out their frustrations upon the earth. They could swear and yell at the hard earth, but it did not care. Only hard work and sweat would finish the job. Each of them was a ranch hand, with deep muscle in not only their arms and back, but in their core, for no gym could imitate the work of a ranch.

As Jacob dug into the earth, the steady rhythm of his pickax allowed his mind to wander. He thought about the conversation he had with Susan. He was thinking about being a priest, and he wasn't sure what he thought about it. The idea had been with him for a few years now, and he had told no one. Rosie's accident made him realize that time was precious, and he needed to face this calling. What would his father think? What would his friends think? What did he think?

As he dug in the hot sun, he came closer and closer to the truth: that he had been called to be a priest and bring souls to Christ. The sun beat down and his muscles ached, but as he thought more and more about being a priest, he was filled with the most incredible peace. Time flew by and every night he came home exhausted, wet with sweat, and hungry. Mama saw his face and wondered. He had a strange peace and strength about him that was new. It seemed to her that for the past few years he had been unsettled and anxious about college. She kept quiet, fed him well, and reminded him to shower before he fell into bed exhausted.

She talked to Paul about her thoughts. "I have a feeling Jacob is considering being a priest."

Paul looked at her with a huge smile and a look of awe. "Really? Our Jacob? A priest? Why do you think so? Has he said anything?"

Anna shook her head slowly, "No. I just see his face."

"Well, I could not be more proud. He is a good son, and I'm sure I don't tell him enough. He is hard-working and strong as an ox. But I've noticed his restlessness." Anna nodded. Paul smiled, then said, "You know when I saw him the happiest? When he was tending to that baby calf I brought in a few months ago. At the time, I thought he would become a good rancher, but maybe it is because he is a good caretaker of souls. Hmm." Paul turned off the light and kissed Anna playfully, "We may have raised a priest, sweet Mama."

Anna kissed him back happily. "A priest," she repeated.

WITHIN A FEW WEEKS, JACOB FINISHED THE WORK. They had done a good job, with thick logs sunk deep into the ground, and stripped tree branches for the rails. The pen was adjacent, with a gate in between. He told Mama it was finished. She brought in all the boys, paid them, and fed them well. When Mama told the girls, they were wild with excitement and talked and signed about the day when they could start working with Pistol. When Papa came home that night the girls clambered around their Papa, all talking at once.

"The pen is done!"

"Can we bring Pistol home?"

"When can we bring her home? We want to train her!"

Papa laughed and said he would arrange it for next week. He said this facing Rosie in case she could read his lips, and he was rewarded with a huge smile. No happier papa could there have been!

Finally, the day came when Papa said they would catch the filly and bring her home. Jacob came with his friends, all of whom were very good on a horse and with a rope. Susan, Jessica, and Sierra were there on horseback as well. Billy and Caz stayed with Mama and Rosie at the pen to make sure everything was ready and to hold open the gate.

Papa let them out in search of the herd and found them near the stream that still had a lot of green grass on its edges. They slowly approached the herd. The horses were curious and came over to say hello to the riders' horses. There was nothing

Echoes of Silence

about the tame horses that alarmed the herd and, as the group moved them, they walked peacefully. They all began to move in closer to the filly. The girls looked at her with excitement. She was so beautiful, and boy, she was fast! As they began to separate her from the herd, she dodged this way and that, her speed no doubt what had kept her alive without a mama to protect her. But there were more riders than her, and Jacob and Papa finally got close enough to rope her. Two riders, two ropes so they could apply even pressure and not hurt her. She bolted from the pressure, but the girls rode up beside her, and she settled down in the presence of the other horses. They rode with her into the pen and then took off the ropes. Billy and Caz were ready and closed the gate behind her. Rosie and Mama watched from the rails of the pen.

Once Pistol was away from her herd, she was in a terrible panic. She ran from one side to the other, crashing into the poles and trying to break free. Everyone held their breath, hoping the poles would hold. But Jacob was a good worker, true and honest. The poles were deep, and they held. Finally, Pistol stopped, head down, covered in sweat and shaking in fear. Everything was new and she was afraid because she could not run, and she did not have the herd to protect her.

They gave Pistol some fresh hay which had been stacked near the pen, but Pistol was not to be comforted. All she had known was now far away. She stood in a corner of the pen and stayed there forlorn and lost. Jessica asked if they could leave another horse with her, to keep her company. Mama answered, "No, she needs to learn to look to us for direction and safety. We will be her only companions and soon she will look forward to our visits. When we start to work with her she will learn to trust us. But right now, she is afraid and just wants to be with the herd."

Papa said, "Okay, time to go home everyone. Let's leave Pistol to herself. We are not helping her by standing around."

The next morning, everyone was excited to see Pistol. Jessica offered her newest bread experiment, and everyone quickly ate a slice covered with fresh butter. Jessica opened the bread to see if the herbs were even throughout, and though they were, the bread was a little mushy in the middle. She would have to think about cooking time. No one except Jessica minded, though; they just wanted to go out to see Pistol.

Finally, they left to see her, talking and excited as they walked to her pen. As soon as Pistol saw them, she bolted and ran around the pen, crashing into it and trying to get away. Mama told them, "Just stand here quietly. Let her know you won't hurt her."

They all stood quietly as Mama instructed. Pistol finally stopped running and stood on the far side of the pen, looking at them warily. Billy asked if he could give her a treat and Mama shook her head. "No. Treats won't help, honey. She is too upset to eat. She just needs to get used to our presence. We will come by here every day, and soon we will make friends with her." They stayed a while, admiring her, and then Mama said it was time to go home. "We will come by tomorrow after breakfast."

Every day they visited and stood outside the pen, letting her get used to them. The first few visits she bolted at the sight of them. Then one day she looked up at them and then continued eating. Mama pointed that out. "See, she is not afraid of us any longer. We are making progress."

One day they arrived and Pistol turned and looked at them when they came to the rail. Her ears were up, and Mama said, "See her ears? Now she is curious about us."

That curiosity was what Mama was waiting for. "There is the thinking brain, right there. It is time."

She went into Pistol's pen and asked Susan to open up the gate into the round pen.

"Don't stand near the gate, just leave it open. Our bodies provide pressure which will move her. Everyone, stand over here, by me. I want that open gate to be a safe, open place to move."

The kids all did as she asked. Then Mama started to move slowly and quietly toward Pistol. Pistol moved away from her, and as Mama moved even more, Pistol bolted into the round pen. Mama instructed Susan, "Now, close the gate after me, slowly and quietly. We want her to know she is safe."

Susan did as she was instructed, but Pistol was too smart and too wild not to notice. She immediately ran around, crashing into the walls, trying to get out, all fight and flight. Mama stood in the round pen and went to the center. She just stood there quietly, with a relaxed body. Sierra noticed how her shoulders were soft and she had a quiet look on her. Pistol ran and ran, and the children watched with awe. Pistol was beautiful in the sunlight, her silver-blue coat sparkled with color and sheen. Her muscles moved easily beneath her coat, for she was very strong.

Then Mama pivoted her right shoulder and hip back slightly, as if opening a gate in space for Pistol to move. Her left arm came out at a ninety-degree angle to Pistol's backside as if to block the way. Pistol loped out easily to the right, all the while keeping an eye on Mama. She explained, "You see, I am moving like her mama would have, or the head mare in her herd. I am opening the door by making room with my body and closing the door from her going the other way.

I am going to let her go around a bit and then I will change direction. By doing this, I am teaching her two things. One, that I am her leader because I can move her body, but also that she is safe because she has a leader."

Pistol loped a few times around the round pen, and then Mama suddenly shifted her shoulders and arms, now blocking off her movement from the right and opening up the left. Mama shifted her weight to her right foot and pivoted her hips and shoulders. Pistol made a quick turn and started loping to the left.

"Do you see how she turned by moving her hindquarters toward me? That was a sign of disrespect. But I will let that go for now. Right now she is running in a panic. I want her to calm down and look to me for direction, and then we will ask for respect."

Finally, Pistol stood and stopped, her head high and nostrils flaring. There was nowhere to go, and nothing was pursuing her. She was smart. She breathed heavily, catching her breath and looking at Mama warily. Mama shifted her weight gently, opening up space to the left. Pistol snorted and then began a slow, magical trot around Mama; she nearly floated, her feet were so high. But this was not the mad panic of before; no, this was the majestic stride of an animal who knows it is strong and is surveying something new. Everyone held their breath with her beauty.

Mama said, "She is thinking now, not just in a panic. I am going to ask her to stop by stepping back and lowering my energy."

Mama stepped back, her body perfectly square to Pistol. Her body was quiet and not demanding. There was no energy in her body. Pistol stopped, facing Mama, and looked at her.

"This is good," said Mama. "She is thinking now. That is enough for now. I want every lesson to be small and focused. Today, we taught her that I can move her, and she is safe. Tomorrow, we will ask her to look to me for direction. Remember, her mama in the herd would determine her speed, every footstep, when she ate or drank, everything. Susan, open the gate to her pen."

Susan did as Mama said, and Pistol went into her pen. They gave her fresh hay and checked on the water. They all walked back to the house. The sun was high, and it was warm outside. They were glad for the cool walls of the stone house.

As they walked home, Susan reflected on how much she missed this and how good it was to be working out in nature and working with a horse. Out here, she didn't have to worry what others thought about what she was wearing or saying. Animals and the land only asked for virtue—the virtues of courage and honesty, kindness and perseverance. If you had those things, the animals and land would reward you. In the city, with friends, it was so easy to get caught up in things that didn't matter. She hoped she could live here and raise her children here.

Mama set about preparing dinner, and the children wandered off to do different things. From the boys' room she heard the familiar sounds of scuffing and banging. She went into the boys' room. "What is going on here?" She saw the bed up on its side, resting against the wall. "Boys! Put that bed back right now. You have some extra energy it looks like?" And she scowled at them. They looked at each other sheepishly. They knew what that meant. More work! Mama let the lesson sink in. "Clean up this room before dinner." Mama walked away, chuckling a bit. Children were not much different than horses—make the right thing easy and the wrong thing hard.

When she came into the kitchen, Jessica was sitting at the table. She asked, "Why do you get upset at me for working slowly? Why does it matter? Why can't I work at my own pace?"

Mama thought for a minute. "Well. Let's see. I think it's good to realize that your natural pace can be faster or slower than any other person. And then you should give yourself enough time to finish a project. But sometimes you need to be able to overcome your natural pace and act quickly. Like if there is an emergency. Or if your sister is almost here." Mama smiled hoping Jessica would smile as well, but Jessica was very serious.

"People get mad at me for going slow, but this way I can be more careful, and I enjoy life more."

"That is fine, honey. I think we all have tools in our toolbox, and one of yours is to be precise. No one makes bread as well as you, because you are careful and do a good job. But sometimes you have to realize that you need a different tool and that one is maybe harder to get. Like working quickly and efficiently."

Jessica sat there at the ancient table, tracing the scars in the wood with her finger. She thought about what Mama said and, nodding, realized Mama was right. She was, however, not sure how she was going to fix the problem.

That night as the family gathered for prayers, there was a flurry of talk about Pistol. Everyone spoke at once, telling Papa about the progress they had made. He reminded them to sign, and the family tried to sign as they talked. It was clear Rosie wanted to talk as well, and this made Papa very happy that he had agreed to this project. He had been worried it was a waste of time. He could have just as easily purchased a well-trained horse from his neighbor who was reducing his herd and had a horse that he could use on the ranch. He knew very well it would be a few years before Pistol could be used as a ranch horse, and meanwhile, she would just be another mouth eating hay in a bad year. But seeing the excited smiles on his children's faces made the sacrifice of having a young horse worth it. They moved to the couches and settled, still talking.

Papa listened and watched the kids signing and talking at the same time. After a while, he said, "Time for prayers" and began "In the name of the Father, and the Son and the Holy Spirit." There was a collective exhale around the room, a gathering of thoughts and minds as they all bowed their heads and prayed as a family.

CHAPTER 15

Space of Quiet

The next morning, all the conversation was again about Pistol. Papa noticed that Jacob was a little quieter and more reserved. He caught Jacob's eyes, and Jacob gave him a look that was profound.

"Jacob," Papa said, "I need to check on some fencing in the back. Will you saddle up and go with me? I think Mama has the new filly quite in hand."

Jacob looked at his father and knew now was the time to talk to him. He nodded.

Father and son rode out across the land. The grass was thick and tall. It was turning gold now and reaching the end of its cycle. It reached up to the horses' bellies and waved heavily in the wind, the wheat stalks full of grain. Papa stopped and dismounted. He stood in the grass, feeling it brush against his hands. Jacob watched his father silhouetted against the morning sun, his broad shoulders strong from work, his legs bowed from so much of his life in the saddle, his hat worn and stained from days of heat and rain. He was a good man, well respected, strong and honest. Jacob wanted to carry on that strength; he wanted his father to be proud of him.

Papa pulled up some of the grass. He ran his fingers through the tip of the stalk and watched the grains of wheat fall into his hand. He left it there for a moment, knowing everything about the grain from its weight. This was the grain that would feed his cattle. It was then that a thought filtered through Jacob's mind. It came softly like the rays of sun through the wheat. "Will you feed my sheep?" Christ's words to Peter, three times asked. And Jacob thought about how bread was made from grain.

Papa walked back and mounted Bandit, his movements quick and sure, the muscle memories of a lifetime. Father and son rode on through the grass and up toward the higher places where the cows would be. There was a peaceful rhythm in the horses' footsteps, the cry of a faraway hawk, and the hum of insects flying about as the sun warmed the earth. And in all that, there was a quiet silence between the two. In the space of that quiet, Jacob relaxed and let out a deep breath. Now was the time.

He asked, "How did you know your vocation?"

Papa was quiet for a while and then responded. "I thought about being a priest. It is the highest calling. But, when I prayed, I felt like there was something else I needed to do. I didn't have any peace about it. I ran into your mother, really by accident, and I was absolutely captivated by her. I knew my life would never be complete without her. I prayed then that God would make it clear to me. When I decided to marry her, I was filled with peace and I guess that was how I knew it was the right thing to do."

Jacob too was quiet for a time. Then he said, "That is what I feel too. An overwhelming peace when I think about being a priest."

Papa nodded. "I think that is a good indication."

They rode in quiet, the horses' footsteps the only sound. Finally, Papa spoke again. "Remember, Jacob, a good man provides and protects those who are in his care, both beast and man. I have done that by taking care of my family as best I can and watching out for our cattle and respecting the land that God has given me. You will do the same as a priest. God will bring souls to you, both in your parish and in your life. You must provide for them as a spiritual father, bringing them the sacraments and also good council. You must protect them from evil as best you can. And never forget the power of prayer."

Jacob nodded. He respected his father and these words meant much to him. Many years later, as he rode from home to home, bringing the sacraments and visiting his flock, he would remember his father's council and take comfort in it.

Papa continued. "You should tell your mother too. We can talk to the priest and see what the next step is. He may want you to go to college first. I am not sure." He was quiet again, and then spoke, his voice heavy with emotion. "Son, I am so proud of you. You are smart, a good workhand, respectful to your Mama, and kind to your sisters."

Jacob nodded, a lump in his throat. He did not know what to say. His father's words meant everything to him. And as they rode, their faces shadowed by their hats, neither could see the emotion in each other's eyes. And this was just as well.

MEANWHILE, AT HOME, EVERYONE EXCITEDLY ATE breakfast and cleaned the kitchen. Sierra and Jessica asked if they could take a chance at working Pistol. Mama, excited as well, said, "We will see how she does. It may be too early.

It's important right now that she does not get confused and our signals are clear."

They all walked out to Pistol's pen. Susan opened the gate and Pistol trotted into the round pen. She was smart and knew what was expected of her. Mama walked in and stood quietly. Pistol made a few languid lopes around the pen and then stopped. She looked at Mama, curious. Mama stood facing her, with her chest perfectly facing Pistol. She turned her left shoulder forward and lifted her arm, while at the same time turning her right shoulder and hip back, opening up a space to the right. Pistol turned to the right and started around the round pen. Mama lowered her arms just a bit and Pistol slowed down. Mama explained, "By putting my arms down, I am lessening the pressure which is sending her around. Now, I am going to switch directions. The more I move her feet, the more I tell her I am in charge, but also the more she will feel safe. I am going to send her back and forth until she starts to look to me for direction, and finally for permission to join my herd."

In one fluid movement, Mama raised her right arm and moved her right shoulder forward and moved her left shoulder and hip back. She also stepped one step in front of Pistol, just to make sure Pistol noticed. In a fluid movement of grace, Pistol turned and trotted out to the left. Mama said, "Do you see how she turned hindquarters first? That was a sign of disrespect. I am going to keep her going at a lope and try again. I am going to make her lope until she shows me respect and asks to stop."

Mama put enough pressure to keep her at a good pace and then turned her again. Hindquarters first again. More loping. "This will be her lesson today. Turn facing me and stop," Mama said.

All the kids sat at the round pen, watching their beautiful mama, her eyes flashing and her body fluid with strength and energy. She was captivating, and they could see in moments like this why their father had fallen in love with her. Her black hair had fallen out of its bun and fell around her face and shoulders like a magnificent horse's mane.

Caz pointed and said, "Look! Mama's hair matches Pistol's hair, black with some grey in it."

Mama heard and smiled to herself. She changed Pistol's direction over and over. She looked like she was dancing with Pistol. To the left, flowing mane and tail, then a moment to change direction, a fluid exchange of balance, and then back again. Pistol was sweating, dark stains on her grey coat. She had one ear on Mama, watching her, listening to her. Mama said, "On another day, I am going to ask her to join up, I will be watching for her to lower her head, for her lips to soften, and then for her to lick her lips. That is when she is asking me if she can come into my herd. But right now, I am just looking for respect."

And then it happened, Mama asked for a change of direction, and Pistol turned, keeping an eye on Mama the whole time. Mama immediately relaxed, dropped her arms, and stood quietly. In that space of quiet, Pistol stopped immediately as well. She stood facing Mama, panting. The two stood and looked at each other. It was magical. No one wanted to breathe. Sierra snuck a glance at Rosie and saw that Rosie was transfixed.

Mama said quietly, "Susan, open the gate. Let Pistol go home." Mama stepped back, releasing Pistol. Pistol trotted quietly into her pen. For the first time, she was relaxed. She went to her trough and drank a long draft. Mama said, "We are going to go now and let her relax and think about what happened."

On the parade back home everyone was quiet. What they had seen was magical. They were enchanted with their mama. Sierra asked, "Next time, can I try?"

And Jessica asked, "Me too?"

"Yes," Mama replied. "You can all try. Now she is ready."

That night after dinner, they sat outside, the little family, under the stars. There was a lot of excited talk as everyone shared about Pistol. After a while there was a quiet that fell over the family. A gentle peace in the twilight of the day. In that quiet, Jacob spoke up.

"I have been praying and I am thinking of becoming a priest."

He looked at Rosie and signed to her. She looked at him with liquid blue eyes and smiled.

Mama said happily, "Jacob! That is wonderful!" She choked up with pride and joy and said, "I am so proud of you. You are a good man, Jacob."

Mama rocked in her chair and, in the space of that quiet, the family sat together feeling happy and hopeful.

CHAPTER 16

The Magnificent Echo

August arrived with oppressive heat. Only at dawn could the little house finally find relief. It did its best to keep cool with its rock and stone, with drapes drawn and ovens off, but by the afternoon it was horribly warm and there was nothing that could be done but wait for night. But it was the nights that never cooled that were hard on everyone.

On one of those nights, Rosie slept fitfully, tossing and turning in the warm room. Suddenly she woke up, covered in sweat, her body alert. She'd had a strange dream. It was a silver puzzle piece revolving in the sky, spinning around and around, beautiful and alluring. And then, without warning, the puzzle piece dropped and fell into place. The land shimmered with beauty, and she was filled with a happiness she could not explain. Rosie lay back in bed thinking about it, watching the stars move in the sky. At last, she fell asleep, waking to bright sunlight and Sierra letting her know it was time for breakfast. But the memory of the dream stayed with her.

Sitting around the table and eating eggs and toast, Mama proposed working with Pistol. Everyone groaned about the heat, but Mama laughed at their grumbling and said, "Pistol doesn't like the heat either. She will tire easier and maybe learn her lesson faster. Today is the perfect day to work with her." The children groaned again at her enthusiasm.

Susan got up and as she collected breakfast dishes, said, "Well, I'm sorry Mama, I am meeting with some friends. We are going shopping and then to lunch. I'll be back this afternoon to help with dinner."

Jacob stood up from the table as well and said, "I'm working with Papa. We are going to move the cattle to another pasture with more water and grass." He grimaced, and Mama could not help but notice how much he looked like his father.

Billy said, "Well, we want to go play in the stream! It's too hot to do anything else!"

Mama nodded and said, "Ok, that is fine. Get your chores done, and you can go."

She looked at the three younger girls, "What about you three?"

Sierra nodded and Jessica said, "We'll go."

They quickly cleaned up from breakfast and headed to the round pen. Mama brought Pistol out and sent her around as before. The heat was heavy, and soon Pistol stopped running. She stood, dark with sweat, facing Mama and waiting for instruction. This is what Mama wanted—Pistol, obedient and calm.

She looked at her girls and said, "Who wants to try it next?"

Sierra was at the gate, eager to take a turn. "I want to try," she said.

Mama smiled to herself at Sierra's eagerness. "Okay, Sierra, your turn."

Sierra got into the pen, her eyes blazing and her face

fierce. Pistol immediately ran around, and everyone shuddered as she ran into the pen, crashed into the wood, and fell on the ground.

"Sierra!" Mama called out, "You have so much energy! You have to learn to control that. Make yourself quieter."

Pistol scrambled to her feet, and everyone was relieved to see she was not injured.

Sierra looked helplessly at her Mama. "How do I lower my energy?" The thought was entirely new to her.

Mama answered, "Think quieter thoughts, slow your body down. Make your breathing rhythmic, and relax your shoulders."

Sierra took a deep breath and focused on feeling calm. She sent Pistol around again, and this time, Pistol took off at a gentle lope.

"Nice, Sierra!" Mama called out. "Good job staying calm. Now ask her to change direction."

Sierra changed her balance and Pistol turned, keeping her eye on Sierra. It felt like poetry. Sierra watched Pistol lope around easily.

Mama interrupted her thought and said, "Now ask her to stop. Just relax and breathe deeply."

Sierra let her muscles relax and exhaled slowly. Pistol came to a stop, facing Sierra.

Mama nodded, pleased. "Nicely done, Sierra. Now release her. Put your head down and walk away."

Sierra turned away from Pistol and walked out of the round pen, thinking about how Pistol had responded when she lowered her energy.

After watching Sierra, Jessica was determined to work with Pistol. "Can I go next?" she asked.

Mama nodded.

Jessica went into the round pen and lifted her arm, but Pistol did not move. Jessica turned and looked at Mama, questioning.

"You have to keep your shoulders square, so you don't cut her off." Mama went into the round pen with her and gently turned Jessica's shoulders to make them straight.

Jessica nodded. She lifted her arm, and this time Pistol moved around the pen.

Mama, thinking all was set, walked out to let Jessica work with Pistol alone. But, as soon as Mama left, Pistol stopped.

Confused, Jessica asked, "Why isn't she moving?"

Mama said, "Send her again. Let me watch."

Jessica tried again and Pistol began to graze, wholly indifferent to Jessica.

Mama nodded, seeing the problem immediately, "You aren't sending her with any energy. She doesn't believe you. Remember, if you were her mother, you would want her to move."

Jessica looked at her Mama not understanding.

Mama tried again, "Imagine when Caz was a baby, and he was about to touch a hot stove. You would tell him, 'No.'"

Jessica nodded. "Now, what does your body look like? What are you about to do?

Jessica thought for a moment and then said, "I'm about to jump up and grab him. I don't want him to burn his hands."

"Right," Mama said. "What are your muscles doing?"

Jessica imagined jumping up to pull Caz from the hot stove. "They are getting all bunched together, like they will spring."

"Yes." Mama nodded. "Exactly. And that is what the

alpha horse does too. She doesn't just pin her ears, her muscles bind up, so she is ready to pounce and punish that baby horse. The warning first and then the punishment. So, when we direct the horse, let them see your energy, let them see your muscles ready to pounce."

Again, Jessica put energy into her shoulders and legs as if she were about to chase Pistol if she didn't move. Then she lifted her arms. This time Pistol moved off, not quickly, but like a child who is reluctant to do a job.

"That is better," said Mama. "But I'm not letting you out of that round pen until you get Pistol to lope at a good pace. Try turning her."

Jessica changed her position and Pistol stopped. Mama saw the problem right away. She adjusted Jessica's shoulders. "If you are not exactly square, then you cut her off and she thinks you want her to stop. Remember, your body is telling her what to do. Your body doesn't lie. Even if you want her to go, your shoulder is blocking her and telling her to stop. She is listening to your body."

Rosie watched. Silent. And unnoticed. Learning with her eyes, trying to remember with her body.

Finally, Jessica figured out her shoulders and, summoning her energy, sent Pistol at a good clip around the pen.

"Change her direction," Mama said.

Jessica, focusing on what Mama had told her, changed position and turned Pistol. Fluidly and gracefully, Pistol turned and loped the other way. Everyone clapped and shouted with joy.

"Very good, Jessica!" Mama cried out. "Now, cut her off just slightly and lower your energy."

Jessica stepped in front of Pistol and then deflated her energy like a balloon. Pistol immediately stopped and looked at her. Jessica smiled broadly!

"Well done!" cried Mama.

As Jessica left the round pen, Mama thought, *Not only is Pistol being trained, but my girls are learning patience and self-control.* She smiled, pleased with the morning. She said, "I'm proud of both of you girls, you did a good job today."

Mama suddenly realized how hot it had become. The morning had slipped away, and the sun was high above them. Mama wiped the dirt and sweat off her face with her shirt tails.

But there was another set of eyes that watched Sierra leave the pen. And those eyes burned bright and fierce. Rosie desperately wanted to do what her big sisters had done. She was tired of being seen as weak and an invalid. She was ready.

Sierra felt that gaze burn into her back, and she turned around. When she saw Rosie's face, she smiled to herself, for she knew exactly what Rosie was thinking. Sierra turned and met her gaze. Challenging her. Daring her. Sierra said, still looking at Rosie, "Mama, wait. I think Rosie wants a turn."

Surprised, Mama looked at them both.

Rosie signed, "Please, can I work with Pistol?"

Mama stood there under that hot sun, thinking. Her heart was beating with both excitement and fear. Did Rosie understand what to do? Did she understand she wouldn't be able to receive instructions? Worse, what if something went wrong and Rosie got hurt? Mama looked at Rosie, her face fierce with determination. Mama also knew that look, for she had seen her little girl fight her whole life to keep up with her sisters. She had waited and prayed for this moment and now it was here. Mama nodded and held the gate open. She watched Rosie as she walked in; her clenched fists, her straight back and jaw set. Mama saw it all and waited.

As for Rosie, she walked into that round pen expecting Pistol to respond like she had with Jessica and Sierra. But Rosie didn't realize the anger that she had been carrying with her. She was frustrated at being an invalid. She was frustrated at being left out of things. She didn't like the chalkboard, and she did not like having to sign. She was angry she was deaf and she hated being separated from everyone with silence.

And Pistol, sensing this anger, reared and neighed shrilly at her. Rosie stopped, stunned. She looked at the beautiful filly and realized, Pistol saw her as a threat. She trembled and tried to calm down. But then Pistol began to run. She ran and ran; head up, nostrils flaring. She would not stop.

Mama could not communicate anything, for Rosie had deliberately turned her back. But Mama understood. Rosie wanted to sort this out herself.

Rosie watched Pistol run. She tried to collect herself. She tried to breathe and then she understood. She was angry. She was really angry, and Pistol could sense it. Rosie was suddenly ashamed. She didn't realize, until that moment, the anger she had been carrying all that time. But it was just Rosie and Pistol in that round pen, and Rosie wanted nothing more than to move that beautiful horse.

If only I could share in that beauty, she thought. *Just to be a part of her strength and power.* She tried to remember again what her father had told her out on that ledge.

The echoes.

She breathed deeply and thought about Pistol. She imagined Pistol reflecting her movements. *Like an echo. Like an echo*, she thought.

And then she smiled, remembering what Papa had told her so long ago. "*Sometimes God surprises us. He gives us a voice through nature. In an echo, your little voice is magnified by those magnificent mountains. In the same way, the horse can magnify your ability and allow you to be more than what you are."*

And now she knew. She had found the key. Within her very silence she could make a song, and this beautiful horse would echo her voice. Even if hers was a silent voice. Pistol would be her silent echo.

She loved that thought and relaxed into the silence. She understood now that she could use her silence to know more, to see more, and to feel more.

And then she remembered her dream, the puzzle piece falling into place and the earth shimmering with beauty. She closed her eyes, took a deep breath, and let her anger go. Let it wash from her body like the water in the spring. Cleansing. Cooling. She opened her eyes and saw that Pistol had slowed down, was nearly floating around the pen. She was watching her. Listening. Ready.

She lifted her arm and stepped to the side, like she had seen her Mama and sisters do. Pistol moved off easily and loped around the pen. Rosie stood looking in amazement, watching Pistol respond to her movements, seeing in Pistol a beautiful, strong echo of her quiet movements. God surprising her, making what was humble grand, just as her father promised. Rosie's heart started to beat with joy. She turned toward Pistol. In one fluid movement, Pistol leaned back on her hindquarters and turned, eyes soft. Watching her, responding to her. Rosie sent her around and turned her again. Pistol loped easily, her mane and tail flying, one eye on Rosie. Her eyes were soft, and her neck arched. She was deferring to Rosie. Responding. Echoing the quiet changes in her body. It was amazing to watch this beautiful horse respond to her movements, her pressure and her release, her give and her take.

She changed her direction this way and then that way, her confidence growing, her smile bigger. The silence was a cocoon around her, just her and Pistol. Every movement of Pistol was a sign, an expression. As if Pistol was speaking to her. And then she saw the soft lips, the lowered eyes, the licking of lips, and Rosie understood, as if Pistol was talking to her. Pistol was ready to come to her. Rosie put her arms down and stood quietly. Pistol stopped just as quickly and turned, facing her. Pistol lowered her head and Rosie relaxed her body. Soft. Accepting. Welcoming.

And Pistol walked forward into that open space. Trusting. Rosie watched in awe. Even in her silence, this beautiful horse responded and obeyed her. Maybe Pistol could even love her.

At that thought, tears flowed from Rosie's eyes. Tears of hope. For until that moment she had not realized that she felt unlovable. Blinded by her tears and not daring to move to brush them away, suddenly Rosie felt something warm and soft. Pistol had walked up to her and put her head on Rosie's shoulder. Slowly, Rosie wrapped her arms around Pistol and buried her face in Pistol's warm neck. The two stood there, the orphan and the wounded.

Mama gasped and held her hand to her mouth. She had never seen such a thing. Rosie petted and cooed at Pistol, and Pistol nuzzled Rosie's hair. Finally, Rosie turned away to look at her mother. Both had tears in their eyes. Pistol, released from Rosie's focus, trotted off and began to nibble grass. Mama nodded at Rosie and opened the gate for Pistol to go back into her pen. Rosie stood there for a moment longer, watching Pistol walk away.

Mama, for once, had no words. They all walked home in silence with light feet and happy hearts. That evening at dinner there was a silence but a silence that was filled with awe and love. Papa wondered, as did those who had not seen, and Mama assured him with eyes full of joy that she would tell him later. For now, it was enough to let the magnificence of the day speak in the silence.

CHAPTER 17

Fair Day

It was the night before the county fair. The town looked forward to it all year. The women perfecting their baking recipes, the kids raising their animals, the men talking about the effort of turning the fairgrounds into a county fair. Some fair weekends were intolerably hot, but this year there was a slight break in the heat and everyone in the county was talking about going.

Jessica was excited to bring her bread to the fair and see what the judges thought. The boys had been carefully working with their goats and now they were stocky little fellows who followed the boys around like puppies. Papa was excited to spend time with the other ranchers talking about cattle and weather. Other years, Jacob had shown a steer, but everyone agreed it was too much after Rosie's sickness.

Mama signed up Apollo to compete in a cutting class. Apollo had an incredible cow sense and was able to anticipate the calf's movements to help keep it in the center of the ring. She competed with him every year, and every year she hoped he might be calm enough to win. Last year he had been so excited by the cheering crowds and the cows that he started to buck and prance and lost track of the cow he was moving. She had confidence that he could do it, he just had to calm down and trust her.

The boys packed their showbox with goat food, grooming brush, comb, halters, and chains for showing. They set aside bales of fresh straw for Papa to put in the trailer. The goats were scrubbed and cleaned so the white glowed brightly and the red was clean and vibrant. They were put in a special "night before the fair" pen that was plush with clean straw so they would not get dirty. Jessica carefully and deliberately gathered her herbs and made her bread. Mama took Apollo out on a hard ride to get his energy out and then washed and brushed him until his golden coat shined like a bright penny. Papa hitched up the trailer, loaded bags of feed, bales of straw, boxes, chairs and anything else Mama gave him.

Susan and Jacob talked about hanging out with friends. Jacob was nervous about telling his teammates about being a priest. Some would understand and some would not. Susan got a little giddy about being at the fair with Joe, wondering if he would kiss her on the Ferris Wheel.

That night, long after the moon had gone to bed, Paul and Anna lay in bed, thinking about tomorrow. At last, Anna asked what they had both been thinking. "How do you think Rosie will be at the fair?"

Papa held her and said, "I am sure she will be fine. She seems so much better, and I am still so amazed at how she worked with Pistol. We will just keep an eye on her. Make sure she doesn't get overwhelmed."

Anna nodded, feeling safe in his arms and strengthened by his conviction.

The morning of the fair rose bright and early. The family was up before the dawn, loading animals, getting the bread ready, and loading up Apollo who pranced like he was going to carry an empress. Mama looked at Papa and he grinned back. He loved that she loved that silly half-wild horse for he knew it was a part of who she was.

As they drove into town, they passed family after family, also leaving with their stock trailers and best homemade goods. Soon it became a little parade of trucks and trailers. It was fair day!

At the fairgrounds, Papa got in line with the boys to sign in the livestock. Jessica was dropped off in front to register her bread. Mama and the younger girls walked Apollo to the horse stalls, with Apollo prancing like the fine horse he was, wanting all the world to know. She put him in, and then went to register him for events.

Susan and Jacob walked away to find their friends. Susan was dressed in her best country outfit, dark jeans, scrubbed-and-shined boots, a belt with rhinestones on it, and a shiny buckle she had won a few years back from sorting cattle on Dash. She had on a brightly colored western top with pearl snap buttons, and had it just opened to see the tank top she wore underneath with a bright conch necklace. Jacob too had his dark jeans, boots, and western top with a buckle he had won roping cattle. They were a fine-looking pair of kids, Papa mused as they walked off into the crowd.

At the livestock entrance, the boys stood trembling, waiting to see what the goats weighed. They had carefully fed them and walked them, hoping they would be the right weight and the right bulk. They had to be between sixty-five and eighty pounds. There was a long line of boys and girls standing anxiously, for this was the culmination of so many days and months of carefully feeding and taking care of their goats. There had been years that someone's goat did not make weight. It was crushing. The child had to take the animal home without competing and his project became a total loss. Billy and Caz stood anxiously in line, Billy biting his nails and Caz moving around kinetically, bumping into things and almost knocking Billy over. The goats gleamed in the light as they were weighed: sixty-eight pounds and seventy-two pounds! They were good!

Each into a stall. They set about trimming their goats, brushing them again, and best of all, visiting with every single boy or girl that lived within fifty miles of the town.

Once settled in, Papa and Jessica went to check in on Mama. She was with Apollo in his stall, brushing him and getting him to a beautiful sheen. Sierra and Rosie were fussing over him, braiding his mane and tail. He stood there with half-closed eyes, loving the attention.

Finally, the animals were set, and the family wandered together down the center aisle of the fair. As they found their friends, each split off and soon it was just Rosie and Mama walking together. Rosie held Mama's hand. There were food stands and stands where local artists sold their creations. Beautiful necklaces or bands for your hair. Pottery and fudge. One booth had delicious cowgirl toffee—it was Mama's favorite. She bought a small bag and enjoyed eating it as she walked. At every booth stood a friend, and Mama visited each one. The crowd grew as did the noise. Mama just soaked in the energy and became more and more animated. With all the excitement, Mama only dimly noticed that Rosie was shaking.

When she looked over she saw Jacob standing with some of his teammates They were shaking his hand and patting him on the back. She wondered if he had told them he was going to be a priest. They were all good boys—some had faith, and some did not, but she knew they respected Jacob.

Mama saw Papa in a large group with the other ranchers and tradesmen from the town. He talked and drank with them, men hardened by weather and hardship, good family men who had sacrificed everything for their families. All of them in their country best: dark jeans, fine-pressed western top with pearl buttons, and a well-worn hat that had seen many a sunny and rainy day. But on this day, they let themselves drink beer and talk and laugh the day away. It was fair day!

Mama found a group of her friends as well and stopped to talk. As she laughed and gestured, hugged and told tales, she didn't notice the hand that quietly slipped from hers. They had been going to this county fair since they themselves were children and never had there been any instance of danger. The children of all ages ran around with their friends, each with a pocket of saved money, each in charge of caring for their animals at certain times, each able to ride on the rides with their unlimited ride bracelet. It was the one day the town could play and visit and eat delicious food and escape from the hardships of life. So, Mama did not think twice when that little hand left hers.

Mama and her friends walked through the different booths. Jessica had indeed won first place for her bread, another friend won first place on her apple dumplings, another friend was second in her fudge. Mama came upon a group of children and saw Jessica in one group or Sierra in another. She saw Susan and Joe walking hand in hand and Jacob laughing with his football friends. Suddenly she realized Rosie was not with her.

She began to look for her, worried. She walked back the way she had come, retracing her steps. When she came to Susan, now with her girlfriends, she asked, "Have you seen Rosie?"

Susan had not and now joined Mama in the search. They came to the boys and asked, and they reported they were on their way to care for their goats, so they all went together. Now they came across Papa, and he joined them. And up by the livestock barn they came upon Sierra and Jessica. Mama did notice Jessica was talking to a boy and she made a mental note to ask Jessica about it later. But still no Rosie. Now they were really worried.

Susan told her friends, and Jacob told his. Papa expressed worry to his friends, one of whom was a sheriff. Pretty soon the county fairground was a swarm of people looking for Rosie. No one. No one could find her.

Finally, Sierra asked Mama, "Was she scared? Could she be hiding?"

Mama immediately remembered that tiny shaking hand. Her heart just sank with remorse. She should have known. Why didn't she realize? Why wasn't she paying attention? Mama told Papa and he too was overcome with guilt. Where had he been? Drinking and laughing with his friends.

Sierra said, "Maybe she went to the barn. To be with the horses. Maybe she is with Apollo."

They hurried with Sierra to the barn. There, curled up in the back of the barn, with Apollo's nose at her side, was Rosie, trembling and shaking in fear. Mama rushed in and held her, swallowing her up in her arms and body. Papa too rushed in and held her as well, and finally that little body stopped shaking. Sierra stood at the doorway, worried but slightly indignant, and signed, "What happened?"

Rosie signed back, "There was so much happening and no sound. I couldn't hear Mama's voice. I couldn't hear people walking around me. I couldn't hear the rides. I felt so lost and confused. I didn't know how to tell Mama I was scared. She couldn't hear me."

At this, tears flowed down Mama's face.

"I didn't know what to do," Rosie continued signing, "but I knew Apollo would protect me. So, I came here. He took care of me."

At that a fresh flow of tears came down Mama's face, but these were happy tears because her silly horse had protected her little one.

Papa signed, "Can you go with me, if I hold your hand? Will you go with me and Mama?"

Rosie nodded. And out they went, Mama and Papa on each side, holding her hand. Sierra following behind, angry that Rosie had run away, angry that Rosie wouldn't talk. Word spread like wildfire that Rosie was found, and all was okay. Beers offered to Papa, an ice cream offered to Rosie, and lots of hugs of relief for Mama.

Mama left to prepare Apollo for the competition. After she left, Sierra took Rosie's hand and took her behind the stadium. When Rosie stopped and looked at Sierra, she could see Sierra was furious. Sierra yelled, "Why didn't you say anything!? Why don't you talk? You are getting us all in trouble! We have to watch out for you all the time. Why don't you talk!? Stop this. You are being a selfish brat and you need to start talking!"

Sierra had tears in her eyes and her face was red with anger. Rosie, only seeing that Sierra was mad at her, started to cry as well. She shook her head; she did not understand. Sierra then pounded out the words with her fists, signing, "Why don't you talk? You need to start talking! I know you can. You've got to stop this. You are going to get hurt or get in trouble and no one will know."

Rosie's eyes flew open. She had not thought outside her own miserable world of silence. Had not thought, even for a minute, how it was affecting anyone else. She signed, "I'm sorry" to Sierra and signed again, "I will try."

Sierra, sorry for her outburst and sorry for Rosie's tears, gave her a hug, took her hand and the two of them walked back to the stands and sat with the family.

They all watched Mama as she came out to the arena to compete. She had on a dark blue western shirt with rhinestones, and she borrowed one of Susan's sparkly belts. She had polished her boots and rubbed her saddle and bridle until they gleamed. The whole family was there, including Susan and Joe, to watch and cheer her on. Even Jacob and some of his friends came to watch "Mama Derrick."

When she signed up, they gave Mama a paper with a number. She pinned it to her back. Finally, it was her turn. Apollo came out into the arena with an arched neck and looking like a cat about to spring. They approached the cattle; she had two and a half minutes to pull out two steers from the group and keep them away. She went into the midst of the cows and picked out a steer. Apollo could read her mind and as soon as she came up to the steer, he nosed that little steer as if to say, "Hey you, I'm coming after you!" The cows went in many directions, but Apollo stayed glued to that one and followed him this way and that. And Mama stayed glued to Apollo. They separated the steer from the rest of the herd and kept him outside the group. There were four men on horses to hold the herd in one place and to help keep the steer from bolting out into the arena. Her job was to keep the steer from going back to the herd. Apollo was brilliant and agile as a cat, dashing this way and then that, outpacing and outsmarting the steer. She went back in to get a second steer. Apollo quickly peeled off the steer Mama had chosen. Mama held on to the horn, and stayed centered so Apollo could do his job. Everyone in the stands cheered for them as the score was announced. Mama had done really well and depending on the other scores might win the buckle.

As they left the arena, Mama rubbed Apollo on the neck. He had kept his mind focused on the task and was the amazing horse Mama knew he could be. He knew he had done well, and as they rode out he began to prance. Mama took a look back at her family and couldn't help but notice Rosie smiling and clapping. She was squished amongst her family, safe and secure, and the sounds didn't matter. She had just watched her mama do a wonderful job and Rosie was so proud of her!

The fair went as it did every year. Local musicians coming out to play as the sun settled into the horizon. Boys and girls linking up, walking hand in hand. The men getting rowdier and the woman more relaxed. Children running around on sugar and adrenaline, and all around the feeling of a good time in a good community.

And somewhere in the night, Joe went up to Susan and asked her to go on the Ferris Wheel with him. As their chair rose into the night, all the lights of the city lay out before them, and the moon rose high above them. As the cool wind played with her golden-brown hair and she looked at him with luminous eyes and soft lips, he could not help himself but leaned over and kissed her. And in that moment the world could have exploded with fireworks for the happiness and excitement in their hearts.

This kiss was not unnoticed by Mama, who leaned over and, in the midst of the crowd, gave Papa a big kiss herself. For it seemed not so many years ago that the man by her side had kissed her on that very same Ferris Wheel. And that kiss was not unnoticed by many of their friends. Then, like an echo reverberating back and forth, their joy spread throughout the fairgrounds causing other lovers to kiss and rejoice in their love. For a kiss between true lovers is a blessing to the world.

Finally, late in the night, the Derrick family said their goodbyes, gathered their animals and gathered themselves, and drove home. Home, where the dogs lay at the front gates guarding the ranch and waiting for their masters to return. It was fair day.

CHAPTER 18

Abigail's Gift

A week had passed since fair day, and finally everything was put away, everyone had slept enough, and the household had recovered from one of the best days of the year. The boys were sad their goats were gone and sold, for they had been working with them every day.

What no one knew was that Rosie, in that barn, scared and alone, had tried talking to Apollo. She knew he would not laugh at her and so she tried to tell him about her fears. But she could not hear her voice and she didn't know if the sound was coming out all wrong. She worried she sounded strange and her words were garbled. Apollo did not care; he only heard the fear in her voice and nuzzled her gently. After that night, Rosie spent many hours talking to Apollo, telling him things and watching his reaction to her words. He was a perfect echo to her spoken word. When she was too loud, he would turn away, but when she spoke just right, he would bring his face close to hers and tickle her with his nose hairs.

That morning, Papa and Jacob had already left to check a spring that was getting low from the drought. Mama and the girls sat around the kitchen table eating breakfast. Mama asked them by signing, "Should we work on asking Pistol to join up today?"

Rosie's grin said everything. Everyone agreed it was a fantastic day to work with Pistol.

Suddenly there was a knock at the door. Susan opened it and there was Abigail. She had her four daughters with her and a nursing baby. She looked distraught. Susan immediately welcomed her in. Anna went to her with a warm hug and admired Abigail's beautiful baby. Without anything being said, Susan put on a kettle for tea while Jessica and Sierra ushered the girls into a room with toys. If Abigail had sons, Billy and Caz would have stayed and played, but their sisters had everything under control. Everyone understood that working with Pistol would be postponed, and if they were disappointed they didn't show it. Abigail's distraught face told them all they needed to know.

Anna offered her a chair at the kitchen table. She brought her a warm cup of tea and some bread that Jessica had just pulled out of the oven that morning. They all knew what to do. If someone came to the house, they were to be offered a place to sit, food and drink, and, if needed, a time for conversation. It was what one did. Sometimes, a visitor had to travel a long distance, and the trip was often not made lightly. Abigail took both, but more for the comfort than hunger.

They sipped their tea and ate their bread in silence. For sometimes silence is a medicine all in itself. The baby cried out to nurse, and as the room was empty, Abigail opened her shirt and nursed without the need for modesty. Her breasts were full, and the baby suckled eagerly. Abigail sighed and Anna could see her whole body relax. The sun shone through the window with long, languid rays upon the young mother and her rounded breasts. Abigail's long hair, lit up by the sun, fell upon her shoulders. Anna thought for a moment that if she were a painter this would be a perfect image of the Madonna. She smiled warmly at Abigail, and that smile too was medicine. Abigail breathed deeply again and soaked up the sunlight, the warmth, the comfort, and the immediate feeling of being loved. It was what she needed this morning.

Finally, she put down her teacup and asked, "How do you do it? How do you go all day with everyone asking and demanding from you? Even my husband comes home and demands his dinner and his quiet. All day long I am giving and giving. There is no one who takes care of me. I miss my mother. She is so far away."

And, with this last sentence, big tears fell down her face. Anna put her hand out to comfort Abigail.

Abigail continued, "My house is falling apart; I don't have any time to clean it. I barely have time to feed anyone, especially myself. And then Doug comes home and is mad at me."

Again, those big tears streaming down her face. Anna got up quickly and brought her some tissues. She knew. She remembered.

The baby finished suckling and looked up and smiled at his mama. He looked at her with eyes so absolutely filled with adoration and love. She returned the look of love and adoration. All the sorrow in that kitchen was gone for a moment. But just for a moment, and then the look again of weary sadness. Babies bring their own reward but their own cross of self-sacrifice as well.

Anna got up, refilled Abigail's teacup, and rummaged through the kitchen, looking for something sweet. She found some ginger cookies and brought them to the table.

Abigail took one modestly and chewed thoughtfully around the edges. Anna sat down again. She took a breath and said a little prayer. How well she knew this young mother's suffering, but what should she say to help her, to give her the courage to continue?

Anna spoke. "It's hard, I know. I remember being a young mother. I knew a woman whom I admired greatly. She had seventeen children."

Abigail gasped. "Seventeen! Really? All her own?"

Anna smiled. "Yes, all her own. She was my hero too. She told me that if I could make it past six children, I would be okay, but before that, it got increasingly difficult. So, there is hope."

Abigail laughed despite herself and said, "So, I just need to make it past six children, and I will be all right?"

Anna laughed too. After a moment, Anna went on. "Maybe talk to Doug and explain how hard it is. Can you explain that you need his help when he comes home? Maybe he can take the kids so you can make dinner? Or maybe he could help with dinner? One of the blessings of having so many children is that you and your husband really need to work as a team. It's like branding day, every day."

Again, Abigail laughed, thinking about the chaos of collecting all the cows in one pen—the babies running and jumping, the young male calves trying to mount the other calves, the mama cows lowing for their babies who are all mixed up in the herd. Imagining that her household was like this every day made Abigail laugh.

"Yes," replied Abigail, "I need to talk to Doug. I don't think he realizes how crazy it's been since the baby was born."

"I will make some meals you can put in the freezer," Anna said. "That will help a bit, and then talk to Doug. He is a good man. I know he will help when he realizes how much you need it. Sometimes as women we think we can do everything and there is nothing like a new baby to make us realize we can't."

Abigail nodded. She realized as soon as Anna said it that she had been proud. She had always kept her house in pristine condition and had prided herself on that. Half of her sorrow was not meeting her own expectations. "I also so much want to please Doug. My mom kept a messy house and I wanted to not be like that. My father would get so mad." Again the big tears. "I don't want Doug to get mad like that."

Mama nodded. "Trust in your husband's goodness. Talk to him. See what he says first. Let him be the one to say he wants this or that, but at least let him know what you are dealing with." Mama reached out again and touched Abigail's arm. "And please, take care of yourself. Take a bath or take a moment to have a cup of tea in the morning. Remember to do things for yourself when you have a moment. If you are falling apart, the house falls apart. You are a good woman and a good mother. Remember that. And…" Mama smiled at the baby. "Enjoy that baby of yours. They give us so much love and joy, take the time to just enjoy him." Mama thought about her eldest son, about to go away, and became a bit teary-eyed. "They grow up so fast."

Anna called in her girls. They came out with Abigail's daughters. "Susan, can you take the girls over there and you all can give Abigail's house a deep clean?"

Susan nodded. She understood. Neighbors helping neighbors.

When Rosie was sick and in the hospital, Jessica had called Susan night after night in tears. It was just her and Jacob trying to run the house while Mama and Papa were with Rosie. Susan tried to help over the phone but was distraught at not being able to come home and help. She was so thankful that so many friends and neighbors had come over to help with meals, help watch Billy and Caz, and help with the animals. The Derricks knew what it was like to feel like everything was falling apart.

The girls clambered around their mama. Beautiful girls, with bright eyes and cheerful faces. Clearly Abigail was a good mother. They asked their mama, "The Derrick girls are coming to our house to play with us. Is that all right?"

Abigail took a long thankful look at her friend and neighbor and smiled. "Yes, that is fine."

All four girls went off with Abigail to help her for the day. Mama sat in her empty kitchen watching the sunlight play along the old tile walls, seeking out the dishes on the shelves, the flowers on the table, all the miscellaneous items that had been left on the counters. She sipped her tea and thought about days gone by, crying babies, toddlers running around recklessly. The crazy days of cooking dinner with a baby on her hip and one clinging to her apron. Those were good days and now they were days long gone. It was a blessing to talk with Abigail and remember her own days with young children. It reminded her of the many blessings she had been given over the years.

Billy and Caz, just in that moment, came bursting in the door full of mud and trouble.

Billy said, "I saw all the girls leave. Can we go to the stream?"

Mama was so comfortable sitting in her chair being melancholic that she considered sending them off by themselves. But then she thought about it and decided to go with them. For these days too would soon be gone. She rose to her feet and smiled. "Yes, let's have some adventures by the stream. It is a beautiful day!"

CHAPTER 19

Rosie's Dance

Sunday morning came bright and beautiful. Papa came out into the kitchen whistling and saying loudly, "Let's make pancakes today!"

Billy was already up and cried out, "Yes, with bacon!"

Caz, not to be outdone, said, "Pancakes with maple syrup and whipped cream."

Sierra heard the commotion from beneath her soft covers and mumbled, "With strawberries." And this woke up Jessica, who leapt from the covers and opened the curtains to the room, letting the morning light spill in. Sierra was surprised. Usually Jessica was slow and deliberate. Jessica looked at Sierra and had the most unusual smile. Yes, the morning had started out well.

Susan groaned and turned over in her bed, for she had been out late with Joe. Rosie sat up as the light filled the room. She yawned and stretched languidly. She closed her eyes, feeling the warmth, feeling the strength in her muscles.

Sierra saw this and felt the healing in Rosie's soul. That simple luxurious stretch was a good sign. Blood moving into all the parts of her body. She still had not uttered a word since coming home, but this stretch made Sierra smile, and she too stretched, enjoying the feeling of her muscles and body after a night of good sleep.

The smell of coffee and bacon wafted through the little house and woke Mama up. Sunlight was streaming through her windows and already the morning felt good. She put on her robe against the morning chill and walked into the kitchen. Paul handed her a warm cup of coffee well laced with cream. Just like Anna liked it. She kissed him and he smiled, perhaps a little too broadly, which Sierra noticed as well. It felt good to see Papa like that, a little out of control, and to hear Mama's playful laugh. Yes, it was a good morning.

The family sat down to eat, sat at the ancient table which Grandpa had made from an old oak that fell one winter. The table had grooves and markings, like an old man that was very wise. They bowed their heads and said grace. Rosie bowed her head with them and was silent.

They ended with a resounding "Amen," and they began to eat, enjoying the bounty of the morning. Pancakes, strawberries, whipped cream, eggs, and bacon, along with fresh coffee and orange juice. Papa looked at his beautiful family, and asked "Well, family, what are we going to do today?"

"Work with Pistol!"

"Play in the stream!"

"Take a hike!"

Papa sat back and winked at Mama and said, "Well, what do you think, Mama? What should we do today?"

She nestled in her chair and said, "Well, how about if we take a hike to the stream, have a picnic, and then on our way home visit Pistol and we can show you how far she has come. Remember how wild she was when you brought her in?"

Papa nodded and thought it was a great idea. He looked at the clock, "Okay, one hour to Mass. Clear your plates. Susan, wash the dishes. Jacob, put away the food. Girls get dressed. Remember, Billy and Caz, you need showers!"

Mama nodded and wrinkled her nose. Showers indeed!

Everyone scrambled and within an hour met again in the living room, dressed in their nice clothes, ready for Mass, boys showered and looking surprisingly handsome. Mama nodded in approval, and they got in the car and drove to Mass.

The gospel was St. Matthew and a well-loved reading: "Look at the birds in the air. They don't plant or harvest or store food in barns. But your heavenly Father feeds the birds. And you know that you are worth much more than the birds. You cannot add any time to your life by worrying about it. And why do you worry about clothes? Look at the flowers in the field. See how they grow. They don't work or make clothes for themselves. But I tell you that even Solomon with his riches was not dressed as beautifully as one of these flowers. The thing you should want most is God's kingdom and doing what God wants. Then all these other things you need will be given to you. So don't worry about tomorrow. Each day has enough trouble of its own. Tomorrow will have its own worries."

Paul and Anna grasped each other's hand. They needed to be reminded of this truth. Paul whispered, "The thing I want most is God's will, my love. We must not worry, not about the drought, or Rosie, or anything else."

Anna squeezed his hand and nodded. Sometimes it was hard, but they had faith and they had each other for strength.

After Mass, Anna noticed Abigail standing and talking with some girlfriends. She had on a bright dress, and she was talking with sparkling eyes and an animated smile. Anna went over and gave her a hug. She stood with the ladies and joined in the conversation. She could see Paul talking with some of the men, so she waited and enjoyed the time with friends. They all lived so far from each other; this was really a special time. Finally, the other ladies left, and Anna looked at Abigail. Abigail hugged her and said, "Thank you. I talked to Doug, and it went so well. He was feeling left out and kind of taking it out on everyone because he didn't want to admit it. When I asked if he could help, he was so generous and immediately said he would. That night we set aside some time just for us. He gave me a nice bath with candles and music. After…oh, it was lovely. It's so funny how when there is a new baby, we can just get lost. Thank you so much. It also felt so good to have the house clean!"

Anna's eyes shone with joy. Someone had given her the same advice long ago and she was so happy she could pass it on. She hugged Abigail again and told her, "I'll bring over the meals this week, so you can just pull something out when things get crazy."

After Mass, the family hiked to Sweetwater and set up a picnic. Mama had prepared a feast and they enjoyed fresh homemade bread, cheese, and meat, with lots of fruit from their garden. Mama had put in some chocolate cake as well. They all ate and talked happily. Rosie had a smile on her face, for she was enjoying the company, the sunshine, and the good food. But she also had a secret. She was no longer afraid of the water. When it was time to go into the river to play, Mama watched Rosie anxiously, but said nothing. The doctor was wrong about Rosie losing her balance and they prayed he was wrong about the water as well. Papa was ready to pull her out of the water if she got confused about which way was up. But watching her ride had given him so much hope.

Everyone jumped into the water and began swimming and splashing. Rosie went into the river, waist high, and began splashing and playing with her brothers and sisters. Suddenly, Rosie dove into the water. Papa and Mama both stood up, but Papa held out his hand and looked at Mama. "Hang on. Let's see what she does."

Suddenly, Rosie came up for air, smiling. Everyone cheered. "Hurray for Rosie!"

Mama and Papa grinned at each other. God was blessing them, indeed.

That afternoon, while everyone relaxed, Mama and Susan sat on the bank, enjoying the sunshine.

"How is Joseph?" Mama asked quietly. Inviting. Not asking too much, but also, most definitely, asking.

Susan smiled in the sunlight and Mama saw that look. She knew the look. She remembered talking to her own mother, sharing that first touch of love. It seemed like a long time ago and yesterday all at the same moment.

Susan said, "I love him. He is so wonderful. He is kind and makes me laugh. He works hard, Mama, like Papa does. He is a good man. I love his family too. His mama is quieter than you, but I like her too."

Susan looked at her mother, trying to express so much more than what her words could say. She looked at her mama for the first time, thinking of her meeting Papa, seeing in him what she saw in Joe.

Susan asked, "Mama, how did you know Papa was the man to marry? You seem so happy together."

Mama laughed, for there had been plenty of fights between she and Paul. But they always resolved them, even if it took years. And in the meantime, both were very careful not to say hurtful things. Yes, they were happy. Mama thought back for a moment. She said, "Well, first of all, marry a good man who has a strong faith. When you are so mad at each other that you cannot see straight, it may be only your faith in God and your accountability to him that keeps you from making a very bad mistake. Second, marry your friend. Marry the man that you can sit with, trapped in a snowstorm, and still enjoy his company. Your father is my best friend, and I love talking with him. Third, marry the man that will defend you and protect you—whether with his actions or his words. And of course, make sure he welcomes the children God gives you."

Susan nodded. She had watched her mother and father her whole life, and while it was good to hear these principles, she knew them already.

Then Mama said, "Why don't we invite him to dinner, let Papa meet him too."

Susan thought that was a great idea.

The sun began its journey back to the earth and Mama declared it was time to pack up their things and visit Pistol. It wasn't too far, but she wanted to show Papa how much Pistol had improved. As they walked, they discussed who would work with Pistol. Everyone wanted to do it. So, finally Papa said everyone must take a turn except Billy and Caz who had not been taught. Susan explained she had not been taught either, and Papa looked at her and asked why. Susan looked him back in the eye and said, "I have been spending time with Joe."

Everyone stopped and looked at Susan. This was the second time she had mentioned Joe and she sounded awfully grown up this time. Papa was glad he had on his hat because his eyes were shaded from the sun and he hoped Susan could not see all the emotions flying through his heart: jealousy, pride, love, and loss. All he could see was a little girl in pigtails telling him about a butterfly she had found. He was stunned and quiet. Susan saw all this, even beneath the brim of his hat. She had known he would react like this and that was why she decided to say it now, while on this glorious Sunday walk.

Sierra took this moment to ask if she could work with Pistol first. Jessica glared at her, because of course she wanted to go first. But Mama said, "All right. Susan, can you open the gate?"

Sierra went into the round pen while Susan opened the gate. Pistol had been left alone for a few days due to the visiting of Abigail and chores on Saturday, and she seemed like she missed the company. She eagerly went into the round pen to be with Sierra. Papa was impressed already that Pistol wasn't flying around trying to get out. Pistol stood at the center and looked at Sierra curiously.

Sierra took a breath, squared her shoulders and sent Pistol around in a gentle lope, just as Mama taught her. Sierra worked Pistol back and forth. Pistol turned with her hindquarters toward Sierra and Papa thought, *Darn it, that horse is being disrespectful.* He had seen plenty of young colts turn with their hindquarters and then kick out at the person moving him. If a horse's hoof hit you, it could cause a lot of damage. One of his neighbors had been kicked so hard his leg had been broken. He looked at Mama, but she gave him a reassuring nod.

Pistol and Sierra continued to work. Pistol started to sweat, and her loping slowed a bit. She turned on the forequarter with her eye on Sierra. Papa thought, *Okay. It's going to be okay.*

Pistol kept going, now keeping an ear and eye on Sierra. Mama suddenly cried out, "Her lip, look! It's soft. Do you see how it is kind of flapping. She is ready to join up. Sierra, watch her, when she starts to lick her lips, she is asking to join up to you. To be part of your herd. Keep sending her around and watch."

Sierra kept her moving, to the right and then to the left. Everyone watched, spellbound. And then suddenly, Pistol began to lick her lips.

Mama said, "Do you see? She is licking her lips. Drop your arms and stand quietly. Lower your head and take all the energy out of your body. Remember your energy kept her moving, but now your quietness will invite her in and let her know she can approach you."

Sierra did as her Mama said and tried to deflate her body. Pistol stopped and looked at her, thinking, watching.

Mama said, "Step back a bit, invite her in."

Sierra did as her mother instructed as Pistol took a step forward. She took another step, licking her lips. Sierra stood in the middle of the arena, astounded and amazed that this beautiful horse would want to come toward her. She listened to Mama's words, but she felt full of excitement and nervousness. Pistol took another look at her and then trotted away. Sierra wanted to cry and scream at the same time. Mama's sharp voice caught her attention.

"She just disrespected you. Step in front of her right now and turn her."

Sierra did as she was instructed, and by the force of her passion Pistol immediately turned around. Hindquarters first. Okay, this part Sierra understood. She focused on sending Pistol back and forth. Mama had an idea and said, "Work on slowing her pace. This will teach you how to lower your energy."

Papa watched, enthralled. He understood generally what Mama had done with Apollo long ago but didn't understand how much it involved controlling your emotions and your body.

Sierra worked and worked on lowering her energy. As she became tired, her mood relaxed and she breathed. Pistol slowed to a collected trot. Sierra gasped. She had done it! She minded her emotions and slowed Pistol to a languid trot. Pistol was almost more beautiful in her controlled movements. Finally, once again, Pistol's lips became soft, she lowered her head, and then began to lick her lips.

"Okay," Mama said, "you know what to do. Slow down and breathe. Lower your head and think quiet thoughts, like you are trying to sleep."

Sierra did as Mama instructed. She actually closed her eyes and let her body go soft. Suddenly she heard something. She looked up. Pistol was walking toward her with liquid eyes. She reminded herself to breathe. And then Pistol came to her and nuzzled her. Slowly Sierra reached out her hand and touched her beautiful, soft neck. She rubbed it as she had seen the other mares rub their baby's neck with their lips. She had tears in her eyes, for not only had she mastered Pistol, but she had also mastered her own reckless passion, and that had never happened before. Sierra breathed deeply, and so did Pistol.

Suddenly, Billy and Caz shouted with joy, and before Mama could silence them Pistol bolted. Sierra looked at her family. She was overcome with pride and joy. Now that Pistol was running around, everyone broke down cheering and Papa was very proud and said so. He declared, "That Pistol is some horse! She is going to make a fine cowhorse, and I'm very impressed with what you all have done with her."

And everyone looked at each other, filled with pride from Papa's praise. But the day was not finished and there was a surprise still ahead. Rosie signed, "Can I go in?"

Mama nodded, excited to show Papa what Rosie had done. Rosie went into the round pen and Pistol stood quietly, watching her. Rosie closed her eyes and focused, remembering the last time she worked with Pistol. Confidence filled her heart. The quiet helped her focus. The quiet was part of the beauty. She opened her eyes and squared up to Pistol. Rosie put out one arm with her other shoulder and hip back, opening up an entrance for Pistol to move. Pistol took off at a gentle lope. Rosie turned with her, amazed again that her body could move this beautiful half-wild creature. She watched as Pistol loped around, her muscles gathering and releasing energy. Watched as her coat glistened in the sun. Feeling the warm sun on her face and shoulders, she felt so alive. So very alive in this moment. Rosie then leaned the other way, changing her center of balance, closing the door with shoulder and hip and opening the other direction. Pistol turned and changed direction. Rosie smiled, her body feeling strong and fluid, like a dance between her and Pistol. The silence increasing her sense of strength and movement. Pistol echoing her movements, making them stronger and more powerful. Pistol echoing the silence and creating a song with her dance.

Papa watched and was overwhelmed by the beauty of his daughter. She was only ten, but she was poetry in motion. Her blonde hair shining in the light, her body moving this way and then that way. The horse's grey coat was almost metallic in the sunlight, muscles rippling as it changed direction with an incredible fluidity and strength.

Rosie paused for a moment and looked at Papa. She mouthed "Echo." He was taken aback. It was the first time she had attempted to talk. The first word, in any form, that had been communicated. He thought for a long time what she might mean, or if he had understood correctly. And then he remembered their time sending echoes across the canyon and wondered if that was what she meant.

Rosie turned back to Pistol and sent her around again, rejoicing in Pistol's response. Rosie turned Pistol, and then she saw Pistol's lip going soft and then Pistol licking her lips. She stopped and made her body quiet and soft. Pistol stopped and faced Rosie, licking her lips with soft eyes and lowered head. Rosie stood there. Quiet. A smile across her face, her blue eyes alert, in the moment and shining bright. Papa held his breath. To see Rosie like this seemed like a miracle he had not dared to hope for. He looked at Mama who nodded and smiled just as big. Rosie stepped back and Pistol began to walk to her and then paused only a moment and put her head on Rosie's shoulder. Rosie put her check against Pistol's soft face, and they stood like that in silence, words not needed or missed.

And then Rosie threw back her head and laughed. It sounded musical and happy. Rosie backed away from Pistol and Pistol followed her. She turned to the right and Pistol, head down, ears forward, also turned to the right. Rosie shifted her balance as though she was playing tag, and Pistol turned in a fluid, snakelike turn, following her. Rosie and Pistol ran around the arena, with Pistol gaining speed, but never going past Rosie. She was following Rosie in a beautiful dance of motion and love.

The family stood around watching in awe, soaking up Rosie's laugh like starving children. Rosie for once had no need for sounds or hearing; it was just her and this beautiful horse dancing in the sunlight on a beautiful Sunday afternoon. The dust rose up in the arena and the sunlight filtered through. Everything seemed surreal and almost magical. Mama remembered a time long ago when she danced with a young, half-wild colt. She smiled and pondered how blessings were given to generation after generation.

Rosie stopped, panting, with flashing blue eyes and rosy cheeks. Pistol came to her and rested her head in Rosie's arms, and Rosie just stood there petting Pistol and letting her breathing slow down. Everyone stood around them with tears in their eyes, their hearts bursting with joy. Rosie turned and looked at her family with a big smile and signed, "We were dancing."

CHAPTER 20

Secret Adventures

The next morning, Susan asked Mama if they could go shopping before she had to go back to school. It was a somber moment, realizing that Susan would leave them once again. Mama looked at Susan. She was tall and confident. Her light brown hair was thick and wavy and fell around her beautiful, blue, almond-shaped eyes. Mama imagined her in a wedding dress, and then pregnant with a little round belly, and then holding a little one. It was all so good and wonderful.

"Mama, can we go?" Susan interrupted her thoughts.

"Yes, yes, let's get started early. Are you ready?"

As soon as they left, Rosie came to Sierra and signed, "Can we see the horses?"

Sierra signed, "Pistol?"

Rosie shook her head and signed, "Many horses."

Sierra smiled mischievously. "Yes, let's go look!"

She told Jessica she was leaving to take a hike with Rosie. Jessica nodded, for she had her own plan of mischief today. Jessica asked Jacob if he could watch the boys, but Jacob had planned a meeting with the priest. So, Jessica went off with the boys, Jacob went off to town, Mama left with Susan, Sierra went off with Rosie, and Papa left for the cows.

It was to be a day of adventures.

ROSIE AND SIERRA TACKED UP GINGER AND RAIN. SIERRA made sure that Rosie got Rain herself and tacked her up. She watched from the corner of her eye, but Rosie knew well enough what to do and using her ears wasn't really a part of it. At first, Rosie felt clumsy and awkward. It was so strange to do all the familiar things without sound. But the muscle memory took over and then she worked easily and swiftly. She was excited to go out on an adventure.

Sierra brought the rifle and ammunition. She tried not to think about a lion sneaking up on her deaf sister. She would just have to be extra vigilant. They rode into the morning sun, feeling the movement of the horses, feeling the sun warm on their shoulders, seeing the beautiful countryside unfold before them. Rosie relaxed in the saddle and enjoyed the feeling of it all. As the land opened, Sierra went into a gallop. Rosie, following Sierra and knowing Rain would not leave Ginger, put her arms straight out. She put her face into the sun and wind, relaxed into the rhythm of the horse's movement, and felt as though she was flying. It felt amazing and it mattered not at all that she couldn't hear! Her body felt strong and alive, her mind was clear and bright, and she felt as though the anger, the fear, and frustration were flying from her body, flying off into the wind and the sun.

Soon they arrived at the spring. They tied the horses up so they could eat fresh grass and, taking the rifle and lunch, they went to the spring. They both stripped their clothes to their bathing suits and went in the water. Rosie and Sierra played in the water, their splashes looking like diamonds in the sunlight. They dove deep into the dark green water and made silly faces underwater as the sunlight set the underwater world on fire. The girls got out and lay in the sun, letting its warmth dry their bodies. Rosie and Sierra laughed and compared tans; Sierra was darker.

Then Sierra heard it and Rosie felt it. They looked at each other.

The horses!

They scrambled, grabbing their clothes, lunches, and rifle, and hid behind the rocks. The horses came, this time languid and confident. The stallion paused only for a moment and then set to drinking. After he raised his head, the rest of the horses approached. Rosie watched, her eyes sparkling with joy. Sierra looked at her sister and felt so happy and proud that she had brought her here.

Meanwhile, Jessica and the boys were having their own adventure. Jessica had determined that she would go work with Pistol and get Pistol to join up since both Sierra and Rosie had gotten Pistol to join up. She was going to go alone, but after walking to the round pen she was happy the boys were there, just in case something went wrong.

She opened the gate and Pistol, welcoming the company and activity, went easily into the round pen. Jessica got in and stood in the middle. She took a deep breath and, summoning her energy, she sent Pistol around. Pistol looked at her curiously and wandered around eating tufts of grass.

Jessica tried again and then lost her temper and shouted, "Go on, you stupid horse! Why don't you go?"

Pistol moved away at the sharp sound, but she was clearly running from Jessica. Jessica felt bad, she knew this wasn't the way to do it. She stood in the center of the pen pondering what to do. Pistol realized Jessica wasn't chasing her and so she too stopped and set to grazing again. Jessica said, "I don't know what to do."

Billy said, "Well, why don't you pretend you're yelling at us to clean the house?"

And Caz said, "Remember what Mama said, that this would be how her mama saved her life? Or something like that? Why don't you pretend it really matters?"

Jessica stood straight and positioned her shoulders as Mama had showed her. She put out her arm and pretended that she was saving Caz from the hot wood stove. She let herself feel the bounding up of her muscles, like she was about to pounce. Suddenly, Pistol set off around the pen, keeping an eye on Jessica. Jessica was so excited she could barely believe it had worked! She moved her body and changed position; Pistol turned and went the other way.

Billy said from the rails, "Bad turn. She disrespected you."

Jessica set her teeth and turned Pistol again. This time Caz, who was chewing on a piece of grass, said, "Wrong again."

Jessica grew insistent and sent Pistol around, now Pistol was going at a pretty good pace. Jessica moved her body quickly and assertively and this time Pistol turned while keeping an eye on her. There was a new head mare in the round pen with her. Jessica was so excited! She was doing it! She couldn't wait to show Mama!

Back and forth the two of them danced, Jessica feeling her strength in her body, feeling the strength in her mind as well. And now the two boys were cheering her on, and Pistol didn't care. This way and that way.

Suddenly, Billy shouted, "Her lips! Look! She is almost ready!"

And then within moments Caz shouted, "She is licking her lips! She is licking her lips!"

Jessica took a deep breath and stopped. Pistol stopped and looked at her. Jessica let her body go soft and supple. This was much easier for her to do. Pistol took a step forward and then another. She walked up to Jessica and nuzzled her, seeking those soft touches she had missed from her mama.

Meanwhile, Jacob stood at the edge of the church, pausing before he walked in. He would not have admitted it to anyone, but he was scared. Scared of the momentous commitment he was about to make. There was something about saying it out loud and saying it to a priest that made it real. He thought about giving up being married and being a father. Thought about giving up riding the range with his father, tending the cows. At that thought he almost went home.

A voice, a memory, sprang within his heart. "Peter, will you feed my sheep?" And then he remembered his father's advice. He would ride the range, bringing the sacraments to the old and sick and visit the members of his parish. And this thought filled him with so much joy that he walked in most eagerly. The priest was there waiting for him and brought him into his study.

The priest started. "Tell me why you are here."

And Jacob began telling the priest about Rosie's illness. About the realization he wanted to save souls. And finally, about the immense peace he had when considering being a priest and bringing souls the sacraments. They talked a long time, the priest and the boy. And afterward, joy and peace surrounded the two in that room. Jacob left with a plan. He would join the seminary, take some schooling with the priests, and continue to discern his vocation. No decisions needed to be made now except to be open to the promptings of the Holy Spirit and follow Christ. All would be made plain.

Susan and Mama did some school shopping and bought groceries for Joe's visit. Susan told her stories about her and Joe. The time he surprised her with a morning hike and breakfast overlooking the plains. How he had been at her side during Rosie's time in the hospital. She and Mama laughed when Susan told her how hard it had been for him to first ask her out. So many precious memories and thoughts shared.

They stopped for lunch at a nice restaurant. A break from burgers when they were all together and usually in a rush. As they ate their salads, Susan sat in the soft sunshine, watching the water play on the glass cups full of water and ice.

Susan asked Mama, "What was it like when you had a baby? How did you know what to do?"

"Well…" Mama was quiet for a moment, trying to find the words to summarize all she had learned over the years. "I guess, it seemed like when that baby was first born, it needed me completely. It was like the goats or the cows. When the baby wanted to nurse, I figured it needed to nurse. When the baby wanted to be held, I held it. That baby was so trusting and vulnerable. All it had was me to take care of it. It could do nothing on its own. If I did not respond, the baby would think the universe had abandoned it." She paused and chose a bite of salad. "I think at around eleven months old the baby starts to get a will."

"What do you mean?"

"Well," and Mama laughed, "the baby wants to eat bugs or grab a knife. It becomes pretty obvious that these are wants and not needs, and that he can't have those wants. So, then you have to say no."

"Is that hard to say no and watch the baby cry and make a fuss?"

"Well, yes. Especially at first, because you are so used to giving the baby its needs. But it's easy when it's a knife or a bug! But the best thing is diversion and then you realize the baby is just exploring how and in what way it wants. So yes, give the baby a toy instead of a knife or a piece of apple instead of a bug. Then you can also teach the child to look outside of immediate impulses and learn to look for better ways to get his needs met."

"Seriously? The baby learns that?"

"Well, maybe not at one or two, but all those reactions are put in the mind, in the subconscious actually, and the child will use that later. Just remember, everything you say or teach the child is how they will talk to themselves or what they will incline to as an adult."

Susan was quiet and thought happily about getting married and having children. She was excited and eager to begin the next stage of her life.

AND PAPA. THE FIRST OF THE CREW TO LEAVE THE HOME that morning. He repaired fencing and could not help but notice the wetlands were drying up. He depended on that snowmelt to settle in the low areas and stay wet, providing grass to the animals. He checked the cows and could not help but notice they were not quite as fat and shiny as they had been in June. His chest tightened under his leather vest. He prayed and asked God for rain but especially for snow. It was the snow that gave the long-lasting water that kept things wet. He would have to start feeding the hay in the barn. He shuddered with the memory of those dead cows in these very fields when he was a young boy riding with his father. And though he swore it would never happen again, he knew all too well he was under the mercy of God. He prayed. Prayed for rain and snow. Prayed for God to protect his family and his herd. Prayed for the souls of his children, that they would find their way, especially Jacob. He would die for them if it would help, but of course it would not. He had to protect and provide, and he knew that all too clearly.

AND SO IT WAS THAT EVENING THAT EVERYONE CAME home and sat around the family table. Everyone wanted to talk at once, except Papa, who was worried, and Rosie, who still would not speak. And Jacob, who was full of joy and peace and did not know the words to express it all. And Jessica, who did not want anyone to know where she had been and had sworn the boys to secrecy. And for that matter, Sierra, who had not gotten permission to take Rosie to the spring. And Susan, who was still shy about Joe.

And so it was that everyone sat at that table full of news and thoughts and no one spoke. Rosie sat there, watching the excited silence, and for the first time she did not feel lost, but in fact felt like she entirely belonged to this family. Mama served a delicious, fragrant stew that had simmered all day while everyone was gone. She served it up in old earthen bowls that had been with the house since anyone could remember. She felt like it was a good day for memories and beauty. The little family ate around the ancient table, from cool bowls of clay, and simply enjoyed the gift of family, love, and presence.

CHAPTER 21

The Cellar's Promise

Now it was time to harvest the garden. At the end of summer, before winter came with its cold and harsh wind, they retrieved every last bit of produce. The leftover greens would be fed to the chickens and then the garden beds covered with a thick layer of old straw and bedded down for the winter.

It was always the sign of the end of summer. Great baskets of apples, apricots, plums, and pears were collected. For vegetables, they brought in snap peas, tomatoes, and squash. They also grew red peppers and cucumbers. Much more than the family could possibly eat at one time. They spent a week canning them and preserving them all year. When the winter winds blew and there was snow piled high around the house, there was nothing like going into the cellar and bringing up a jar of brightly colored fruit or vegetables. It was like a taste of summer. Mama had learned from her mother and loved doing this with her children.

The kitchen was full of jars, pots, and beautifully colored fruits and vegetables "Susan and Jessica," Mama instructed, "you sterilize the jars in hot soapy water and rinse them well. Keep them in hot water until we are ready. When you are done, fill the pot with water. Remember: enough to cover the jars."

Susan and Jessica did as she said. They had done this every year and knew well the process. Jessica carefully placed them in a rack so the jars wouldn't touch the bottom of the pan.

"Okay, Sierra, you and the boys fill each jar. We will do the fruit first, and then the vegetables. I will be washing them and preparing them. Billy and Caz, remember how to remove the air bubbles and seal them up?"

Both boys nodded.

Sunlight streamed through the kitchen, lighting up the sparkling jars, shining through the steam. The kitchen was filled with the fresh smell of sweet fruits and spicy vegetables. Mama took the onions and garlic and tied their long green stems together into a beautiful braid. They would hang in the cellar as well, giving off a tangy smell. Mama also took all the herbs, cilantro, and lavender and tied them in large bouquets with burlap ribbon to be hung and dried.

Finally, it was done. A beautiful bounty of food that they had grown, and they could eat all winter.

Caz asked, "But why can't we just buy this from the grocery store?"

Mama tied the last of the lavender, the fragrance surrounding her like an aura as she answered, "Because this is what we grow ourselves. We can take pride in our work and know we grew it from our own land."

And Billy added, "Plus, it's healthier. Right, Mama?"

Mama stood up, nodded, and stretched out her back. "Now," she said, "let's have some lunch! I'm starved. After lunch, we will take these down to the cellar."

They pulled out Jessica's fresh bread, cheese they had made from the cows' milk, and slices of fresh beef. After lunch, they headed down to the cold root cellar. There was a door in the kitchen that went to the cellar so they could go there when the winter winds blew hard and snow fell thickly. The cellar was a wonderful, dark place, with an earthy aroma and a coolness that embraced them as they descended the wooden steps. Papa had put in a freezer and a heavy wooden butcher table down in the cellar as well. This is where he would butcher the meat and store it for the family. Many a deer had been laid out and processed on that table. They used very sharp knives and Papa was severe in his instructions with the knives, for they would cut off a finger so clean and fast it wouldn't even hurt. Papa had all his fingers, but they knew some ranchers who did not. The idea terrified them, and they were always very careful.

But today they laid out all the jars and bouquets of herbs on that table. They pulled the jars that were still on the shelves out as well. Then they put the new ones in the back, with the label and the date showing forward. Then they put the old ones in the front to be used first. They stood back and admired their work, a colorful and edible mosaic that would feed them all winter.

Mama instructed them as she did every year, "If someone comes to us hungry and in need, always remember we have this bounty and we will share it with them. We give thanks to God for his blessings and generosity. Our cellar is full of food, and we will be fed when all the earth is asleep. That is the cellar's promise."

And with that she closed the heavy wooden door. They walked back up the steps, another little parade. They were proud of what they had accomplished but also a little melancholy. This march back up the root cellar stairs marked the end of summer. A time of change. Susan would be returning to school, Jacob would be leaving soon, and the warm summer days would come to a close, bringing winter, dark, and cold.

That night, Papa came home from dinner and was in a dark mood. Everyone sat around quietly, not knowing what to say. Even Rosie noticed and looked at him with questioning eyes. They said their prayers solemnly that night and Anna waited for a chance to talk to Paul alone.

As the children got ready for bed, Anna asked Paul, "Do you want to take a walk?" He looked at her and nodded, his face showing the weight of his worries.

Together they walked out past the gate, alongside the rambling stream. And, as the sun set in the sky, she asked, "How was your day?"

"Fine," was his only response.

Anna was quiet. Up over the rise of the hill, the fields lay out before them. She watched as he breathed deeply, and his shoulders relaxed. And still, they walked. Finally, Paul spoke.

"Luke wants to borrow some hay; he needs seven tons to get him to the fall. My cattle will starve if I give him that."

Anna gasped, "Oh. What are you going to do?"

Paul shrugged, "He really needs hay and doesn't have the money to buy it. He is in trouble. He's planning on bringing his cows down to his lower pasture, but there isn't enough grass there to feed them. It's only a temporary solution. What he really needs is hay and then to get his cattle sold early."

Anna took his hands and said, "Okay, let's pray."

Paul said, "Dear Lord, my friend is in trouble. He needs hay badly, and I want to help him. Please help me know what to do."

They continued to walk in silence and finally came to the grove of aspen and turned around. The moon was rising in the sky and lighting up their path. Finally, Paul took a deep breath.

"Okay, this is what we are going to do. I am going to talk to Doug and some of the other ranchers. I can give him some of that hay and maybe others can help too. We can supplement with grain. Others may be able to do the same. He may have to sell early, but we can give him enough hay to make a profit. And then we pray that we can make it through the winter with what we have."

Anna took his hand, and they walked the last part of the way, hand in hand, comfort and strength uniting them, shrouded in faith. It was neither the first nor the last time they had had to trust God to do what was right.

CHAPTER 22

Joseph's Approval

It had been decided that Joe would come for dinner on Sunday night. Papa said he would grill fresh steak and Mama would do the fixins. Papa was nervous because he didn't really want this young man to take away his daughter, and he could see plenty well where this was going. He also loved his daughter and wanted to be supportive of those she cared for. So, he was torn. And he didn't like it. He grumbled about it all day and it was even worse when Mama and Susan laughed at him.

"No respect," he grumbled playfully.

Susan was nervous because she wanted Joe to be welcomed, to see how wonderful her family was, and she hoped that they all liked each other. But in the back of her mind, she wanted Papa to grill Joe and maybe make him a bit uncomfortable so she could see what he would do. She told Mama this and Mama said she would say something to Papa.

Mama was nervous, because telling Paul to come up with questions made Paul even more cranky and he would not take suggestions from Mama.

Jacob was nervous because Joe was an incredible athlete and strong student. He really respected Joe and didn't know what Joe would think about his decision to be a priest.

Rosie was shut down almost completely in anticipation of a stranger, and no one really expected anything more or even really tried to convince her otherwise.

Sierra was ready to bolt, and really it was only thinking about Pistol bolting that made her stand her ground.

Jessica was determined to cook, so she never made it out of the kitchen, and the boys snuck out the back door to the stream.

Mama surveyed her landscape and said a little prayer. *We all had better get used to this*, she thought. *I have three more daughters!* This made her laugh, which everyone heard and helped lighten the mood.

Right on time, Joe arrived. It was painfully clear the poor boy was a nervous wreck. The Derrick family were well-respected ranchers, and Paul Derrick was known to be not only a good man but a fierce one as well. The Cross brand was widely respected as some of the best beef raised in Wyoming.

Joe had flowers in his hand and wore a freshly washed and ironed shirt. Mama and Susan could see he had ironed it because there were strange creases here and there. His face was scrubbed clean, and his hair newly cut. Susan had put on a pretty dress and curled her hair. She ran to him and gave him a kiss on the cheek. This made him blush so badly he nearly dropped his flowers. Mama hurried to get them from him. Susan held his hand until she saw Papa's face which was positively glowering at the two. Joe dropped her hand, went over to Papa and, looking him in the eye, shook his hand.

"Hello, Mr. Derrick. My name is Joseph Bollinger. I am so happy to meet you."

Papa shook his hand and said, "Hello, Joseph."

There was still a bit of tension, and so Susan came over to Papa, kissed his cheek, and said, "You can call him Joe."

Susan's charm and Joe's respectful greeting did the trick. His face relaxed and he nodded at Joe. Papa offered Joe a beer, and even though Joe would have liked nothing more to calm his nerves, he shook his head. He was twenty-one but not much more.

Papa said, "Well, I'm going out to grill. You can join me if you like." And even though Susan was a more pleasant option, he followed her father out to the grill.

Papa turned towards Joe with a severe look, as if challenging him. "She really likes you, you know."

Joe looked Mr. Derrick in the eye and said, "I love your daughter, Mr. Derrick. I have known her for a long time, and this past year have really gotten to know her better."

There. He'd said it. He could think of nothing else to say at the moment. He had rehearsed it so many times, and it never came out this blunt and this unplanned.

As for Paul, he was struck by both the forcefulness and sincerity in this young man's declaration. It was the honesty and commitment that he was looking for. "Well, the steaks are ready. Let's go inside and see what the women have put together." And he almost winked, because, despite himself, he was starting to like the boy.

Once inside, Mama looked at Papa and said, "Well, did you ask him questions? Do you approve?"

Papa looked at her. "I like him." And left it at that.

Dinner started out awkward, but Susan and Mama were charming. When Jacob saw how nervous Joe was, he too lost his awkwardness, and they talked about football, classes, and classmates. Joe asked Jacob what his plans were now that he had graduated.

Jacob paused a moment and then responded humbly, "I am very interested in becoming a priest. I am going to attend the seminary next year."

Joe looked at Jacob with penetrating blue eyes and said, "I thought about being a priest as well. It is the highest calling. But I think God has other plans for me."

And here he looked at Susan with unguarded love. Jacob immediately felt he had gained a brother, while the rest of the family smiled and nodded. Mama looked at Papa and they both remembered, in a flash, that time so long ago, when Papa had come to her house calling and looking for her father's approval.

Before Joe left, he handed Susan a small box. She flushed and opened it. It was a band of leather with a snap and two hearts engraved on it. "Did you make this?" she gasped. "It's beautiful!"

He nodded and smiled happily and put it on her wrist. She held it beneath her hand and then looked at it on her wrist. "Thank you. I love it."

He gazed at her and could think how much he wanted to kiss her, but the rest of the family came pouring out the door and began to admire the wristband. He said goodbye and, with a wave of his hand, was off.

That night, as they were getting ready for bed, Anna suddenly laughed.

"Remember when you came to my house for the first time? You looked like an untamed grizzly bear that had been nearly drowned with scrubbing."

Paul laughed and said, "I resent that comment."

Mama went on. "My father was so distressed by your energy and drive."

Paul said, "Your father was a very elegant shopkeeper from New York with a very wild daughter." Paul laughed suddenly and added, "I actually feel sorry for your father. What must he have thought, trying to raise an accomplished daughter and instead having this near-wild creature who crawled around rocks looking for horses."

Anna threw a pillow at him. "I was accomplished! I could dress up nicely, play the piano. I was…educated."

Paul went around the bed, caught her up, and said, "All I know is that I managed to capture the prettiest girl in all of Wyoming."

And with that he threw her on the bed, kissing her. As for her, she did not mind. No, not at all.

CHAPTER 23

Pistol's Lessons

The next morning the schedule was clear, so they all went to see Pistol. Pistol was very happy to see them and neighed at their arrival. This put everyone in good spirits.

Mama said, "Okay, we are going to put a halter on Pistol. Who wants to work her until she joins up?"

Jessica was very excited to show Mama, and Mama agreed it was her turn. Jessica got in the round pen and Susan opened the gate. Susan was practically humming; she was so happy about the dinner with Joe. She sat on the rails, watching with a dreamy look on her face. Sierra thought it was ridiculous, but Jessica wished she could be more like Susan.

Pistol trotted in. Jessica summoned up her energy and put her arms out to move Pistol. Pistol looked at her, confused. Jessica panicked and thought, *What's wrong? I practiced this!*

Mama said, "Pay attention to your shoulder. You are blocking her passage. She is smart and very sensitive. She is waiting for you to open the gate. Turn your shoulder back a little."

Jessica understood and moved her shoulder back. Pistol immediately set off on a trot. Mama was impressed.

"Nice job. Okay, now turn her. Remember to not only change your arms but your shoulder and hips as well. Horses don't have arms, so you need to think about what your body is doing."

Jessica did as she was told and was pleased when Pistol changed direction.

"Okay, now speed her up," Mama said.

Jessica remembered "saving Caz from the wood stove" and felt her energy rise. Her body became more alert, more forward-facing, her arms higher, her shoulders bigger. And with that, Pistol went into an energetic lope. Jessica was so pleased with herself she could have burst.

Mama said, "Nice job! Wow! I'm impressed!"

After a few runs around the pen, Mama said, "Okay, her lip is getting soft, she is keeping her eye on you. As soon as she licks her lips, stand quiet, and lower your energy."

Jessica did so and Pistol stopped. Jessica stepped back. Pistol began to walk toward Jessica, licking her lips and looking to be petted. Jessica was bursting with pride and so happy to show Mama she could do it!

"Very nice. Now I am going to have you do this because you are so quiet. Take the halter and rub her very gently with it." Mama handed her the halter and went back to the rail. "Start on her shoulder and then up her neck, across her withers and down her back."

Jessica did as Mama instructed, and Pistol stood quietly.

"Now take the halter and carefully put it on Pistol. First, put the strap around the neck, then slide the loop around her nose. That's it, nice and quiet." Mama came up gently and quietly. She took the short rope connected to the halter in her hands. It had knots on it so it wouldn't slide through her hands. "Now go ahead and tie the halter on."

As soon as Jessica tightened it, Pistol felt the pressure and bolted. Mama was ready. She held the rope tightly. "Jessica, go to the rail."

When Pistol came to the end of the rope, she reared and shook her head. She knew she was trapped, so she panicked. Mama just held the rope and did not move. Pistol came back to the ground and bolted again, first to the left and then to the right. Mama's muscles bulged and strained, but she did not let go. It was an amazing sight to see Mama's body strain against a seven-hundred-pound horse and to see that horse using everything it could to plunge and pull against that rope. Dust rose in the air, hair and mane flew, and the sun filtered through the dust, causing strange shadows and light. Then suddenly, all was calm. Pistol came to her feet and stopped fighting. Immediately, Mama let the rope loosen. And Pistol realized the reward. She put her head down and licked her lips. Mama came up to her and rubbed her all over with the rope, just so she would not be afraid of it. Pistol stood there shaking but quiet and finally she relaxed.

Mama took off the halter and said, "That's enough for today," and opened the gate for Pistol.

"But I want to try it," said Sierra.

"Tomorrow," said Mama, and that was that.

Mama could see Sierra was upset. She went up to Sierra and said, "Look, I know you wanted to put the halter on Pistol. But there will be other times." Then she chuckled and said, "Look, just like Pistol has to move when we ask her to move to be a part of our herd, so when you are a child, you have to obey your parents. Do you think Pistol has any idea why we are moving her back and forth in silly, round circles? She doesn't see any lions or threat. There is no food or water. But she has to trust us, that we know what is best for her, even if it doesn't make sense. You also have to trust your parents. Even if it makes you feel like you are going in a circle for no reason. And by the way, we also have to trust God even more! So, let your parents make the decisions and treat them with respect. And when you are an adult, you must trust God and go to him for direction."

Sierra laughed despite herself, because she did, in fact, feel like she was going around in circles for no good reason. Then she said, "You want me to lick my lips!?"

Mama laughed and put her arm around Sierra's shoulders. "Exactly!"

The next day everyone was eager to see what Pistol would do. Mama went in and after Pistol joined up she rubbed the halter on Pistol's neck. Pistol did not mind and seemed to enjoy it. Then, Mama tied the halter on Pistol and nothing happened. Pistol was shaking a bit, but she stood still. Mama rubbed her all over and petted her until Pistol relaxed. Mama said, "Today we will teach Pistol to walk."

She walked to the side of Pistol and put a little pressure on the line. She explained, "What I am going to do is a lot of little arcs and disengage her front legs."

Sure enough, Pistol moved her front legs and stepped to the side.

Mama said, "As soon as she steps over, I am going to immediately release pressure. That lets her know that this is what I wanted her to do. Remember, her Mama would put pressure on her with her body or ears or mouth and as soon as the baby moved, she would release that pressure."

Mama went to the other side of Pistol and did it again. But Pistol did not move. Mama explained again, "I am not going to do a tug-of-war; instead, I will try something else. I am going to disengage her hindquarters and get some movement from her. As soon as she moves, I will release pressure right away by loosening the rope."

Mama did this over and over, little arcs all over the arena, and pretty soon Pistol was taking steps with Mama when she asked.

"Sierra, I'm going to let you go next, just like I promised. Start with sending her around and asking her to join up with you. Remember: lower your energy when you are asking her to stop and then walk toward you."

Sierra asked Pistol to move out and here Sierra's energy really worked well. Sierra had such a beautiful command over her body, and she simply had to bend this way and that for Pistol to change direction. Pistol immediately showed her respect and turned, keeping an eye on Sierra. But now was the test.

"Okay, now lower your energy, relax your body, lower your head, lower your shoulders, bend your knees. Now breathe."

Pistol stopped and looked at Sierra. Sierra took a step back and had to remind herself to breathe as Pistol began to walk toward her. Sierra could barely look up, she was so internally excited, but she kept her breathing quiet and Pistol continued.

"Now rub the halter on her shoulder first, then her neck, and then across her withers. Nice and easy, head slightly down, nothing exciting here going on."

Sierra did as her mother told her.

"Now put the halter over her nose, gently, and the strap over her ears and, don't tense, tie it." Then Mama reminded her, "Lower your gaze. You are staring at her."

Sierra dropped her eyes and remembered to soften and

lower her shoulders. *Breathe*, she told herself. Pistol let her put the halter on.

Mama said, "Okay, time to ask her to walk. We want to get her body moving and not just have a tug-of-war. Take a step to the right with her so she moves her shoulders. As soon as she takes a step, then release all pressure."

Sierra did as her mama said, and Pistol took a step, moving her feet.

Mama said, "Okay, now move off to the left and move her that way. She is a little sticky on the left so you might have to move her hindquarters."

Sierra did as Mama said, and soon Pistol was walking in little arcs all over the round pen and soon just walking with Sierra.

"Nice job! She is smart and you are being very patient and consistent. Always remember your job is to keep calm, ask clearly, and make it easy for the horse to do the right thing."

Mama smiled; she was enjoying this so much. She loved explaining horses' movements to her children. As a young woman she had so loved learning about working with horses from the trainer. And now, as a mother, she could see the body language that a mother and child use to communicate.

Rosie signed and Mama saw it only in the corner of her eye. She would have to get used to watching for that. She was so used to responding to the voices of her children. Rosie signed, "Can I try?"

Mama nodded and then signed, "Remember what Sierra did? I won't really be able to give you instruction."

Rosie nodded and signed, "Okay."

She got into the pen and Sierra handed her the rope. Sierra looked at her and said slowly, letting Rosie read her lips, "Rub him down first so he can get used to you and the rope."

Rosie nodded. She took the rope in her hands. She was quiet and gentle, so Pistol relaxed with her. Rosie rubbed her down just as she had seen Mama and Sierra do, first the shoulder, then the neck, then across the withers. The silence let the world around her disappear. It was only her and Pistol. Pistol relaxed and her eyes went soft. She was enjoying it! Rosie saw this and continued to rub her, along the flanks, the belly, the forehead. Rosie's calm demeanor was magic on the horse.

Rosie took a step to the right. When Pistol felt the light pressure on the line she turned to the right and Mama was delighted to see Rosie release pressure right away. Mama could see that Rosie's deafness had already taught her to be more aware with her eyes and body. Rosie began to walk around the arena in arcs, with Pistol following, each step more willing. When Rosie stopped, Pistol stopped. Rosie looked at her family, standing there along the rails, cheering her on, and she just smiled. A broad, big, happy smile. Mama came into the round pen with her and gently took the rope. Rosie went back out with her brothers and sisters. Susan looked on from the gate, and no one noticed the tears in her eyes. Rosie's deafness had seemed more abrupt to her because she was away at college and so her healing seemed even more amazing and important.

That night during dinner everyone wanted to talk at once, and Papa made them sign so Rosie could be a part of the conversation. There was plenty of skipped words, but enough that Rosie could see what everyone was saying. She joined in as well, signing away. Papa watched his family, pleased.

After dinner, Paul asked Anna to walk with him. The moon was low, and the stars were brilliant. A cool breeze brushed away the heat of the day. They walked in silence for a while, enjoying the land. Finally, he spoke.

"We are in trouble, Anna. I don't know if I have enough hay and I've used up our savings for grain. Maybe I shouldn't have given the hay to Luke. I don't know. The grass is almost gone, the springs are low. We need to pray for that rain. Maybe God will even give us that snow! My God, that would be wonderful."

He sighed, for even in the saying of it, it was a prayer of faith and hope. Anna took his hand and said, "Let's pray now."

And they walked hand in hand, praying and asking God for help. She thought about how they had worked with Pistol earlier that day to walk with them, trusting them. She thought to herself that they needed to walk with God and trust him. Even if it felt like they were going in little arcs, half this way and half that way. All the time.

The next morning, Papa rode off, his face grim and fierce. Only Mama saw him and again she prayed. It was going to be hot that day and hot for the next ten days forecast. Nothing was looking good. She sat at the old worn table and wondered about the heartache they shared. Sometimes life was not easy.

The children spilled out into the kitchen and asked about seeing Pistol. Susan had a breakfast date with Joe, and Jacob was visiting the seminary. Both of them had eyes full of hope and love, and Mama wished with all her might she could protect them from the sufferings that they were bound to experience. She wished her mother and father were alive, that she could go to them for comfort, and suddenly she felt very alone. She said a prayer again, and then got up and made breakfast. A quick one so they could work with Pistol early.

The six of them went out to work with Pistol. Mama could not help but notice how low the river was. The children noticed her mood and were more quiet than usual. They figured it was the heat, for already at nine in the morning it was near one hundred degrees. They went to see Pistol and were all encouraged by her happy neigh. She came trotting out to meet them, and Caz snuck her some carrots when he thought Mama wasn't looking. Of course, Mama saw, but she said nothing for the time being. Not right now.

"Today," she said, and she signed also while the children all watched her, "today we are going to teach Pistol how to pivot on her front and back legs."

She worked with Pistol until Pistol joined up and stood quietly with her, trusting and respectful. Mama put on the halter, carefully rubbing her first. Pistol was smart and stood quietly. Mother touched her front shoulder. Pistol's skin flicked but she did not move.

Mama explained, "She needs to understand the difference between not being afraid of my touch and learning that my touch is directing her. I am going to increase my pressure until she moves. I want her outside front leg—the one closest to me—to cross over her inside front leg. So, now I'm going to put more pressure in my pointing."

Suddenly, Pistol licked her lips and crossed her front feet over, pivoting on her forequarters. Mama immediately pulled her finger away and petted the filly.

"Now, I am going to do the same with her hindquarters."

Pistol again was confused and had to rethink what was going on. Mama was patient and kept on the pressure until Pistol moved her hindquarters. With her hindquarters, she did not cross her legs over but kind of hopped sideways.

Mama did it again and again until Pistol crossed her legs. Mama immediately released pressure and praised Pistol. Pistol licked her lips, and her eyes grew soft. She understood.

"Everything you do on one side, always do on the other. The other side of a horse is a completely different horse."

Mama went around the horse and, going to the front, asked for the pivot. Pistol practically flew across the arena. Mama held on to the rope until Pistol stopped, looking at her and breathing heavily.

"I don't understand," said Jessica. "Why did she react so strongly?"

"Because it is her other side, and she literally sees things differently from each eye."

Mama brought her back and squared her up again. She tried again. This time, Pistol pivoted nicely and had no problem with her hindquarters.

"That is all for today. It is hot and she was perfect." Mama said. "Let's go back to the cool house."

They walked back and Sierra finally said, "I guess when Rosie got sick, we had to pivot."

Mama stopped short and looked at Sierra. "Yes. Yes. Explain what you mean."

"Well, we were all going along with our family, thinking things were the way they were—you know, Rosie could hear, and we were all doing all right. Then God took away Rosie's hearing and we had to pivot. We had to adjust. I imagine it was hard for Pistol to move like that, and it was hard for us to adjust to Rosie losing her hearing. But maybe if we trust God more, like we want Pistol to trust us, then maybe it wouldn't be so hard."

Mama hugged her, and with tears in her eyes she said, "Yes, Sierra. I think you are right."

Susan came home looking very pretty and in a lighthearted mood. She sang as she cleaned the kitchen and got lunch ready for Papa. When Papa came in he was done for the day.

"I'm going to go to town and get feed and supplies," he said. Mama nodded and handed him a nice lunch with a cool glass of iced tea, just how he liked it.

Just then the phone rang. Anna picked it up. It was Joe calling asking to speak to Mr. Derrick. He sounded very serious and very nervous. Anna handed Paul the phone and held her breath. Paul was still hot and sweaty from the morning work and not in a great mood. He stood with the phone to his ear and nodded.

"Okay. Yup, Sure. Two o'clock," he said, and then he hung up the phone. Everyone was watching. He looked at Anna, his face grave. "Joe wants to talk to me. He says he has a question."

Anna put her hand on his arm and said, "Paul, be nice."

Paul grumbled, "Why do you say that? I'm always nice."

Everyone looked around the room and could barely suppress smiles. Susan went about the house cleaning and singing. Everyone else took bets as to what was going on. Jacob also came home in a good mood, and when they told him about the phone call he chuckled and went in on the bets. Three bets—Jacob, Jessica, Sierra—that he was asking to propose, and two bets—Billy and Caz—he wanted to go fishing.

Papa came home with a truck full of supplies, and after he had unloaded them he came into the house. He saw seven faces looking at him. He smiled despite himself and chuckled. "I gave my permission."

Everyone talked at once.

"Was he nervous?

"What did he say?"

"Did you ask him questions?"

"Did he want to go fishing?"

Papa laughed and said, "Yes, poor lad was shaking, he was so nervous."

And Jacob thought, *Gee, the big high school quarterback shaking.*

"Yes, I asked him questions," Papa continued, "namely how he planned to provide for our daughter."

"Well," said Anna, "what did he say?"

"He said he is going to be a lawyer. Can you imagine that? He is going to law school in the fall. Said it should be about three years, but if Susan will have him they can get married while he's in law school."

Anna held her hand over her mouth and said, "Did you ask…?"

Papa smiled and kissed Mama on the cheek. "Yes, Mama, I know what you are thinking. I asked him and he said he hopes to practice in town. He knows how much Susan loves living in the country and would not take her away."

Anna laughed a bit, then said, "Well, that is great news!"

Then Papa turned and said, "And no, boys, we didn't talk about fishing. But I hear from Susan he is an incredible fisherman, so maybe you can ask him that yourselves."

The boys ran off outside, yelling gleefully. If all that happened here was that they had gained a brother, they were pretty happy with the situation.

That night, alone in bed, Paul and Anna talked, as they did on so many nights. Paul said ruefully, "I can't believe our baby girl is getting married. She just seems so young to me."

Anna said, "Do you realize I was the same age when we got married? I was younger when you asked my father if you could marry me."

This seemed astounding to Paul. He remembered how beautiful Anna was. Those fiery blue eyes and jet-black hair and those long legs. He turned and kissed her. She was the same woman he fell in love with. No, better! She had given him seven beautiful children. She had run his household and she had become a magnificent woman. He said none of this and just looked at her with a look that she could gaze into forever. She once heard a phrase, "Our love could burn down cities," and that was how she felt when he looked at her like this. She kissed him back most amorously.

CHAPTER 24

Heat Wave

Day after day of extreme heat followed. It was too hot even to swim, and the kids just sat inside feeling miserable. Poor Papa had to ride out and check on cows and fencing and always came back red and exhausted. The small streams had dried up and even the river was perilously low. The grass was thin and in some places the ground was just dirt. All the ranchers were in trouble, and they talked about this in the cattle meetings and coffeehouses. The bank was no longer giving out loans because it too had been through this and knew that, if it got bad enough, ranchers would lose their cattle and not be able to pay off their loans.

On Sunday, the families went into town and went to Mass. There, every man, woman, and child got on their knees and prayed for rain. Their worry and fear drawing dark lines in their faces. They came before God in the most blessed sacrament and asked for mercy. They confessed their sins and begged for mercy. The priest's heart, breaking for the sorrow and fear in his flock, offered up sacrifices to the Lord, also asking for mercy. The whole town cried in one voice for help.

One evening, Mama could see that everyone had had enough of sitting in the house. She suggested they get up early the next day and have a breakfast picnic and a swim at Sweetwater. They asked if Papa could join them, and he thought he could. They woke up at dawn, and while the air was still cool they paraded to the river. The water was deep enough to go under, and they all stripped down to bathing suits and played in the water. Rosie and Mama got in too and they all splashed and laughed. Afterward, the sun started to fill the sky and with it came heat. Being wet, it felt good for the moment.

Papa said he had to go to a Cattlemen's meeting where they would discuss weather and ideas to keep their ranches working. As he got dressed, it was as if he put on his armor against the world and his face got very grim. No one liked to see him that way, but Mama understood and was glad. For that determination had pulled them out of many a bad situation. She kissed him goodbye as she always did, and off he went.

After breakfast, Mama asked if they wanted to try something new with Pistol. Everyone agreed very happily. As they walked to Pistol's pen, Susan and Jacob took the time to enjoy every minute of their time with the family, for both would be leaving soon.

Mama explained as she walked, "Horses don't naturally back up. They pivot to the right or to the left and then they bolt. So, we are going to ask her to use her thinking brain and teach her how to back up. There are many benefits. First of all, the horse learns even more respect for you. Second of all, it develops her hindquarters. And finally, it is a good tool to make her stop reacting and to think."

Mama entered the round pen with Pistol. Pistol whinnied and came up to Mama to be petted. Mama put on her halter and then began to touch her all over. Mama petted her, across her back, down each leg, under the belly, over the eyes, and down the nose. Pistol was no longer afraid and loved the grooming. It was what her mother would have done. Now Mama stood in front of Pistol and pointed at her chest. She had the line loose and would use it only if Pistol bolted. Mama made a clicking sound with her tongue and focused on Pistol's chest. Pistol understood the pressure but did not understand what was being asked. She turned away and Mama brought her back with the rope and started again. This time she touched Pistol's chest and clicked again, directing her energy at her chest. Pistol leaned back on her haunches and Mama immediately removed the pressure.

Rosie and Sierra went to the opposite side of the round pen so they could read Mama's lips. Rosie had gotten better at reading lips. If she didn't understand something, she could ask Sierra.

Mama relaxed and explained, "She didn't step back, but she didn't leave, and she did lean back. So, she is understanding a bit more. That is why I rewarded her with the release of pressure. Remember, we are going to use this same pressure and release when we ride."

Jessica and Sierra nodded—they remembered their lessons that day they rode with Mama in the aspens. Mama once again stood in front of Pistol and pointed at Pistol's chest. Pistol leaned back and Mama touched Pistol's chest.

"I'm not touching her chest hard, just applying more pressure than pointing."

Pistol leaned back more but did not step back.

"It's hard for her to understand stepping back. Remember, it's not natural. I'm going to put more pressure on her chest now."

Echoes of Silence

And Mama tapped Pistol's chest, still staring at it. Finally, Pistol picked up a foot and stepped back. Mama immediately released pressure and praised her.

"Some days I quit at the first sign of understanding, but Pistol is still listening, her ears are still on me, so I'm going to try again."

She set up Pistol again and pointed at her chest, clicking again. This time Pistol took a step back all on her own. Mama stood up, released pressure, and praised and petted her.

Sierra asked if she could try it. She got in and, taking the lead rope, pointed it at Pistol's chest. Pistol, feeling her energy, turned to the right at a near bolt. Sierra put her back and tried again. Again, Pistol bolted. This happened over and over. Sierra lost her temper and yanked the rope, smacking Pistol on the neck.

"Sierra! That was not right. Pistol is trying to understand what you want, and you are giving her confusing signals." Mama got in the pen. "You don't want to punish her for trying. You want to make the right thing easy." Mama adjusted the length of the rope. "Now, if she chooses the wrong thing, the rope will go tight, and she will run into it. If she does the right thing, the rope will stay loose." Mama's tone was sharp. "You have to keep calm and let her figure out the right thing to do. Take a breath and try again."

Sierra tried again and when Pistol went to the right or left, the rope went tight and pulled against her.

"That's right. We are going to do the same thing when we ride. Make the right thing easy and the wrong thing hard."

Sierra, sweating and working hard to control her emotions, tried it again and suddenly Pistol backed up three steps. Everyone cried in joy and Sierra made sure the rope was loose and then praised Pistol.

Mama said, "Good job! Now let's all go home and relax."

When they got home, Papa was sitting at the table with notepads and a calculator. Mama looked at him. His face was devoid of expression. He looked up at his wife.

"I am trying to calculate feed and trying to decide if I should take the steers early to the market or wait until the fall. If I wait, they will be bigger, and I will get more. If I take them now, I don't have to feed them. The worse question is gambling on the weather and trying to decide if I should sell any of the cows."

Mama sat with him quietly. She prayed for his discernment. "What are other ranchers doing?" she asked.

"The bigger ranches are holding out for rain. The smaller ranches are selling three months early. In fact, I'm taking the oldest three to help Luke gather his cattle tomorrow so he can sell. Anna, this is awful."

She asked, "How are the cattle prices?"

"Well, that's the thing. Even though many ranches are selling now instead of in the fall, the prices are not bad. It's a good thing the market goes across the country and kind of balances out."

"Any idea of prices in the fall?" she asked, knowing he could not possibly know the answer to that.

Paul shook his head absentmindedly. Then, having made a decision, he said, "I am going to wait. I still have some grass in the field and hay in the barn and, as long as I do, I can feed the cattle and hopefully get a better price later." He put his pen down and carefully gathered his papers and calculations. "Let's go to bed. I am up early to help Luke."

The next morning, Papa was up early and Mama went into the kitchen to make coffee and breakfast. Susan, Jacob, and Jessica were already up getting dressed. They ate breakfast quickly. Even though Papa's mood was serious, they were excited to go and work cattle. Papa said out loud so they could all hear, "Thank you, Mama, for the breakfast." And everyone nodded, their mouths still full of food.

She kissed Papa as he went out the door and said, "I'll be there in a few hours with food and the kids."

They got the horses, saddled them, and loaded them in the trailer. They drove to the Mavericks' ranch just as the sun was lighting up the sky. Luke was there with a hard face. He gave directions, three men in a group. They would find cattle and bring them into the holding pen. There they would pull out the weanlings and older cows. The animals had been castrated, wormed, and branded in the spring. Luke had already decided how many were going to market. It was a serious business and every rancher had made his own gamble.

They rode out in groups of three just as the dawn began to lighten the sky. Papa rode with Susan and Jessica, while Jacob rode with Cody and Mr. Johnson. The horses were fresh and eager to work, for they did not know it was three months too early. They did not know there was a drought. They were happy to be out working with their partners, men the horses had known all their life. The horses tossed their heads and pranced a bit. The men sat easily in the saddle. Many of them had ridden before they could walk, as fathers proudly placed sons and daughters on those patient steeds who understood their job was to keep that little one safe.

The earth fell away from them in terrible barrenness. The grass was eaten to a stubble and, in some places, there was only dirt. It was awful to see, and Paul shuddered, remembering the bones and the crows from a time long ago. The sky spread out above them like a pale canopy of blue. The day was already hot, so they went to the coolest places—

riverbeds, outcroppings of trees, the shadows of hills. And sure enough, there were the cattle, in small groups. The men pushed them gently, so none would bolt. And the cattle, well used to man and his horses, moved along with gentle lowing. And then the riders noticed something—a little cloud on the horizon, tinged in silver and gold. No one said anything, but it was their business to notice. The sky had been without clouds for too long.

Once they were in at the Mavericks' holding pen, then came the business of sorting them. The first job was to sort the cattle by age and size. They had a large pen with a small gate which led into another pen. There was a man at the gate ready to close it. A rider cut off a small group and brought them to the gate, and then, quick as lightning, the rider cut off the cows to the left and another rider came up behind to push the weanlings in through the gate. The first rider sent the cow into a third pen where all the cows would go, and a man at that gate closed it behind her. One by one they were sorted. They sorted into groups: the sick that needed care, the older and the weanlings to be sold, and the cows that Luke would keep for breeding. He kept careful track of the cattle by their ear tags—when they were born, how their birthing went, and generally whether he liked the cow or not.

The cattle were sorted. Those going to sale were in a pen to be picked up the next day and taken to market. The young calves would be purchased as feeders, and another ranch would take on the job of feeding them and then selling them as adults, while the older ones would be purchased for meat. Wives came with food to share and, even though Luke was selling early, they could celebrate because as long as a man had cattle, he had a livelihood. Before they ate, every cowboy took care of their horse first. For their horses were their partners, and none of this was possible without the horse. The horse was taken to a shady spot, his cinch loosed, and then they made sure it had cool water and, depending on the time of day, hay to eat.

Mama arrived around noon, driving with all the food and bringing the four youngest. Upon arriving, Mama went with the women and helped get things ready, for when the riders stopped they would be famished.

That night the families sat around on a crazy variety of chairs and ice chests, eating and drinking, telling stories and bolstering their courage. How many more ranches would sell early? Each had to make his own calculated gamble. Wives and girlfriends talked and shared tales of homemaking and not a little laughter on behalf of their men whom they loved fiercely and would do anything to support. The children played games, many of them trying to rope a log or an unsuspecting dog. The horses sat quietly, enjoying the cool evening air, resting and knowing they had done a good job. Somewhere in the night a coyote called out or a man exclaimed a little too loudly or a baby cried to a hushing mama. These were the nights that held them tight. In hard times and good times they were there for each other, for without each other they could not do the incredible work it took just to raise cattle and give the country beef. They were proud of what their lives, their jobs, and their cattle produced. They bred them and raised them to be the best they could be. It was what they lived for and what they died for. And what thanks did the man in the grocery store give as he grabbed a steak on his way home from work? It mattered not, for the rancher's reward was on nights like these when he could look out on his herd and be proud of what he had raised.

CHAPTER 25

A Bear in the Deadwood

The next morning, as the eggs were scrambled and the sunlight fell across the kitchen, Papa asked Jacob to help check cows. Jacob was sitting at the table, his brow furrowed.

"I told Cody I would help him dig a ditch for a water line, but I would rather go with you."

Papa looked at him seriously, "Son, a man is only as good as his word. If you said you would help him, you need to do that. If you start going back on your word, you won't have anything left in you but backup."

Jacob nodded. He knew. He had heard this too many times. He shrugged his shoulders, drank his coffee. "Well, that's where I'll be today then."

Papa turned to Mama and Jessica. "Well, ladies, how about it? Are you up for going out back and checking on cows?"

Jessica was delighted. She finished the eggs and left them on the counter for anyone's helping. She put her hair in a ponytail, pulled on her boots, went outside, and got the horses ready. Mama was riding Rain. Her favorite, of course, was Apollo, but he had thrown a shoe and couldn't be ridden. Jessica was riding Dash and Papa was riding Bandit. Off they rode into the rosy dawn. It was still a bit cool, and the horses were ready for work. They walked a good distance for it was going to be a long, hot day, and they wanted to take care of the horses.

Papa explained, "There is a small group of cattle that went into the rocky ground where it is cooler. They are not with the rest of the herd, and we need to check on them. If there is not enough grass, we may have to bring them down with the rest of the herd. I don't like them being alone."

They rode out of the flat plains and into the rocky high ground. Around rocks and over fallen trees. Papa explained, "This is called deadwood. It is layer after layer of broken and dead branches. Look how far down the horse's hoof goes when he steps. The horses can work their way through these layers of branches, but if a horse panics and runs, he can easily break his leg. We'll go nice and slow. We have all day to get there, and I don't want any accidents."

Jessica nodded, remembering Mama's story of Apollo.

All of a sudden, there was a crashing of branches. Papa called out to Jessica, his voice strong and commanding, "Stop the horses and sit quiet, Jessica. Just breathe."

A huge bear came crashing through the brush. Papa became calm as ice, for he had seen bad accidents with bears. If they were lucky, it was just foraging around for berries and would leave them alone. Dash started to get antsy and started to stomp and dance in place, looking like he was ready to bolt. They were deep in the deadwood, and if Dash bolted he would break his legs.

Mama said with a terrible calmness, "Jessica, sit back in your seat, use your legs and back him up a few steps. Just like we practiced. You've got to get him thinking and listening to you."

Jessica did as she was told, and Dash backed up, stepping carefully through the branches. It was enough to settle him down.

The bear, as Papa predicted, wandered off. After they watched him leave, they proceeded forward. Mama rode up next to Jessica.

"You did a good job. Do you know why I had you back up Dash?"

"So I could get to his thinking brain?"

Mama nodded. "Yes, that horse has to trust you. When you asked him to back up, it forced him to change from being reactive and trusting his own instincts to trusting and listening to you."

Jessica nodded and they rode on. Then Mama spoke thoughtfully, "You know, we ask these huge animals who can fight and who can run to stop and sit quiet when a predator comes by. It's totally against their instincts. And we know that if we do, its most likely that bear will just ignore us. But the horse doesn't see it that way. He thinks he should run or fight. A horse won't win a fight with a grizzly bear. And if he runs with all that deadwood on the ground, he could easily break a leg. He doesn't even know he has to trust us because he can't see ahead and doesn't know about the deadwood. So we, as rational creatures, have to lead him and keep him safe."

They continued across the valley and up into the higher country, the horses bobbing their heads with bridles jingling. The land was open, and they could see for miles over the valley. The air was cooler here and they enjoyed the relief. Jessica was happy to be with her parents. Times like this were rare. She wondered whether or not she should tell them about Karl. She really liked him but didn't know what they would think.

Mama was quiet for a while, and then she continued. "We have to trust God like that. Sometimes he asks us to do things that seem scary, and we want to run or fight. But he sees what is ahead and what is behind. And our job is to trust him. If these beautiful, big animals can trust us who are smaller and weaker than they, then how much more should we trust God, who is infinitely good and infinitely powerful?"

Jessica decided to trust her Mama and told her. "I like a boy. His name is Karl Sanders."

Mama rode quietly, trying to decide what to say. "Oh. How did you meet him?"

Jessica kept her nervousness down and said, "At 4-H Club meetings. He is raising goats and helping the younger kids. He is a great guy, Mama."

Mama smiled at Jessica, looking at her and realizing that she too was becoming a lovely young lady. But before anything else could be said, Papa cried out, "I see them! Over here!"

They broke out into an easy lope. There were about thirty head, happily sitting in the cool shade. The only problem was that the terrain was high tundra with only scraggy dry bushes. The cows would starve up here, but they didn't have the common sense to go down where there was food even though it was hotter.

Papa said, "I will push them forward. Jessica and Anna, you each take a side."

The three of them started to move the cattle. Suddenly a small calf bolted right in front of Jessica. Jessica turned Dash and ran after it. Papa was closest to her and followed, shortening the distance. Mama decided to follow as well. And so it was that all three came upon the most remarkable scene.

CHAPTER 26

The Circle of Love

That morning, Joe put a small box into his saddle bag, along with a clean blanket, some cheese and bread, and some fresh cider. He was shaking and nervous. Today was the day. He had finally earned enough money to buy the ring and he had gotten Mr. Derrick's permission. Now he was going to do it. Change his life forever. He wouldn't have had the courage except for his love for Susan. He could not imagine life without her. He called Susan the night before and asked if she would meet him that morning at the crossing of their roads and go on a picnic. She agreed and, feeling like it was a special occasion, put on a pretty blouse with flowers and fluttery sleeves. Of course, she wore her jeans and old boots, but a nice blouse and some lipstick made her feel pretty. She looked at the horses remaining in the pen, not Apache or Pilgrim. Apollo had thrown a shoe. She could take Ginger. She saddled the horse and, meeting Joe, they rode high into the hills. Dawn was just breaking, and the air felt fresh and crisp. Out in the plains, they raced each other. Ginger, being very fast, outran Joe's horse. When they stopped, breathless, Joe looked at her, her eyes bright and her chest heaving with the thin mountain air. He could barely believe he was asking this beautiful woman to be his wife. It was all he could do to not kiss her right then and there.

He put his head to the task and chose a place to set up his picnic. They tied up the horses, and as he spread everything out on the blanket, Susan was filled with so much happiness and joy. What a wonderful surprise from Joe!

They sat on the blanket, eating a bit of cheese and bread, laughing and talking. More than once, Joe looked at Susan with such an overwhelming desire to kiss her and hold her. He leaned toward her and started to kiss her when suddenly a small calf came racing past her. She started to stand and Joe, without thinking, pulled her back to him.

And it was in that very moment that Papa rode down onto their little clandestine picnic with Mama and Jessica following. Papa came into that glen like a rider of black death. His face was dark and fierce. Both Susan and Joe stood up in a moment. Susan wanted to stand in front of Joe to protect him, but Joe had the dignity to stand in front of her. He said, "Hello, Mr. Derrick. This isn't…uh…what you think it is."

Papa, momentarily considering trampling the boy with his horse, bellowed, "This is exactly what I think it is! Pack your things and leave now, before I help you to leave."

Joe, with shaking hands and feet too big for his legs, quickly collected everything he had packed. He knew exactly what it looked like when he pulled Susan to himself, and he would have been lying if the thought had not crossed his mind. He was angry at himself and would have been angry at Mr. Derrick but didn't dare. He quickly jumped on his horse, took another look at Mr. Derrick, and looking for a retreat but finding none, rode at a respectful lope down the valley, his face a bright red.

Watching him ride off, Papa then glared at Susan and told her to get on her horse and help him move the cattle down the hill. They brought the calf back to its mother and then spent the afternoon bringing the cattle back down to the herd. Other than Papa giving out instructions, it was a quiet and awkward afternoon. Susan was miserable.

Papa rode to Mama and said, "You'd better talk to her. I'm so mad I could rip something apart. I trusted Joe to take care of my daughter, and this is how he behaves."

Mama considered how to calm her husband while at the same time trying to think about what to say to Susan. Hadn't they had enough talks about modesty and avoiding the occasion of sin? And then in a moment, she remembered the small box on the blanket. *Oh dear. Oh dear,* she thought and giggled a bit to herself. *He was going to propose!*

As they neared home, the cows began calling to each other, and now the cattle joined each other and merged once again into a single herd. Papa rode ahead to make sure each animal was accounted for and safe. Mama told Jessica to stay with Papa in case he needed her. And she and Susan pulled back.

"Susan," Mama said, trying to keep neutral. "What were you doing on the mountain with Joe?"

"I don't know, Mama. Joe asked me to meet him. We weren't doing anything wrong." Susan blushed and Mama looked at her. Susan said, "Well, we kissed."

Mama sighed. "Is that all? You understand how imprudent it is to be alone for so long? It is a temptation for you both. Also, did you tell anyone where you were going? What if something had happened? I know you love him, but you still need to be prudent. Also, your father is furious. You are going to need to talk to him."

Susan put her head down. She knew Mama was right. And even though she didn't say it, she had seen that look of desire on Joe's face. All he had done was kiss her, but she could tell he wanted to do so much more. It was exciting and scary all at the same time. And, in her excitement, she had forgotten to tell anyone where she was. She said, "Mama, Joe kissed me, and it was very sweet. But I understand what you are saying. I'm very sorry."

Mama and Susan caught up to Papa and they rode beside each other to the ranch. They all saw Joe standing there, looking fearfully resolved. As they approached and slowed to a stop Joe got on his knees and said, "It might as well be this way. Susan will you marry me? I love you more than anything. I would walk through hell for you. I would stand up to the most fearful man for you." And here he cast a glance at Papa. "I will die to protect you. Please marry me."

Susan jumped from her horse and leapt into his arms and said "yes." Mama sighed happily with tears in her eyes. Papa just glared at him. He didn't want to admit it, but darn, that boy had guts. Papa dismounted and, looking the boy in the eye, said, "What were you doing on that mountain with my daughter?"

Joe stood up. Now holding Susan's hand, he looked his future father-in-law in the eye and said, "I asked Susan to join me so I could propose to her. I got distracted by her beauty up on that mountain and kissed her. But that is all."

Papa stared him hard in the eyes, and when he saw that the boy returned his look, Papa nodded. Then he reached out and shook Joe's hand. "Welcome to the family, son. We are glad to have you."

Joe smiled broadly and shook Papa's hand vigorously.

THAT AFTERNOON, MAMA AND THE GIRLS WERE IN THE kitchen together, cleaning and preparing dinner. Susan was humming happily as she worked, pausing every so often to look at her ring. There had been a chorus of cries from her sisters when Susan came home with a beautiful, simple ring on her finger. They asked to tell the story, and each time Papa was fiercer, Joe was braver, and the whole event more charming. Mama was making two roasted chickens for dinner with all the special fixins. Mama brought in fresh herbs from the garden, and as she washed and cut them long afternoon rays of light streamed through the windows while the herbs filed the kitchen with fragrance. Susan, looking at her ring, asked Mama, "How should a woman keep charge of her home? I mean, there is so much talk about empowered women and I'm just not sure what is right."

Mama moved on to preparing the fresh vegetables as she thought how to explain the delicate balance of obedience to her husband and being a strong woman. For both were necessary. She made sure she was facing Rosie so Rosie could read her lips. There was no way she could sign all this, and she wanted to include all the girls.

"The man is the head of the household, but he delegates the running of the home to his wife. A woman usually has a better sense of the relationships within the family and can help the family work together. She knows the children in an intimate and very particular way, so she can help the children to grow in virtue and wisdom and keeps the home clean and ordered."

"Okay," said Susan. "How would you explain what makes a strong wife?"

Mama rubbed the fresh herbs over the chicken and put it in a pan with the vegetables. She squeezed lemon juice over the top of the chicken and over the vegetables, then put the lemon in the chicken itself. She put it in the oven and, closing the oven door, she stood up and said, "First and foremost, a woman must be strong in overcoming her own vices, maybe laziness or vanity. Maybe a desire to be admired or to be the center of attention. Always remember the first step in holiness is to have self-control and humility. This takes a lot of strength. But a woman must also be strong in how she raises the children. She must have the courage to tell a child if they are doing the wrong thing, she must not be afraid that a child won't like her if she asks for virtue. Many times, a mother has to reprimand a child even if she knows the child will be angry or upset."

Mama paused a moment, looking out the kitchen window into the hills, then said, "There is a deeper strength a woman must have. She must have a spiritual strength that holds up not only her family, but her husband too. When he is weary and discouraged, a strong wife must have a deep trust in God. She must be able to pray for him, pray for his courage and his wisdom, even if she is tired or hurt."

Billy and Caz came in just then and opened up the fridge, looked for something to eat. Finding some cheese, they closed the door and leaned against it, watching and listening.

Seeing the boys there, listening, Mama smiled at her children with a twinkle in her eyes which they knew well, and she began. "It's like with horses." The children laughed; Mama loved using horse stories to explain things! "Marriage is like two horses pulling a cart. First of all, you want to marry someone who pulls the same speed as you. You can't have an Arab and a draft horse—they will always fight because they work differently. But once you choose your spouse, then you need to work together to pull. It doesn't do any good if you use your strength to fight the other horse—the cart will go nowhere and everything will break. Much of the time, you pull together, each with their own job—the man to protect and provide, the woman to love and to guide.

Billy laughed, "Hey that rhymes! Did you mean it?"

And Caz bent over laughing. "Anyone want a peanut?"

Mama smiled and the girls snickered. Mama went on. "Some of the time the wife pulls harder, some of the time the husband pulls harder. Some of the time one of you is nearly dead with worry, fear, sickness, and then the other has to pull not only the cart but the other horse as well. That is how a strong woman works in a marriage."

The girls nodded. They understood the analogy all right, but they were not sure if it helped them understand marriage.

Munching on the cheese slice, Caz said, "I don't understand. Where is the cart going?"

Billy looked at him disdainfully, "Heaven, silly. Where else would it go?"

Caz pushed him and Mama shooed them toward the door. "Off with you! Go out and feed and see if your father needs any more help!"

The boys left, banging against the walls and leaving a trail of dirt from their shoes. Mama watched them leave with a smile on her face. Mama turned back to the kitchen and her daughters. She began to clean the counters with the lavender soap they had made. The fragrance mixed in the kitchen with all the smells from the dinner preparation—fresh rosemary, garlic, and lemon. The girls sat comfortably and let the smells of the kitchen, the soft light, and their mother's advice wash over them. It felt very comfortable and safe there in that kitchen, and they wished it could be like this forever.

Mama told them, "Dinner will be ready in about an hour. Get your evening chores done now, so we can relax after dinner."

As everyone left the kitchen, Susan stopped Rosie and signed to her, "Please won't you say something? Please, before I leave for the year, can you tell me you love me? Anything. I miss your voice so much, Rosie. I've loved watching you laugh and smile, but I know you can talk, and I don't want to miss it."

Even if Rosie could not read Susan's lips, as she had started to do, even if Rosie could not read the movements of her hands, as Susan had started to learn sign language, and even if all these things had not been expressed, Rosie well knew what Susan was asking. For it was the last thing. The thing she was most afraid of. Speaking out loud. And though she loved Susan with all her heart and was so very grateful for her friendship, she could not do it. Talking with Apollo had not been enough. Working with the horses had not been enough. Laughing in joy was not speaking. And so, she shook her head while big tears of sorrow fell from her eyes. Susan could see the conflict in her little sister's face and simply responded with a big hug. She whispered in Rosie's ear, "I know you can talk. I know you will, when it is the right time. And I will be waiting to hear about it."

But Rosie could not hear her, feeling only the whisper of air on her cheek, like the tiny wings of a hummingbird. She hugged Susan fiercely, hoping for some of her courage.

Echoes of Silence

Just then Papa came in. Joe had stayed to help Papa do some work, and by the time the work was done there was only good will and hunger. Jacob came in as well, and when he looked at Papa he said, "Ditch is dug."

Papa nodded at him. Jacob smiled; no more words were needed.

Mama's roast chicken smelled amazing and the boys washed eagerly. It was a wonderful celebration and dinner, full of love and joy. Susan played the piano afterward, a beautiful, lilting sonata. Rosie walked over to the piano and, placing her hand on the piano, suddenly realized she could feel the music! Her eyes opened bright, and a big smile lit her face with joy. Everyone smiled and enjoyed the moment.

That night as the family prayed, with one more in their circle, the stars seemed to shine brighter than before. Susan looked around and thought, *This is my circle of love.*

CHAPTER 27

The Quiet Grumbling

Sierra woke up sad and despondent. Today was Susan's last day and Jacob was leaving a few days after that. It would feel very sad and empty in the house. She couldn't imagine how they had made it without Susan, and now Jacob was leaving too! Sierra trudged around the house grumpily. Mama was melancholic as well, and Jessica just baked like crazy. Both Susan and Jacob were slowly packing things and had made runs to town to buy things they would need. They were sad to leave but also excited. Susan would be with Joe at college and Jacob would start at the seminary. Both were looking forward to their vocations. Susan thought about her talks with her mother and was glad she could ask her for advice. Jacob was happy for his father's strong example, but it was up to him to figure out how to serve a parish with that same strength.

Mama put her coffee cup down and said, "Hey, let's go work with Pistol today and put a saddle on her. Maybe even put a leg on her."

Everyone was happy with the distraction. The day was miraculously a little cooler, so they took a welcome break from the small house.

The early morning air felt refreshing, and the boys ran and played in the stream. They all walked together, enjoying one of their last hikes together. Pistol whinnied happily for them, and they now were all able to go in the pen with her and love on her. She was quite used to both the attention and the chaos. She was smart and she loved her little family. Mama went through the regimen—joining up, pivoting, walking forward, and backing up. Pistol looked happy to please and excited to be working. Mama thought, *She is going to be a good little horse. Better than Apollo. I started him too late, and he is still half-wild.*

Mama held the rope and picked up a blanket. She rubbed it on Pistol and at first Pistol flinched but then stood quietly. Mama rubbed the blanket over her back, along her haunches, over her withers, under her belly, and even over her face. Pistol was calm. Then Mama, still holding the rope of the halter, showed Pistol the saddle and let her smell it. Pistol seemed indifferent. Mama put it on her back, carefully and slowly, and then cinched it up. Everyone assumed Pistol would continue to be calm. But when Mama pulled the cinch up tight against Pistol's belly, she bolted. The saddle immediately fell to the ground and Pistol quickly pivoted as if a cat had landed beside her. They had not noticed until now, but Mama was hanging tight to the knotted rope, so when Pistol bolted she quickly came to the end of the line and then reared up. Mama stood quiet until Pistol calmed down. She brought her back and picked up the saddle again. Now Pistol was highly suspicious of that monster and shied again, but Mama followed her with the saddle until Pistol saw it would not hurt her.

Mama showed her the saddle and this time Pistol was calm, trusting Mama but not quite the saddle. She was able to cinch it this time. Then, she let Pistol go and sent her around the round pen. Mama was calm and did not act surprised when Pistol bucked and then bolted when the stirrups hit her side. Mama let her go around for a while until Pistol realized the monster on her back, grabbing her sides, was not hurting her. Mama explained, "You see, that is what a lion would feel like. Jumping on her back and then grabbing her sides. So, her instinct is to bolt and buck to get it off. She just needs to realize for herself that it will not hurt her. And look, she is slowing down now."

Mama turned her the other way and around she went, but now at a mindful lope rather than the crazy running. Mama turned her back again and Pistol began to use her thinking side of the brain because she knew what was going on. She put her head down and licked her lips. Mama stopped and relaxed. Pistol stopped, waited, and then came up to her. Mama petted her and rubbed her everywhere. "Okay, who wants to put a leg on her? I am going to hold her so she doesn't bolt."

Sierra offered and Mama was glad because Sierra was not only the most agile, but the most aware of her body position and weight. Sierra came in, shaking with excitement. Mama stopped her.

"Stop right now. Collect yourself. Take a breath. Slow your breathing. If you approach her like that Pistol will think there is danger. Remember she is reading from you what the situation is. You are the head mare to her."

Sierra stopped and rolled her shoulders, took a deep breath, and slowed her breathing. It worked. She could feel her muscles relax. She softly approached Pistol and petted her. Then, with measured strength, put her foot in the stirrup.

"Now lean over the saddle so your weight is distributed."

Sierra did so, and Pistol only looked back at her as if to say, "What are you doing up there?"

"Okay, well done. That is enough for today. Nicely done. Nicely done."

They walked back to the house, the summer heat already bearing down on them. As they walked, Billy and Caz ran up to Rosie. They stood on either side of her. Billy touched Rosie on the shoulder, so she looked at him as he signed, "Why won't you talk already? What's the big deal."

Rosie looked at him, astonished and angry. But before she could respond, Caz bumped her so that she fell into Billy. She glared at him, and he signed, "I don't care if you sound dumb. I sound dumb. What's the big deal? I heard you talking to Apollo in the barn. Who cares how you sound?"

Rosie glared at them both and was filled with so much anger she ran home and into her room. Mama came up to them and asked, "What did you say to Rosie? What is going on?"

The boys grumbled and said, "Nothing."

When they all got home, Mama went into the girls' room and saw Rosie there, her knees drawn up close to her chest. Mama signed, "Are you okay?"

It was clear she was not, but Mama was hot and tired and so when Rosie nodded, Mama just closed the door behind her and went back to cooking dinner.

At dinner, they sat together and ate Mama's soup. A last meal for the family to eat together. Rosie was quiet and very sullen looking. Mama was distressed. Susan was thinking about Joe and was quiet. Jacob was thinking about the choices he was making; all his friends were going off to college and he was feeling the weight of his decision. Billy and Caz were upset about what had happened with Rosie and felt bad about it.

Finally, Caz asked, "What food would you take on a deserted island if you could only take one meal?"

Everyone had a different answer—some sweet and some savory. After everyone answered, Caz said triumphantly, "I would take Mama's soup. It has everything you need—meat, vegetables, and water. You could live forever on Mama's soup."

Everyone looked around the table and nodded—it was one thing they could all agree on.

After dinner they went outside to pray. The sky was bright red and orange with a strange light. They watched the sky darken and it felt foreboding. A last meal, a last sunset. Mama rocked in her chair. The moon rose into a cloudy sky. It looked haunting and mysterious as the clouds flew over the moon, some dark, some light. The little family sat in quiet for a while, just enjoying each other's company.

At last, Papa said, "Let's pray. Dear Lord, we pray for our family, for our friends and neighbors. We pray for those who have asked for our prayers and for those who have no one to pray for. We pray for Susan and Jacob especially as they go and learn your will for them. We pray for Mama that she is strong, and for Sierra and Jessica and Rosie. We pray for Billy and Caz. And Lord, help me to love you and obey you. Help me to know what is right and to lead my family toward you. Help me to protect my family, especially against this drought." He sighed and then began the rosary with the sign of the cross. "In the name of the Father, and the Son, and Holy Spirit."

They each made the sign of the cross with bowed heads and humble hearts.

After prayers, everyone said goodbye to Susan. She would be leaving early in the morning. Jacob was quiet, he was the next to go. It seemed so strange they were growing up and leaving the house. He felt oddly protective, knowing that soon he would be gone, leaving only his young sisters and little brothers. *Well,* he thought with a sigh, *I will have a few more days with the family. I will ask and see if there is anything I can do to help before I leave.*

Susan drove away early that morning, just as dawn was beginning to wake. The sky was ugly and red. She let herself feel melancholy for a while. Then, as the sun rose and the sky slowly lightened, she thought about finishing her final year of school, seeing all her friends, and of course being engaged to Joe, and her mood lightened considerably.

The day started out hot and humid. It sucked away their energy. Susan was gone and they all felt her absence. They closed the curtains in the house to keep it cool and spent the day cleaning and getting the girls' room back to just Sierra, Jessica, and Rosie. A bed tucked away; a closet filled once again. It felt lonely and sad to take away Susan's place in the room. No one thought about Pistol, and Rosie was still moody.

That night, after dinner, Rosie went to her room while Sierra and Jessica washed dishes. How had they managed with Susan gone? It felt so normal having her home. And now she was gone again.

"Plus," said Sierra, "she's going to go and get married and leave us."

Jessica was washing dishes and water was flying everywhere. She argued, "Look, Sierra, don't say that. They might live near us, and we will still see them."

Sierra slammed pots around. "It won't be the same and you know it." The only response was a quiet grumbling.

Jacob heard the slamming of the dishes. He came into the kitchen and laughed when he saw the bubbles and water all over the floor and counters. He came rushing over to Jessica and swept her up in a big bear hug. She pounded on his arms and pretended to bite them. Her eyes were sparking fire as Sierra watched, astonished. It took a lot to make Jessica upset. But finally Jessica relaxed, and Jacob put her down. He knew her perhaps better than anyone, knew her deep moods that took a long time to be expressed. He knew she needed to laugh more than anyone.

Jacob asked, "What's going on here? You all are feeling sorry for yourselves."

Sierra and Jessica now both glared at him. The truth was harsh. Billy came into the kitchen then and asked Jacob, "Can you tell us a story?"

The girls looked at him with hopeful eyes. *Yes*, they both thought, *a story would be just the thing to distract us.*

Jacob opened the fridge and, finding some squash bread, sat down with a plate and the butter. Putting a generous amount of butter on a piece of bread, he chewed thoughtfully.

"Remember the time when we came home from Easter Mass, and our cows were out on the road?"

They all nodded, smiles filling their faces.

Billy said, "And Papa said we had to take care of it right away so they wouldn't cause an accident."

Jessica smiled and said, "And Mama said we didn't have to change because it was so important to get it done."

Sierra said, "So we jumped on our horses with our Easter dresses and our nice shoes. Well, I pulled mine off."

Then Jessica added, "We rode out to the road, trying to move the cows. Other neighbors came out to help us and soon there was a whole parade of people, blocking other driveways and trying to move the cows down the road to our front drive where we could turn them in."

Jacob was smiling to himself, watching the eager faces of his siblings recounting the story.

Billy cried out, "But remember the cows started running and kicking up their heels, and we were worried they would run past our gate? But Caz was there all along with a wheelbarrow full of hay."

Caz, hearing his name, popped his head into the kitchen and said, "It's what Jessica told us to do when any of the animals got out. Go get feed!"

Jessica looked at him with a smile and nodded and said, "Well, it worked! All the cows followed Caz right down our driveway and we got them in the front pen."

Sierra laughed, "Our new Easter clothes were covered in horsehair and mud, but Mama didn't mind. She was so glad the cows were safe."

Jacob took another bite of bread and smiled with a twinkle in his eyes. "But then Papa said we had to find out where they got out."

Sierra cried out, "So we all marched down the fence line, still in our Sunday best, and found where the cows had pushed a fence down low and that is where they got out. Papa said it had to be fixed that day, even though it was Easter Sunday!"

Jessica said, "Mama said we had time to go change first, so we did. But all our clothes were already ruined. We went down to the low fence with all our tools and more fencing. Jacob, you and Papa pounded the fence posts, while the girls attached the fencing to the posts. Then Mama pulled the fence with the truck."

Sierra said, "Everyone wired the fence to the t-posts and made sure it stayed tight."

They all nodded; it was good to work together as a family.

Caz started to jump up and down. "But then! The mud fight!" Everyone laughed with him. It was the best part of the memory! "I don't remember who threw the first mud ball, but pretty soon everyone, even Mama, was throwing mud, and then the mud fight turned into a wrestling match and everyone was in the mud."

Billy exclaimed, "And then we saw Papa kissing Mama and they were all muddy!"

Everyone laughed again. Jacob stood up, rolling up his sleeves, and put on some music on the radio.

Caz asked, "Did we ever do an Easter egg hunt?"

Billy answered, "No, we never did. I wonder if the eggs were hidden or not. Maybe they are still out there."

The music filled the kitchen and they all began to sing as they cleaned the kitchen, enjoying their time together and their memories.

There was one, however, who had not joined them. Who had heard neither the clatter of dishes, nor the laughter. She did not hear the music or the storytelling. She sat alone in her room feeling sorry for herself and wondering why God had done this to her.

AFTER PRAYERS, AND ONCE EVERYONE HAD GONE TO BED, Paul and Anna sat outside talking. Paul asked, "Why won't Rosie talk? I don't understand. What is going on? Are you trying to talk to her? What do you do during the day to help her talk?"

Angry at the accusation, but also frustrated with Rosie, Anna held her tongue for a moment and then she said, "I don't know. I don't know why she won't talk. Paul, what do you want me to do? I can't make her talk. There is plenty of talking in the home, if that's what you mean!"

Paul said nothing. What could he say? He was frustrated that Rosie wouldn't talk even after all this time. He blamed himself and he blamed Anna. He blamed the doctors, and he did his best not to blame God. Rosie was doing so well in everything else, but he wanted to hear her voice again and there was no reason he shouldn't. He was silent in the darkness. Anna could feel his anger and his silent grumbling came across loud and clear.

CHAPTER 28

The Hunt Which Saw Too Much

Susan had gone and now Jacob was making final preparations to leave as well. That morning, the house was melancholy and Mama was downcast.

Caz suddenly cried out, "When Jacob leaves, we won't have a big brother!"

Billy groaned and hit his chest. "What will we do without a big brother? Who will protect us?"

"And play silly games?" cried Caz.

Suddenly Billy said, "Wait! What about Joe? He can be our new big brother!"

Caz perked up. "Yes. That is a good point. But we still have to wait nine months for him to come back."

Jacob, overhearing his two brothers, felt his heart swell with love for them. He rushed into the room and gathered them both in his strong arms and, carrying them around the room, said, "Well, I haven't gone yet, and I won't be far! So, you just better watch out before you replace me that quickly!"

The two little brothers laughed and happily pummeled their big brother as he carried them off to the living room and they wrestled on the carpet.

Papa watched them, laughing, "We could use some fun." Then he announced, "I think this is a great day for hunting."

Billy and Caz came running into the kitchen with cries of joy. Jacob followed, hair mussed and shirt half off. Mama looked at them and laughed. Papa continued, "Jacob, what do you think about building some bookshelves for Mama so she can get her books organized?"

Jacob looked at his mother and said, "That is a great idea. I've been wanting to do something extra before I left, and I know how much that means to you."

Mama smiled at all her men, both big and little, and said, "Thank you."

Papa selected a rifle and ammunition for the hunt. Mama made a nice lunch for them with enough water for the day. They saddled Bandit, Pilgrim, and Apache and rode off at a nice, evenly paced walk, giving the older horses a chance to warm up.

Mama worked with Jacob on where to build the bookshelves. He went off to get wood and supplies leaving Mama alone with her books. She started the dusty project of pulling books out of boxes and putting them in different piles. So many books. Children's books that she had read to them when they were little, books she had read herself as a child, books she and Paul had read together. So many wonderful memories and thoughts. Covered in dust and memories, she was glad for the distraction. It was a perfect parting gift before Jacob left.

Jessica, Sierra, and Rosie went into their room and all sat on the bed. They felt even closer together since Susan had left. They were conspiring. Sierra signed, "Let's go to the spring and see if the herd of horses come. Papa is gone, so he won't know, and Mama is too distracted."

Rosie nodded, her sad eyes now bright with excitement, "Yes, and it's so hot outside, lets swim."

Jessica said, "Okay, but shouldn't we tell Mama where we are going?"

Sierra hushed her. "No! She won't let us go! Don't say anything!"

They agreed and told Mama they were going to Sweetwater. Mama was buried deep in books, and just nodded absentmindedly. They packed a lunch and plenty of water. Sierra signed to Rosie, "Are you okay without a saddle?"

Rosie nodded. Sierra had figured out how to carry the rifle scabbard across her back and Jessica could carry the lunch and water in a backpack. After putting on bridles, they rode off on Ginger, Rain, and Dash. It felt exciting to be out alone and they immediately broke into a gentle lope. Rosie, with a mischievous grin, broke into a run, passed Sierra and Jessica, and the race was on! Rosie hadn't ridden at a fast gallop since before she got sick. The wind stung her face and the pounding of the horse put her into a soundless trance. It felt like all her troubles were flying away from her.

As they approached the spring, they slowed down and were relieved to see the pool was still full. They brought the horses so they could drink and cool off. There was still some fresh grass around and the horses very greedily grabbed and munched it. They loosely tied the horses and, taking off shoes and shorts, dove into the water. It was cool and refreshing, for the day was quickly becoming hot. They swam and played and dove all morning. Sitting on the soft grass, they got out the lunch. Afterward, they lay on the bank and closed their eyes, nearly sleeping in the warm sun. They did not notice the clouds building on the horizon.

MEANWHILE, PAPA RODE OUT WITH HIS YOUNGEST TWO boys. This ride had been a long time coming, as the boys had been clamoring forever to learn how to hunt. As Papa rode, however, he could see his cows were losing weight and the grass was nearly gone. "Dear God," he prayed, "please bring rain and snow. Help me to trust you." Then he said to the boys, "We are going up in those hills where there are still springs with water and green grass. There will be deer up there. Always watch out for bears or lions though. You hear me?"

Both boys nodded and grinned.

Papa went on. "Billy, you are going to shoot the deer if we find one. Caz, I want you to watch and learn. You are still too young to hold the rifle."

Caz wasn't too happy about that, but he knew it was special to be going with Papa and hunting, so he said nothing.

Up in the highlands, the trees were turning orange. Fall was finally coming, and Papa prayed again for winter to come quickly. *Hopefully*, he thought, *God listens to Mama's prayers.*

It was so hot that a September snow seemed impossible.

As they went higher up, it was a little cooler and they found a nice spring where they could water the horses and eat lunch. They had been riding for a few hours and were very high up. They were surrounded by tall pines and aspens. After a bit, they left the horses and went to a spot that Papa thought would be a good place to wait.

Down below, Jessica, Sierra, and Rosie played and rested, still hoping to see the horses. Suddenly they heard the pounding hoofs of the horse herd. They stood up, noticing for the first time the dark clouds on the horizon. That storm looked angry and was coming on quickly. They could see as well that the horses were running from something.

But Rosie, instead of hiding, ran out into the open to see them. Sierra followed her, protective. Jessica stayed and watched from the rocks. Once out in the open, Sierra could see why the horses were running. There was a lion following them, jumping from rock to rock. She was looking for the slowest or the weakest in the herd. That lion terrified Sierra. She had seen what it could do. She called out to Rosie, but of course Rosie could not hear her. Jessica stood up and saw the lion as well. It was coming closer. She waved her hands at Rosie, calling out in desperation. Rosie's attention was on the horses and so she did not see anything else.

But someone else did see.

Papa sat with his boys in the high hills. He helped both boys set up the rifle on the trunk of a fallen tree. He explained while they waited, "You are going to aim for just behind the shoulder. Remember to breathe."

They sat in the leaves and grass, deep amongst the trees. They enjoyed the quiet. Birds became used to them and started to sing. And still they waited. At last, a beautiful young buck walked by, headed to the spring, just as Papa had anticipated. He knelt behind Billy to help brace the rifle. Billy took his safety off, lined up his shot, and fired, remembering to breathe. He gasped as the buck fell. The recoil hurt his shoulder.

Papa said, "You pulled the trigger too quickly and the rifle moved. It wasn't a clean shot. Watch."

Just as he spoke, the buck got to his feet and wandered off, clearly injured and disoriented.

Papa said, "We need to follow him and bring him down. It's not fair to have him running off injured."

They trudged through the thick underbrush, following the chaotic and bloody tracks. Papa came upon a ridge and noticed a movement below. He stood on the edge and looked out across the valley. He could see everything. He could see Rosie out in the field watching the horses, he could see the lion following the herd, and he could see Sierra and Jessica trying to wave a warning to Rosie. He was consumed with anger. It was exactly what he had been afraid of.

"What the hell was Anna thinking?" he muttered between grinding teeth.

There was nothing, absolutely nothing he could do. He stood and watched, frozen. Billy and Caz came up to him and immediately saw what he was looking at. For once in their lives they were absolutely silent. It was too terrible that they were up there and could only watch.

"Can you shoot the lion, Papa?" Caz asked.

Papa knew he could not, but he lifted the rifle to his eyes. No, he couldn't take the shot, it was too far away. He put the rifle down.

The clouds came in boiling and dark. The wind picked up, blowing in unpredictable gusts. Suddenly they heard thunder from the darkening skies, but there was no rain. This storm had not been forecast, but out on the plains they could build up surprisingly fast. Papa regretted that they were so high up. Many of the trees were brittle from the heat and lack of rain. They stood there on the edge of the mountain in the strong wind and continued to helplessly watch. Suddenly a bolt of lightning flashed in the sky, frightening the already stampeding horses. Now Rosie was directly in their path!

MEANWHILE, THE LION WAS MUCH TOO CLOSE, AND Sierra ran to get the rifle. Turning away from Rosie, she ran back for it. That lion would see Rosie as much easier prey than a horse. Rosie, finally seeing the lion, started running back to her sisters, across the open field. Jessica watched Rosie running, watched as the lighting struck the earth, and watched as the herd veered away from the lighting straight toward Rosie! Suddenly, Rosie tripped and fell on the ground just as the herd was getting closer.

PAPA, BILLY, AND CAZ SAW ROSIE FALL AND WERE NEARLY weak with fear. They could not imagine their beautiful Rosie being crushed by a stampeding herd. It was just too awful. Sierra had gone for the rifle, and it was only Jessica that could help. Jessica, who was slow to decide and slow to react.

Then, they watched in amazement as Jessica, without hesitation, ran to her. Now both of them were in the path of the crazed horses. Jessica helped her up and, grabbing her hand, the two ran for the nearest outcropping of rock, scrambling and cutting their legs on the sharp rocks as they climbed to safety. They made it to a flat part of the rock just as the horses rushed by. Jessica and Rosie, not knowing where Sierra or the lion were, made their way back to their horses. Sierra was there with the rifle, had loaded it, and was aiming at the lion which had just turned toward them all. Sierra look a shot at the lion and missed. But the lion did not like the sound of the rifle and slunk off into the rocks to hide. The girls ran to their horses, mounted, and took off at a gallop. The horses were already skittish and dancing from the panic of the fleeing herd, the lightning, and the smell of the lion. Jessica rode behind Sierra and Rosie to make sure they were not unseated, as they were all bareback. But they had good seats and flew across the range.

As they approached the house, they slowed down. Mama heard the gallop of the horses and when she came out to see what was going on, she could see the panic and fear on their faces.

"Where were you?" she shouted, all her composure gone. "What happened? Are you okay?"

Rosie was dark and sullen, and neither Sierra nor Jessica could decide what to tell her, so they remained quiet. They all dismounted and began grooming the hot and sweaty horses. Finally, Jessica looked her mama in the eyes and said, "We are all right. We need to take care of the horses." And then, wanting to deflect attention away from her and her sisters, she added, "Also, there was dry lightning. I hope it doesn't start any fires."

Papa, meanwhile, saw all that happened and saw the three girls ride away safely. He dropped to his knees; the relief was so great. He said a prayer of thanksgiving and thanked God that his family was safe. And then he realized what he had seen. Rosie riding like the wind, bareback and with perfect balance, just as she always had. All he could think was that they were going to be okay. He was so grateful for this, and without him realizing it tears appeared on his eyes and his eyelashes fluttered, thinking it was a leaf that had fallen upon them.

Billy asked about the deer, and Papa shook his head to clear it and focus his attention to the task at hand. They found the deer nearby. Billy had grazed him just behind the shoulder, enough to wound him but not kill him. Papa focused on his sons. "Do you see how the recoil caused you to move the rifle slightly? You have to hold it tight. Rest it on a log if you need to." Papa handed Billy the rifle and told him to finish the deer. "Shoot him here, behind the shoulder, and you will get the vital organs but not scatter bone into the meat."

Billy took a deep breath, steadied his hands, and shot the deer. It was hard to see the deer go from being alive to being dead. It felt so final. But it was also horrible to see the deer thrashing and in pain.

Papa said, "Much better to take them down with a clean shot so it does not suffer."

Billy nodded solemnly.

Handing them gloves, he showed them how to field dress the deer. As they worked, Papa spoke. "I want you to clear your mind right now. This deer gave its life so that we could live. His blood is on the ground. It's a little like Christ, dying so that we can live. Every time you kill an animal, have thanksgiving in your heart. And when an animal is in your care, take care of it and respect it." They continued to cut and process, and Caz winced a few times. Papa noticed this and said, "We forget when we are in a grocery store where our meat came from. There is no smell, and no blood. Just clean white aisles and fluorescent lights. It is not easy to take a life, even if it must be done for our survival. Always remember that when you are holding a gun it can take a life, and that is no small thing."

Both boys nodded.

The work was much harder than they thought it would be, knowing this beautiful, live creature was dead from Billy's bullet. Papa said, "We will take this meat and put it in the freezer, and we will remember that God gave us this bounty. And if someone should ask for food, we will be generous. I have had to ask for food as well."

The boys nodded again, feeling the seriousness of what Papa was saying. Life was hard, and it was good to remember to be both humble and generous. Papa handed the antlers to Billy.

"These are yours. They will always be special. Your first buck."

They hung the meat and the antlers on the saddles. Billy was bursting with pride. Papa then looked both boys in the eyes.

"Remember, you work as a team, and sometimes your brother will get the shot and sometimes you will. But you always help each other. Do you understand me?"

Billy and Caz nodded and never forgot that lesson.

Papa and the boys came home and carefully put away the horses.

"They did a good job for us. Take care of them. Groom and brush them, clean out their hooves, and make sure they have hay," Papa said.

Jacob came out to meet them and help process the deer. They washed the meat in an outside sink and then carried the deer into the cellar. Laying it on the old wooden table, they processed the meat, first into quarters and then into cuts of meat that Mama could use. The boys were hungry and tired, but Papa explained that if they did not tend to the deer meat now, it would rot. Hunting wasn't just shooting a deer; it was taking care of the meat as well.

They finished cutting the meat, wrapping it, and putting it in the freezer. Exhausted and proud, they climbed the cellar stairs to the house. Mama had dinner ready but looked white and strained. Sierra still had not answered her questions and Jessica was sullen. Jacob was almost done with the bookshelves and went to finish them before dinner.

Papa walked in the house and asked about the girls. "Are they all right?"

Mama just shook her head.

Papa, not knowing what that meant, looked at her harshly. "Are they okay? Did they make it back safely? I saw them ride home."

Mama looked at him queerly. "What do you mean? Did you see what happened? Because I don't know anything."

His breath became slow and measured. "Where are they? Are they okay?"

Scared now, she looked him in the eye and said very clearly, "They are okay. They are in their bedroom. But they won't tell me what happened."

Papa walked to the bedroom. Mama felt guilty about her lack of attention. She should have asked more questions about where they were going. She had been distracted by the books, but more than that, she had wanted to take the time to feel melancholy about her oldest two leaving.

Opening the girls' door, Papa said in a terrible voice, "You want to tell your mother what happened today?" And by the look on his face, they knew in an instant that he knew.

They came out looking sheepish and stood before their mother. They told the story, and Mama burst out, "You told me you were going to Sweetwater! And instead, you took Rosie to the spring?"

But they had left the part out about the lion. Papa looked at them harshly. "Tell her about the lion."

The three girls looked at each other, sick. Papa had SEEN IT?

Mama was horrified. "What do you mean about the lion? My God, Paul, what are you talking about?"

And all she could think was that she was glad to be hearing this with her three girls standing before her. Heads down, the girls told her the whole story. Mama's face went white, and she just sat in a chair looking at them with such anger. They were truly ashamed. They could see in her face the danger they had put themselves in, and now that they were home safe, their minds could process how badly it could have all gone.

Papa told them in his terrible-and-yet-calm voice they would each get a belting.

"You knew better. You put yourselves in danger. You lied to your mother about where you were going, and so help me God, you are never to do that again!"

Papa was fair in his belting, not a wild barrage of blows done in anger. No, he gave each girl a hug, looked her in the eye, told her what she had done wrong, and how many blows she would get. The belt hurt and afterward they had red welts. But they knew they deserved it.

Papa had a hard time giving Rosie a punishment, but he would be a hypocrite if he did not punish her as well. Just because she couldn't hear, did not mean she was free to do what she wanted, much less put herself in danger! So, he swallowed his pity and gave her the belting as well. Afterward, she looked him in the eye, and he could see thankfulness in her eyes. It surprised him. She finally felt like she was one of the girls again and not just an invalid.

Papa and Mama went outside. Dinner was forgotten, and Billy and Caz, who were hungry, foraged in the kitchen like orphans.

"My God, Anna, you can't imagine what it was like having to watch all that and not be able to do anything about it. I am angry at you also for letting them go."

Mama started to protest but there was no point. She nodded, silently accepting some of the blame. Then he said in an even more quiet voice, his eyes sparkling with happiness. "Rosie can ride like the wind! Bareback!"

Mama gasped and her eyes flew open. "She can? You saw her?"

She smiled and Papa smiled back. And even knowing how worried they both had been, he had to say it. "Anna, the children are getting older and more independent. We have to teach them how to be safe. They brought the rifle. They kept their wits about them, and they managed to be safe. We have to not only thank God for that but realize that we raised them right."

Anna nodded. It was true. She couldn't keep them as children forever.

Just then, Caz poked his head out. "Can we eat dinner? There is nothing to eat in the fridge and dinner smells amazing. Also, did Papa tell you Billy shot a deer!?"

Mama looked at Papa who smiled despite himself. "I almost forgot." He stood up and, taking Mama's hand, said, "Let's eat dinner."

They called the girls out from their rooms, and Papa gave them each a hug. He said, "Okay, you know what you did wrong, and you received a fair punishment. But tell me what you did right."

They looked at him quizzically, and Mama said, "We can talk over dinner."

They sat round the table, and Billy and Caz excitedly shared about their first hunting trip and shared what Papa said about the deer. Then Papa looked at the girls and said, "Now you tell me about your adventure, and tell us the good and the bad."

The girls told their story, and as they told it they realized that although they had made some bad choices, they had made a lot of good choices as well. And as the voices went on, chatting happily and sharing thoughts and ideas, the sun slowly fell around that happy little family.

The beasts in the field and the barn, however, felt none of that peace, for they knew what was coming.

CHAPTER 29

Fire Storm

The next morning started heavy with humidity, heat, and dark clouds. The earth was restless and uneasy. The wind blew in terrible gusts and Papa rode out and checked on his herd. They were huddled in the shelter of a hill, restless, trying to get out of the wind and the storm they knew was coming. Everyone worked to secure any loose items. Mama started a stew over the fire. There was a good chance they would lose electricity in this storm. As for Jacob, he was glad he was home, glad he had one more storm to help his family through before he left.

As the afternoon wore on, it became darker. Suddenly there was a terrible crack of thunder which shook the windows, and a bright streak of light shot across the sky. Rosie did not hear it, but she felt the vibration and saw the light. She looked around with big eyes.

"Lightning," Papa said, his voice heavy with worry. "It's dry lightning. Oh God. It's so dry out there!"

Mama groaned. What could be done? They stopped and said a prayer asking for mercy. What they did not realize was that there had been forty-two strikes of lightning that afternoon and each one had started a fire. The fire service was completely overwhelmed and unable to respond adequately.

They sat under the porch as another clap of thunder shook the house and seemed to split the sky. Almost immediately, a bolt came down from the sky and hit the barn. It nearly exploded in flame. Mama stood up and gasped, her hand over her mouth. "The animals, the hay!"

But it was worse, because everything in that barn was for their ranch. They heard the scream of frightened animals. "Oh my God," Mama moaned, "The animals! Please save the animals. Nothing else matters."

Papa cried, "Jacob! Get the pump! Have your mother hold it in the river. I'm going to get the animals!"

And with that, he ran toward the barn.

Jacob knew what to do. They had talked and planned for their worst nightmare—a fire in the house or barn. They had a pump system which they could put in the river. It was heavy and inadequate, but it was something.

Mama told Jessica, "Call 9-1-1 now. Keep the children here. Do not leave the house unless the fire comes this way. If it does, go to the river and sit in it."

Jessica bolted into the house to call 9-1-1. The call was taken, and information received. She went and stood outside with Sierra, Rosie, and the boys. She told the boys, "You stay with me. You hear me?"

The boys were startled by her forcefulness and stayed glued to her side.

Mama ran to the river and helped Jacob set up the pump. She stood in the riverbed and made sure the suction hose was under water. Jacob pulled the heavy hose toward the barn, spraying the ground as he went. Papa was at the door, trying to pull out the horses, but they were frantic with fear and would not leave. They could hear the scream of animals and Mama could barely hold back her tears. At the house, Jessica and her brothers and sisters openly cried in horror, for now they could smell the rank odor of burning flesh and hair.

Sierra wanted to run away. It was so awful and terrible. She closed her eyes and told herself to breathe. Just breathe. Caz took her hand and looked up to her for assurance. He was scared. That brave little boy had never seen anything so terrible. For the first time, Sierra was glad she had not run away and realized how selfish it was to leave the family that loved her and even needed her. She squeezed Caz's hand and forced herself to smile. "It will be all right, Caz. God is good and Papa is very strong."

Jacob handed the hose to Mama and went to help Papa pull animals out of the barn. Papa cried, "I can't get through the front of the barn, the fire is too much! I'm going to go to the back of the barn and tear out the walls, maybe I can get them out the back.

Jacob cried, "Let me help!"

Papa stopped and looked at him. Papa saw only a man, and one that would protect his family if something happened to him. "No." He put his hand on Jacob's shoulder and said, "I need you to keep spraying water and to protect your Mama and brothers and sisters."

Jacob swallowed his fear and nodded bravely. And with that, Papa was gone to the back of the barn. No one could see him.

Mama suddenly remembered there was gasoline in the barn. She cried out, "No! Don't go. It doesn't matter!"

But Papa could hear nothing over the growl of the fire, the scream of the animals, and the howling wind. Suddenly there was an explosion. Jacob was thrown on the ground with his jacket on fire. Mama ran to him and helped put it out. She brought him into the house to see how bad the burn was. Pulling the smoking jacket off, she saw that Jacob's arms were burnt. With a fearful shudder, she wrapped them in gauze, wondering all the while about her husband.

Suddenly the front door opened with a wave of heat and stench.

Papa came in. He bellowed with a horrible sneer, "Wife!"

As he stepped into the light, the children gasped. He looked more devil than father. His black hair stood straight on end, blown by hot wind and flames. His eyes were red and bloodshot from smoke. His face was black and on the side of his face there was a horrible burn, making his face look even more twisted and grotesque. He snarled, his black lip curling up like a wolf, "You better talk to that God of yours!" He spit black, vile mucus on the ground and continued, "Because he's not welcome here any longer!"

Everyone whimpered. They had never seen him like this before. The children went behind Mama who just looked at him with horror. She could only imagine what he had seen, but oh! It was terrible to see her good husband so totally lost to anger and blasphemy. Jacob stood next to her, not understanding who this man had become, but well understanding his role to protect his mother.

"Everything is gone!" Papa cried out, his burnt face twisting in both wrath and despair. "The hay, the animals, the barn. It's all gone! What kind of God would do that?"

His words were terrible, and Mama and the children stood there, afraid. For if the shepherd is afraid, the sheep will scatter.

But there was one who was not afraid. There was one who saw suddenly in herself her own sin, her sin of pride and selfishness. Until now, she had not spoken because she could not hear her voice and she was afraid. As she recognized her own fear, she saw her father's fear. And she cried out to him, begging him to find hope, as she herself had had to do. She ran to him, clutching his burnt coat with her small fists.

"Papa," she cried. "It's not true! You have not lost everything. You have us! We are here together, and we are safe!"

Everyone stopped. They looked at her. For a moment, it was as if there was no fire outside. Nothing but the sound of her voice. And though it was thick from lack of use, it sounded to each of them like beautiful chimes in the spring wind. Papa fell to his knees, and tears fell from his eyes, the salt in them singeing his wounds. But he did not notice. He saw nothing but his beautiful daughter who had at long last spoken. She fell into his arms and hugged him. Hugged the burnt coat which smelled of dying animals, hugged his weak and ragged arms exhausted from trying to save their livelihood, hugged the man who was hurting so badly he no longer saw the face of God. She understood so well the hurt and despair, the anger, and the fear. She wished only to give him strength and courage. He knelt over her, sobbing in sorrow for his lack of faith, and sobbing in thankfulness for her voice. Soon everyone was hugging Papa and crying along with him.

Suddenly, Billy and Caz came running in. "It's raining," they cried out, "and it's cold!"

They all went outside, and sure enough, it was raining. Pouring rain! It did not take long for the fire in the barn to be extinguished. Then Mama caught a glimpse of Apollo, standing alone, looking out toward the hills from whence he had come. She held her breath, wondering what he would do. In a moment, he turned around and came toward them, but then was out of sight behind the barn. She wondered about the rest but did not ask. Her family was safe and that was all that mattered.

As they stood in the rain, they suddenly saw the goats, followed by Apache and Pilgrim. Those two wise horses did what they knew how to do and herded the goats to safety. Soon the other horses came following, burnt but alive. They had been out of their minds with fear from the flames, but when the gasoline exploded, the back of the barn blew off. They would have died in the flames, but when the two old horses pushed out the goats, those horses followed them. And then Mama saw Apollo come out from behind the barn as well, prancing and tossing his head, helping to herd the goats and well pleased with himself.

The animals went to the garden, eating whatever they could find, as though nothing had happened at all and someone had left the gate open. They had some burns, but they were eating, and that was a good sign. That little family just stood there and laughed and laughed while the rain poured down and washed their wounds.

Papa said, "Right now, right here, we kneel and we pray. We ask God to forgive our sins, especially mine, and we thank him for his blessings." And as they knelt in the wet ground to pray, the rain suddenly turned to snow. Mama's prayers, made long ago, had been answered!

Papa took Mama's hand, helped her to her feet, and they all danced as a family, right there in the mud and falling snow. And Papa knew that his prayers made long ago in the hospital had indeed been answered, though he could never have guessed that this was how it would come to be.

The Yellowstone Fire was one of the worst fires in Wyoming and was finally stopped on September 11 from a quarter inch of snowfall.

Epilogue

Once again, the little family sat around the fire, burning bright within the old hearth, and talking and sharing their blessings. Jacob was at the seminary, Susan was finishing school and planning a wedding. Scars had healed both in body and in soul, but that is the way of suffering united to God's grace. Rosie was speaking now, all the time, and though the thickness in her voice never quite went away, her bubbly spirit had returned, and her eyes once again sparkled brightly.

The news of the terrible fire spread far and wide, and farmers from all over the nation shared their hay with the Wyoming ranchers. Ranchers bringing multiple trailerloads of hay could be seen driving over multiple state lines with huge signs on their sides saying, "Headed for Wyoming." Neighbors helping neighbors. The community came together to help build each other's barns or homes, and those who had not lost a home or barn in the fire helped donate wood and supplies. There were church bake sales and car wash fundraisers, BBQs, and raffles. Mothers and daughters cooked elaborate feasts and shared them at each barn raising, and those without faith reconsidered their position. How did so many endure such suffering and still keep their faith? And where did the charity and joy come from?

Suddenly the wind shook the house. As snow blew against the windows and piled high along the house, Papa joked, "No one get sick tonight, please. I don't want to drive in this."

Everyone laughed.

Billy asked, "When are you going to take us hunting again?"

Caz joined in with a cry of agreement. Papa promised he would take them in the spring. And when Rosie asked if she could go too, no one knew whether to laugh or just say yes. That Rosie—she was afraid of nothing!

As for Pistol, just as Papa predicted, Pistol became an excellent cattle horse, and just as Mama hoped, she carried grandbabies around in her old age, carrying them like the treasure they were.

Papa said it was time to pray, and once again, as they had for so many nights and so many years, they sat beneath the old cross carved in the wall and began "In the name of the Father, and the Son, and Holy Spirit…"

THE END

About the Author

CHRISTY WALL is the author of the much-loved book, *The Greatest Battle* (Luminare Press, 2022). She has also written many articles describing her life on the family ranch. She and her daughters have trained young horses for more than ten years and have seen the profound impact horses have made on the human soul. When Christy is not painting with words, she uses her camera to capture the beauty of family life with light and color.

www.ingramcontent.com/pod-product-compliance
Lightning Source LLC
LaVergne TN
LVHW021802060526
838201LV00058B/3203